LAST MAN TO DIE

Also by Michael Dobbs

HOUSE OF CARDS
WALL GAMES

LAST MAN TO DIE

Michael Dobbs

HarperCollins
An Imprint of HarperCollins*Publishers*

R66425

First published in 1991
by HarperCollins Publishers,
77–85 Fulham Palace Road,
Hammersmith, London W6 8JB

9 8 7 6 5 4 3 2 1

A CIP catalogue record for this book
is available from the British Library

ISBN 0-00-223839-X

Photoset in Linotron Trump Medieval by
Rowland Phototypesetting Ltd
Bury St Edmunds, Suffolk
Printed and bound in Great Britain by
HarperCollins Book Manufacturing, Glasgow

To the memory of my Father.

And to all those who came before.

ACKNOWLEDGMENTS

Much of the original idea for this book began with my father and his vivid memories of wartime London. We spent many enjoyable hours talking of his days as a young policeman. During the course of writing, he discovered he was dying, yet the knowledge only gave added urgency to his enthusiasm for sharing. He didn't live to see the book completed, but it couldn't have been done without him. So this book is dedicated to my father. I'm glad we had the time to share.

Others have helped, and as always in researching a book, I have made both enjoyable discoveries and new friends. I am indebted to Karl Wahnig for his experiences of active service on a U-boat; to have survived was remarkable, to have retained his sense of humour even more so. I am grateful to many others for their assistance and patience, particularly those at the Imperial War Museum, the Commonwealth Graves Commission, the Royal Navy Submarine Museum at Gosport, and M. Bernard Hine for his thoughts on fine cognacs.

Much of the action and argumentation outlined in this book took place, particularly the fierce disagreements between Eisenhower and Churchill as to how the War should be brought to its end. But this is a work of fiction and, I hope, entertainment. It is also a work of love, for my father.

M.J.D.

PROLOGUE

It was a filthy way to die, he told himself.

He had imagined death would be something rather grand. A few immortal last words that friends would discuss and applaud as they chewed over his life and his incalculable contributions to the public weal. A dignified passing wrapped up in the warm blanket of public approbation before he slipped off to some altogether more elevated plane. He had never imagined it like this.

When the doctors told him that, at his age, there was little more they could do, he had thanked them, smiling to show that it was just another challenge. After all, it was going to be their loss rather than his. 'Can't complain. Had a good innings,' he reassured them, comforting himself with the image of a final walk back to the pavilion accompanied by the applause of the crowd and congratulatory obituaries in *The Times* and the *Telegraph*. There would even be a thanksgiving service at St Martin-in-the-Fields, he hoped. Not that either of his two former wives would attend; they preferred to forget rather than forgive. And there were no children. Pity, really.

Only now had he begun to have twinges of regret, to feel the need for support as disease gnawed away at his bones and his self-confidence. He had returned to his old haunts, the scenes of his previous battles and many victories, wanting to relive them one more time. His first stop had been at his ancient public school perched on the Sussex Downs where his intellectual agility had first developed a true cutting edge and his singular competitiveness had marked him out as a boy who would go far. But he recognized no one; only the young headmaster had shown any interest and that had faded rapidly with the realization that there was to be no endowment cheque in exchange for the tea and wholemeal biscuits. He hadn't bothered going back to his Oxford college; nowadays his old university sanctuaries all seemed to be given over to women and he hated that. Women had never been more than a distraction for him, rarely pleasurable, inevitably expensive and ultimately always irritating.

So he had come to London, an uncommon event since his retirement some years before. Even that had changed. People hurried by unaware of him, while the traffic ground to a halt. Whitehall, which had been the playing field for much of his career, hid distant and austere behind the new security and surveillance systems. Downing Street, where during the war he had lived and slept and, in the days of defeat and despair, had even thought he might die, was cordoned off by huge iron gates. He couldn't even get close. No more crisp salutes from the duty policeman, no more satchels full of papers marked 'Top Secret' and smeared with the dust from Churchill's cigars, only barriers with hidden cameras and windows covered by heavy curtains to catch the shards of glass, just in case.

He had sought refuge in the all-male preserve of his club. Here at least nothing appeared to have changed. He had sat in his favourite armchair at the Athenaeum for the entire afternoon before realizing that his friends were no longer there and the few acquaintances who recognized him had no time for a decomposing old man with no future. Someone he thought he knew had approached him purposefully from the other side of the room, but solely to ask whether he had finished with the newspaper. Only the steward in the coffee room seemed happy to speak with him, and he didn't have English as a first or even third language.

He had sat, a frail figure dwarfed in an armchair of ancient, cracked leather, knowing the world had already passed him by, and whether he was yet willing to let go or not was of little consequence. He no longer belonged in this world. He

10

was an anachronism, of less importance to his fellow man than the battered armchair he occupied or the newspaper he was reading. He was an old man watching his body slowly being eaten away, feeling the strength drain from him a little every day and discovering that dying was a lonely and humiliating business. Suddenly he didn't feel brave any more.

So he had come to Berlin. Or, more precisely, had been dragged there. He had never before been to Berlin, yet, as he began to suspect that the mincing clerics he despised might after all be right, that he should prepare to account for those things he had done, so a sense of guilt had risen inside him. Guilt was a new feeling; he didn't know how to handle it. It implied fallibility and a concern for the judgement of others, characteristics for which he was not noted. He had always worked behind the scenes, wielding his influence away from the public eye and never having to answer to any other than a handful of the good and great, and the justification of acting in the national interest had always excused a multitude of sins. Yet as death loomed, the excuse seemed no longer enough, not for what they had planned for Berlin. He had always avoided the place, not wishing to allow any measure of doubt into the comforting certainties of his life, but those certainties were being corrupted along with his flesh and it had become almost inevitable that he should fly here, a last attempt to atone on earth for the things he had no desire to answer for in another place.

Sir William Cazolet Bart., KCMG, CB, CVO etc., former adviser to Prime Ministers and *éminence grise* of the British Establishment, whose informed if unattributable counsel had frequently been sought by monarchs, judges and editors, sat on the upper deck of a bright green tour bus as it barged its way around the sights of Berlin. Most of the other passengers were still in shirtsleeves, enjoying the last of the September warmth, but Cazolet was wrapped up tight in hat and scarf. His circulation had gone and his long, thin fingers showed like white bird's claws as they gripped the seat in front for

11

support against the swaying of the bus. He shouldn't travel until next spring, one doctor had advised. There's no point in waiting, another had countered, you won't be here by then.

Berlin was not as he had imagined. The western half was tinselly, garish and loud, while the east still bore the scars of the attempt to build nirvana out of concrete. 'Directly ahead you shall see the Brandenburg Gate,' intoned the courier, 'built in 1791 to act as a toll gate at the western end of Unter den Linden. It was here on 13 August 1961 that the first stones of the Berlin Wall are being laid. The statue of the goddess of Victory on top was firstly naked, but was quickly covered up, and then taken for a few years to Paris by Napoleon . . .'

The bus lurched to the right and the Gate was no longer in sight. An overweight American in the next seat who had been sleeping off lunch gave a belch as he came to life and muttered something in the ear of his equally substantial wife. She ignored him, burrowing into her guide book, double checking everything they were told by the courier with an air of unremitting scepticism, as if anxious to ensure they were getting their money's worth. She saw Cazolet staring. 'Yes?' she said aggressively as if welcoming the opportunity to engage in combat with someone new, before being distracted once again by the voice over the loudspeaker.

'The low grassy mound you are seeing in front of you is all that is left of Hitler's infamous Bunker, which was blown up by the Russians after the war. It was from this point that Hitler and his generals directed the campaign in its last few months, and it was here that he and his mistress Eva Braun committed suicide in the closing days of the war, she by poison, he by shooting himself . . .'

Up to this point the fat American had been far more engrossed in her guide book than the real-life sights of Berlin, but now she stared out of the window, leaning across the girth of her husband to get as close as possible. ''S no bigger than a Little League pitcher's mound, Leo,' she snorted in contempt, digging her husband in the ribs before snapping her guide book shut and burying her nose in a slimming magazine. Leo, grateful for the respite, went back to sleep.

Neither of them noticed Cazolet's reaction. He was sitting to attention in his seat as though he had been reprimanded, his head swivelling on its scrawny neck to ensure that his eyes stayed fixed upon the grassy knoll for as long as possible. When at last it vanished from view, the old man slumped back in his seat, a puppet with all its wires cut. His face, already pale, had become chalky white beneath the parchment skin, the only sign of colour being the blue veins throbbing at the temples. His breathing was anguished, the air being forced through thin, downcast lips. There was sweat on his brow and the dim eyes stared straight ahead, taking in nothing, lost in a distant world of their own. He took no further interest in the tour and showed no sign of leaving the bus when it reached its final stop. The courier had to shake him by the shoulder to rouse him. 'Must have had a turn,' the courier muttered to the driver, relieved that the old man was able, albeit with difficulty, to disembark and so release him and the tour company from any further responsibility.

It was not until the following day that Cazolet seemed to recover. He forsook the formal guided tours and instead commandeered a taxi. 'Take me to old Berlin,' he instructed. 'I want to see the city as it was, before the war.'

'What's left to see? Try a picture library,' the driver muttered.

But Cazolet had insisted, so the driver, encouraged by a substantial tip paid up front, had driven east and north, across the line where the old Wall had once divided the city, into the working-class district of Niederschoenhausen. As the sights of the tourist brochures slipped away behind them the shrunken figure in the back seat seemed to come to life. 'Slow down,' he ordered, peering closely out of the window as they came off the highway and began to bounce along streets of bare cobblestone.

For some while they crawled between the rows of austere, gloomy tenements that huddled along either side of the road.

There was little life to be seen. The only greenery grew out of the cracks in the cornicing that hung, often precariously, along the frontages, and the few people he saw on the streets had expressions which perfectly matched their dismal surroundings. Many of the buildings were in need of substantial repair, with dripping algae-covered water outlets and cracked window panes, or bits of board and cellophane where windows ought to have been. The ancient ravages of war could still be seen in the pockmarks which were spattered across the façades. There were gaps between houses where buildings had once stood but where now there was nothing but a wilderness of weeds doubling as a burial ground for old cars. Everything seemed worn out, of a past age, just waiting to die. At last, Cazolet told himself grimly, he had found a place where he belonged.

He stopped outside the shop for no better reason than that it appeared to be the only place open. It loosely described itself as an antique shop but the goods were more second-hand than aged. As he opened the door, a bell jangled overhead producing not a bright song of welcome but a choking sound, a stiff rattle of discontent as if complaining at being disturbed. Cazolet guessed it had been that way for a long, long time. The shop was cramped and narrow, like a railway carriage, with a thin corridor down the middle between bric-à-brac and dusty oddments which were piled with little apparent logic or order along the shelves and on top of the collection of dark tables and bureaux that had been pushed against the walls. The best of what there was seemed to be in the front window, a large blue-and-white Nanking temple vase which was a modern reproduction, he guessed, and a nineteenth-century mahogany upright clock with an intricate brass face but no back panel. It had been disembowelled and the movement lay on the floor beside it. Both vase and clock bore a substantial layer of dust, as did the owner, who appeared from behind a curtain at the back of the shop wiping his hands on a tea towel. He had a stomach which his grimy undervest and leather belt had difficulty in containing, and

14

from his scowl and the grease that had dribbled on to his chin it appeared as though he had been disturbed in the middle of eating. He was somewhere in his mid-sixties, Cazolet estimated. As always when he met a German of his own age, Cazolet wondered what the other had done during the war and what secrets and torments hid behind the watery, suspicious eyes. He would have been about fifteen by the end of the fighting. In Berlin that was old enough to have been conscripted, to have been sent out with nothing more than a couple of grenades and a busted rifle to face the Soviet tanks and the peasant-conscripts who swarmed behind, to have fought for Berlin street by street and sewer by bloody sewer, to have killed and to have been killed. Many much younger than fifteen had known that. In those days, death in Berlin had recognized no distinction between the innocence of childhood and culpability for having been born a German. Yet this German had survived to become old and fat, and that alone was enough to ensure he should never be taken for granted.

The shopkeeper said nothing, standing silently in the back of the premises smacking his greasy lips and staring, as if he reckoned Cazolet might be on the point of running off with his precious stock. Cazolet refused to be intimidated. He liked this place, its jumble of artifacts, its mustiness, its uselessness. He moved through the shop, pulling out drawers, inspecting battered brassware, smudging the dust off prints before settling into an oak dining chair, testing it for comfort. Had it been one of six it might have fetched a reasonable price but on its own it was simply old – a survivor, Cazolet reflected, which made it something special in Berlin. He was astonished to discover himself feeling a sharp twinge of envy. Of a chair. Bloody fool! he scolded himself, once again rehearsing the arguments as to why he had nothing to fear about tomorrow, whatever it might bring.

It was as he was sitting in reflection that he saw the photo frame. It was blackened with age and dirt, and from behind the smeared glass stared the image of a young German military

15

recruit from the last war, his brave smile and crisp Wehrmacht uniform typical of countless thousands of photographs that had adorned mantelpieces and bedside tables in bygone days. The photo itself held no fascination for Cazolet; it was the battered frame that grabbed his attention. He reached out and took it between both hands, his thumbs rubbing the tarnished metal, trying to reveal the gleam of silver which he guessed lay beneath the oxide. Up the sides and along the bottom of the frame he found small decorative filigree executed in a different metal which beneath the dirt and soot looked like dull brass, and directly in the centre at the top of the frame was a small, slightly jagged hole, as if some further piece of decoration had been pulled away none too carefully. It was staring at the hole that brought it back. A memory, vague with distance and time. He thought he knew what should have been there, but surely it couldn't be . . . With a thumbnail he scratched gently at the filigree, but already he knew what he would find. Not worthless brass but the yellow lustre of gold. Now he knew for certain what was missing. He turned the frame over and with some difficulty began releasing the clips that secured the photograph inside the frame. His hands were trembling, and not solely with age.

The shopkeeper had come over to inspect what he was doing. 'Careful!' he growled.

'This is not the original photograph,' Cazolet snapped. 'This is a war-time piece, without doubt, but the frame was made for something else . . .'

The shopkeeper began to take a keen interest; perhaps he could do business over this piece of junk after all.

'You see the hole?' continued Cazolet as the back came off and his frail fingers searched for the edge of the photograph. 'I think there used to be a little gold swastika here. These were specially produced and given away . . .' He sucked in his breath as the old photograph came away to reveal the original still lurking behind.

'Bollocks,' muttered the German.

' . . . by Adolf Hitler himself.'

16

They could both see the face, magisterially staring left to right into a distance he imagined to be filled with endless victories.

'This is quite rare. It's even signed!' Cazolet was rubbing furiously at the grime on the glass with a spotless white handkerchief.

'Five hundred marks,' the shopkeeper barked, rapidly recovering his composure.

'Oh, I don't want to buy it. I have no need . . .' But Cazolet could go no further. His words died as his vigorous cleaning of the glass revealed not just Hitler's spidery signature but also a dedication. His breathing was laboured as the excitement and the exertions began taking their toll. The frame trembled in his hands as he held it up to his old eyes. He blinked rapidly, giving the glass another polish with the now-stained handkerchief and holding it up once more for inspection. The metal seemed to be burning in his hands, as if grown white hot with a mystical energy all its own. The Englishman was one of life's professional sceptics and even as he had contemplated his own death he had found it hard to believe in religion, but every day for the few months that remained to him thereafter Cazolet would look at his hands expecting to find stigmata burned deep into his palms.

'Oh, sweet Jesus,' he gasped as at last he deciphered the scrawled dedication. 'Can it be . . . ? After all these years of not knowing. He made it. *He actually bloody made it!*'

The old man's hands gave another savage shake and the silver frame slipped from his fingers, falling to the floor. There was a loud crack as the glass shattered.

'That's it,' snapped the German. 'You'll have to buy it now.'

Part One

ONE

March 1945

It wasn't much of a prison camp, just a double row of barbed wire fencing strung around a football pitch with guards occasionally patrolling along the path that ran between the rows. In the middle were twenty or so dark green army bell tents serving as the sole source of shelter for the 247 German prisoners. There were no watch towers; there hadn't been time to build any as the Allied armies swept up after the Battle of the Bulge and pressed onward through Europe. It was one of scores of transit camps thrown up, with little thought of security, anywhere with space enough to provide primitive shelter for prisoners on their way from the war zone to more permanent accommodation. No one appeared keen to escape.

The great tide of captured Germans washing up against British shores had all but overwhelmed the authorities' ability to cope. After all, with the Allies racing for the Rhine, there were other priorities. So guarding the camps was not a job for crack troops but for new recruits, with little experience and often less discipline. That was the trouble with Transit Camp 174B, that and the complete absence of plumbing.

The camp, on the edge of the windswept Yorkshire moors, was run by young Canadians, freshly recruited, ill-trained and with a youthful intolerance which divided the world into black and white, friend and foe. They weren't going to win any campaign medals on this battleground, and perhaps it was frustration and a feeling of inadequacy that tempted

21

them to take out their aggression on the prisoners. In most camps the commanding officer would douse any unruly fires amongst the hotheads, but in Camp 174B the CO's name was Pilsudski, who came of Polish parents out of Winnipeg. And after reports began filtering through of what the Russians had found as they raced through Poland, he didn't give a damn.

The trouble had begun two days previously when the camp's leading black marketeer had come to grief. He had never been popular, but he had his uses. 'I'll do a deal on anything,' he used to brag. He could obtain a surprising variety of necessities from the guards and would get a reasonable price for anything that the prisoners had to sell – watches, wedding rings, wallets, even their medals. It made the difference between surviving and simply sinking in despair into the mud. He was also a bum-boy and sold himself, and the rest of the inmates were willing to put up even with that – until one of them discovered he was also the camp 'stooly' and was selling information to the Canadians about his fellow prisoners. The guards found him late one night, crawling through the mud and screaming in agony, with every last penny of the substantial sum of money he had scraped together shoved up his ass.

Perhaps the incident would have passed without further consequences, for the stool pigeon was no more popular amongst the guards, most of whom thought he had it coming. But it was not to be. Pilsudski received a report of the previous night's incident moments after hearing on the radio of what the Germans had done before their retreat from Warsaw, and how little they had left standing or alive. Before the war he'd had an aunt and aged grandmother who lived in an apartment on the leafy corner of Aleja Jerozolimska and Bracka streets; now, apparently, there was nothing left, no apartment, no corner, no street, no trace of the women. It was the excuse he had been looking for, the opportunity to revenge in some small way the horrors that preyed on his mind.

22

There were nine tables set up in line on the small parade ground. Before eight of them the camp's entire complement of prisoners was standing to attention in a cold drizzle; behind the ninth, which was raised on a dais, sat Pilsudski surveying the scene. The senior prisoner, a commander in the German Navy who leaned heavily on a stick, was remonstrating with him.

'So, Commander, you want to know what this is all about, do you?' Pilsudski was saying, staring down at the German officer like a vulture from its perch. 'Well, I'll tell you. Last night someone broke into the office here.' He waved towards the primitive wooden construction which, before the sports area was commandeered, had served as changing rooms and a small grandstand. 'And I want to know which of your men did it. Pity you Germans don't seem to be able to control yourselves,' he added, the morning's news still much on his mind. 'Some property's missing, so we're going to look for it.'

Already the commander could hear the noise of wrecking as guards went through the tents overturning beds, tearing palliasses, emptying kitbags and the other hold-alls in which the prisoners kept their meagre possessions, ripping everything apart. He knew that anything of value would be gone by the time the prisoners were able to begin picking up the pieces.

'But the offices are outside the wire. My men could not possibly have . . .'

Pilsudski's eyes narrowed; there was venom in his voice. 'You're surely not trying to tell me that Canadian soldiers would stoop to theft. No, Commander, it's you Germans who've had all the experience of theft and pillage and rape, everywhere you've been in Europe.'

'This is completely unjust,' the German protested, propping himself up unsteadily on his stick. He was clearly a sick man, and in some considerable pain after standing for nearly an hour in the drizzle.

Pilsudski's swagger stick came crashing down across the

23

table. 'Don't talk to me about justice, you Nazi bastard. If I make you eat shit, at least that's more than most of your prisoners got over the last six years.'

With considerable effort the German pulled himself up off his cane and stood erect, looking at Pilsudski, his defiance visible through the rain that dripped off his cap and down his face. 'I am a German officer. I most strongly protest.'

'Listen, sauerkraut. You started it. You lost. So shove it.' Pilsudski jerked the middle finger of his right hand into the face of the commander, before turning from him in contemptuous dismissal. 'Sergeant. Search the prisoners!'

At the command the first man in each line of prisoners was prodded forward by the guards until they were standing in front of a table. After considerable further prodding with the muzzles of the standard-issue Lee Enfield .303s they began taking off their clothes, item by item, and placing them on the tables.

'All of 'em, buster,' one of the guards screamed, giving a reluctant prisoner a savage dig under the ribs. He smiled arrogantly through a mouthful of gum while the German slowly obeyed until he had joined the seven other prisoners standing naked in front of the tables. The guards went through their clothes, indiscriminately filching cigarettes, wallets, combs, even family photographs.

The search seemed to be over. Nothing incriminating had been found, and the sergeant was looking in the direction of Pilsudski for further orders. At last, with a bitter look which seemed to bring together all the strands of anger and frustration burning inside him, Pilsudski nodded.

Each of the prisoners was thrown forward across the table, his head held down by one guard as another, hand encased in heavy leather glove, spread his legs and violated him. One of the prisoners began to emit a low howl of anguish but quickly choked it off. Why give the guards still further satisfaction?

'You are . . . tearing up . . . all the rules,' the commander began, barely able to find words as he struggled to contain his feelings. 'What in God's name do you think this is?'

'A medical inspection. For piles. If anyone asks. Which they won't.' Pilsudski's manner was cold as the wind. He didn't regret a thing. 'By the way, one of the prisoners is excused. The queer. I understand he's been comprehensively inspected already.'

'I think I understand.'

'Sure you do, Fritz. How do the rules of war go? To the victor the spoils. To the losers, a finger up their ass. And it's a damn sight less than you bastards deserve.'

'You have already defeated us. Is that not enough?'

'No, not by a long chalk. I want the entire German nation crawling on its hands and knees, begging for mercy, just like you left that faggot the other night. I hope I make myself clear.'

There was no point in further protest. The German turned on his heel and joined the end of one of the lines.

It took more than two hours for the guards to finish their work, and the drizzle continued to fall as the parade ground turned into a sea of slime. There were tears mingling with the rain that flowed down the cheeks of many of the Germans, tears of degradation and humiliation, tears of despair at having been captured, of having let down their colleagues and failed their country. But most of all there were tears of guilt at being survivors when so many others had found the courage to do their duty to the very end. In laying down their arms they were guilty of desertion, of having betrayed the womenfolk and children they had left behind. As Pilsudski knew, capture and defeat had already stripped them of their sense of manhood, and almost every one of the men on that parade ground secretly believed he deserved the punishment being meted out to him. Pilsudski might be a vicious bastard but, as losers, theirs was the greater sin.

Such feelings of personal guilt are the general rule for

25

prisoners of war. But to all generalities there are exceptions. And in Camp 174B, the exception was Peter Hencke . . .

'It's an unpalatable prospect, Willie,' the Prime Minister growled, breaking a lengthy period of silent contemplation as he searched for the soap under a thick layer of suds.

William Cazolet took off his glasses and gave them a vigorous polish to clear the condensation. He felt such a fool on bath nights. In the fortified Annexe off Downing Street where the Prime Minister spent much of his time, the ventilation was close to non-existent because the windows were permanently enclosed in thick steel shutters. It made the bathroom hot and steamy, just as the PM liked it, but for visitors – and there usually were visitors on bath night, even female secretaries taking shorthand – it could be an ordeal. It was one of the many eccentricities of working and living with Winston Churchill.

'What prospect is that, exactly?' Cazolet asked, leaning forward from his perch on the toilet seat in an attempt to restore the circulation to his legs. It could be uncomfortable sitting at the right hand of history.

The Prime Minister grumbled on, almost as if talking to himself. 'There was a time, not so long ago, when the British were the only players in the orchestra. We were on our own. Our empire provided all the musicians. I conducted, even wrote most of the score. My God, but we made sweet music for the world to listen to.' There was no hiding the pride in his voice. 'Had it not been for us, Europe would now be listening to nothing but the harsh stamp of German brass bands. D'you know, Willie, I've never liked brass bands. All huff and puff without any trace of tenderness. Could you ever imagine Mozart composing sonatas for brass bands?'

He paused to scrub his back and puff fresh life into the cigar which had been lying sad and soggy in an ashtray beside the soap dish. The Old Man was lacking his usual jauntiness tonight, the secretary thought. Cazolet was only twenty-eight, a young Foreign Service officer thrust by the opportunities and shortages of war into the tight-knit team of prime ministerial assistants who were responsible for taking care of the Old Man's every need, transmitting his orders, acting as a link between Downing Street and the mighty war machine over which he presided, ensuring that he took plenty of soda with his whisky and, if necessary, putting him to bed. Some couldn't take it, working round the clock in the cement cocoon of the Annexe and the War Cabinet Rooms beneath, without sunlight or sight of the world above, discovering what the weather was like only through bulletins posted on a board in the corridor, subjected to the Old Man's vile temper and suffocating in an atmosphere of constant cigar smoke. But Cazolet had taken it, and it had given the young man an uncanny aptitude for reading the PM's thoughts.

'I've always thought the American military display too great a fondness for brass bands,' Cazolet prompted. 'Very loud. No subtlety.'

'But my God, how we needed them, and how generously they have given. Yet . . .' There was an unaccustomed pause as the Old Man searched for an appropriate expression, hiding behind a haze of cigar smoke. 'It seems we are destined to march behind one brass band or another, Willie,' he said slowly, picking his words with care.

Cazolet wiped the condensation from his glasses once more while he studied the other man. He saw not the great war leader, the stuff of the newsreels and propaganda films. The Old Man was no celluloid figure in two dimensions, but a man full of self-acknowledged faults which at times made him impossibly irascible even in the same breath as he was being visionary. The spirit had always seemed unquenchable, yet the body was seventy years old and was visibly beginning to tire. What else could one expect after six winters of war? Flamboyance and strength of character were not enough any longer to give colour to the cheeks, which were pale and puffy. Too many late nights, too many cigars, too much hiding underground. Of everything, simply too much.

27

'How was Eisenhower?' Cazolet enquired, anxious not to allow the PM to slip off into another empty silence. Anyway, it was time to probe. The PM had been unusually reticent and moody since his meeting with the American general on the previous day, and Cazolet could sense something churning away inside.

'He is a determined, single-minded man, our general,' the Old Man responded. The deliberate way he punctuated the words did not make them sound like a compliment. 'The very characteristics that make him such an excellent military leader make him nothing of a politician. And he is American. He thinks American. He listens too much to Americans, particularly his generals, most of whom seem to have gained their experience of battle out of books at West Point. They are all quartermasters and caution. I judge an officer by the sand in his boots and the mud of battle on his tunic rather than the number of textbooks he has managed to pacify.'

The PM contemplated the moist end of his Havana, deliberating whether it was yet time to call for its replacement. Since his heart murmur three years earlier his doctors had told him to cut down, to cut down on everything except fresh air and relaxation. Idiots! As if the greatest danger facing the British empire was a box of Cuban cigars and the occasional bottle of brandy.

A potent mix of smoke and steam attacked Cazolet's lungs and he stifled a cough. 'They say Eisenhower can be weak and indecisive, that he listens to too many opinions and carries the impression of the last man who sat upon him.'

Churchill shook his head in disagreement. 'If that were so we would not be at odds, since I would be constantly by his side, ready to sit upon him at a moment's notice.' He patted his paunch. 'And I would make a very considerable impression!' He broke into a genial smile, the first that evening. He was beginning to feel better. To hell with the doctors. He lit a fresh cigar. 'Don't underestimate the general, William.

He is not weak. A conciliator, perhaps, who prefers to lead by persuasion rather than instruction. But above all he is an American. Americans are boisterous, unbroken, raw, full of lust and irresponsibility, goodheartedness, charm and naked energy. And above all they haven't the slightest understanding of the significance of Europe. For them it is little more than a bloody battlefield on which they have been called to sacrifice their young men twice in a generation, some troublesome, far-flung place on a foreign map. That's why they deserted us after the last war. They threw away the victory then; we must not allow them to do so again.'

'What do you want from them?'

'There are many things I expect of our American friends – ships, arms, food, money, *matériel*. But one thing above all they must give me, Willie.' His blue eyes flared defiantly. 'They must give me Berlin!'

The blackout curtains were drawn tight around the luxurious manor house adjacent to SHAEF forward military headquarters in newly-liberated France. It wouldn't do to have the Supreme Allied Commander shot up by some Luftwaffe night-fighter, not when he was having dinner and, with growing agitation, giving forth of his own version of the previous day's meeting.

'Would you believe the man? He tried to scold me. Said I was smoking too much, that it was an unforgivable extravagance at a time of general shortage. Damn nerve!' General Dwight Eisenhower started to chuckle in spite of himself. He regarded the PM, half-American on his mother's side, as something of a father figure and so tolerated the older man's bombastic and occasionally patronizing manner. He was no less a chain smoker than Churchill, yet even in his addiction he revealed his modest, less flamboyant character. Strictly a 'Lucky Strikes' man.

Eisenhower paused to indicate there was a serious point to his tale. 'Extravagance! I told him I was willing to be extravagant with everything but men's lives. Yet he still insists on taking the most ridiculous risks . . .' The general shook his head sadly, staring into the flame of the candles that lit the beautifully laid dinner table separating him from his companion. 'The Brits are running out of time. The longer this war goes on, the more bitter the final victory will be for them. They've been bled dry; Britannia with her wrists cut. They've got neither the stamina nor the resources for much more of this. It's making the Old Man impatient, rash.'

The genuine regret in Eisenhower's voice was not lost on his companion, who was British, and who mistook neither the irony of sitting in a Europe only recently freed from German occupation, surrounded by seemingly endless supplies of vintage champagne, nor the absurdity that war seemed to be fought either from foxholes or from the luxury of liberated French chateaux. 'So what did you tell him?'

'Just that. He was being rash. So then he got het up and said risks had to be taken, it was the art of war. Art, for Chrissake! I told him that dying isn't an art but a ruthless damn' military science.'

'You would have thought that after Gallipoli . . .'

'At least at Gallipoli he was taking risks with British and Australian lives. Now it's American lives he wants to put on the line.' He stubbed out his cigarette as if he were crushing bugs, grinding it to pulp in the crystal ashtray. 'You see, he wants Berlin. A final masterstroke to crown his war, so he can lead the victory parade through the captured German capital.'

'What's wrong with that?'

'Oh, not a lot, except the military value of Berlin doesn't amount to a row of beans and it would cost at least one hundred thousand casualties – American casualties – to get there before the Russians. Can you imagine how tough the Germans are going to be fighting for their own capital? Good Christ, we're not ready, we might even screw it up just like the British did at Arnhem, through sheer over-eagerness. If

they pushed us back in front of Berlin it could mean t͟
dragging on for months!'

The telephone interrupted them for the fourth time sin͟e
they had sat down to dine, and Eisenhower jumped to answer
it. This proved to be a mistake as his weak knee gave him a
savage reminder of its presence. He had injured it some
months before in Northern France when, driven by impatience to return to his headquarters, he had commandeered an L-5 spotter plane. It had turned into near-disaster
as in rapidly deteriorating visibility Eisenhower and the pilot
had been unable to find the airfield and were forced to make
an emergency landing on a foggy beach. Fortunately it hadn't
been mined, although the despairing pilot didn't know that
at the time. Eisenhower escaped with no more than ripped
ligaments and a fearsome bawling-out from his concerned
staff. The knee had slowed him down but it hadn't cured his
impatience; even as he talked on the telephone his jaw was
chomping with frustration.

'OK-OK-OK, run up the white flag. If State insists it's vital I
see the Crown Prince – where'd you say he was from? – you'd
better fit it in. Then you go and ask the State Department, very
politely, if they'd mind putting a cork in their courtesy calls
and letting us get on with winning this goddamned war!' The
grinding of his teeth could be heard across the room. 'And one
more thing. No more interruptions, eh?'

He hobbled back towards the table, massaging his knee,
but as he drew back his chair he seemed to double up and a
further flash of pain crossed his face. Chronic indigestion.
When in England he had blamed it on the endless diet of
Brussels sprouts and boiled cabbage which seemed to be
standard fare in London, but in France he had run out of
excuses. They didn't eat boiled cabbage, and the pain was
getting worse. The strains of war were plucking at him,
demanding that he ease up. Yet how could he? There was a
war to be won. So his knee swelled and his habitually high
blood pressure hit new peaks and he lost still more of his hair.
And he could really do without this run-in with Churchill.

31

'For Chrissake, he's being preposterous. Even if we do take Berlin, we can't hold it. We already agreed at Yalta that it'll be in the Russian zone of occupation after the war. So five minutes to hold Mr Churchill's victory parade and then we hand it back. That's about twenty thousand US casualties for every godforsaken minute. A high price for an old man's ambition, eh?'

The ridiculous British were always interfering, rattling their teacups, demanding his time, trying to appropriate his resources, questioning his judgement, amateur strategists all. It had been the British who in the previous autumn had urged him into the attempt on the bridges at Nijmegen and Arnhem. He had been weak, and agreed to it against his better judgement. Nearly ten thousand Allied soldiers taken prisoner. To satisfy the vanity of a handful of men. It had been a mistake, and a costly one. No wonder he couldn't sleep nights. He wasn't going to be bullied into a similar blunder again.

He swirled the whisky around the glass, watching the candlelight catch the finely cut patterns in the French crystal, wondering what his troops in the field facing von Rundstedt had eaten that evening, and envying them their simple tasks of war. 'I'll not let the old men of Europe play their games with my troops,' he said quietly. 'My duty is clear. To win this war, and to win it with the minimum loss of Allied lives. If lives are to be lost, frankly I would rather they were Russian than American or British.'

There was no response. Perhaps he had gone too far. He felt the need to justify himself. 'There's something else. Something pretty scary. Our intelligence guys believe Hitler may be planning a retreat from Berlin to the mountains in Bavaria and Austria, a sort of Alpine redoubt. He moves everything he can in there and conducts endless guerrilla warfare. God, it would be tough rousting him out of there. The war might never end.'

'But is that likely?'

'Were all those panzer divisions he conjured up out of the

Ardennes just before Christmas likely? Those tanks came out of nowhere, caught us napping. That man's full of surprises. He's fighting for his life; he's not going to roll over just to please Churchill.'

'So . . . ?'

'So to hell with what the Old Man wants. We don't push all our troops in the north. We advance in the south, to cut off any chance of Hitler's retreat to the mountains.' He drained the glass. 'And if it means Stalin taking Berlin and half of Europe, it would be a pity. But not a great pity.'

'What a way to run a war!' Churchill exclaimed, more soapy water splashing over the side of the bath and dripping on to the carpet.

Cazolet looked despairingly at his suit, the razor-sharp creases of half an hour ago now a sorry tangle of damp wool.

'Some intelligence men sitting on their backsides in a Zurich bar hear whispers about a mountain fortress and all our plans are cast aside. For mere tittle-tattle and rumour!'

'But surely there may be something in those reports,' interjected Cazolet. He could always recognize when Churchill's enthusiasm ran away with his prudence, particularly late at night.

'Let us suppose, let us for one fraction of a moment suppose . . .' Churchill responded, his jowls quivering with indignation and stabbing his cigar like some blunt bayonet in the direction of the younger man. 'Let us suppose that the same American intelligence experts who just two months ago so lamentably failed to spot thirty-one mighty Nazi divisions massing in the Ardennes to launch the Battle of the Bulge were, on this occasion and in spite of their track record, right. So what? What can Hitler do in the Alps? Let him have his caves, let him freeze in the winter snows just as he did on the Russian plains. He can do no real damage in the mountains. But Berlin . . .' At the mention of the word, his voice lowered, the brimstone being replaced by an almost conspiratorial timbre. 'Berlin is the key, William, the key. Without it, we shall never find our way out of darkness.'

The waters heaved and parted as Churchill raised his considerable girth out of the bath and gesticulated for Cazolet to hand him a tent-size cotton towel. 'It is quite simple. Either we take Berlin, or the Russians will. They are certain to take Vienna, Budapest, Sofia, probably Prague. Almost every one of the great capitals in Central Europe will be occupied by the Red Army. If he gains Berlin, too, Stalin will have his grip around the heart of the continent. I have to tell you, Willie, I do not trust him. He talks of friendship, but every time Comrade Stalin stretches out his hand to me, it always seems to be reaching directly for my throat. We went to war all those pain-filled years ago to preserve freedom in Europe against the threat of National Socialists. Are we in victory to throw it away at the feet of Bolshevists?' Churchill was rehearsing another of his speeches, as he was wont to do with his close colleagues, while he towelled himself dry. Suddenly he stopped, distracted, and sat naked on the edge of the bath.

'And behind us, here in London, I fear the worst, Willie. Some time before the end of the year we must hold an election.'

Cazolet couldn't help interrupting. The idea seemed too absurd. 'Surely after all you've done the electorate must support you?'

'I love them, with all my heart I love them, but I have little faith in their gratitude.' He sat silent for a moment, drawing in his chin until it became lost in the loose folds of flesh. He tried to hide the misting in his eyes, but there was no mistaking the catch of emotion in his voice as he resumed. 'My own father was one of the great statesmen of his age. Yet, at the height of his powers, they threw him to one side. They broke his heart on the great anvil of politics . . .' Tears were starting to roll down Churchill's cheeks as he stared into a past of pain and humiliation, even as Cazolet recognized the hyperbole and inexactitude. Churchill's father had been a drunken womanizer, a rotten husband and even worse father, and had died at a young age of syphilis. Perhaps that was why the son had to work so hard to weave the legend and why he, at least, had to believe so passionately in it.

'No. All triumphs are fleeting, Willie. One cannot expect gratitude, and I do not. After the last war we promised them homes fit for heroes. They're still waiting, and while they wait they discover American troops laden with fresh fruit and chocolates, things they haven't seen for years. Soon they will be asking why Americans do better for themselves while fighting a war than their own government was able to do for them all through peacetime, and I'm not sure I have the answers.' A frown split his forehead. 'Elsewhere it is still worse. Europe is ruined. A tinder box of deprivation and misery. Stalin and his acolytes could rule from the Urals to the Atlantic, even here in London. Everything we fought to save consumed by Bolshevism. So, you see, we need Berlin. The battle for Hitler's capital is the most important contest of the war. Sadly, it seems we shall have to wage it against our American allies.'

There was a glint in his pale eyes, revealing the boyish enthusiasm of which he was so capable – or was it the desperation of an ageing, ailing leader? Cazolet was no longer sure.

'I have made up my mind, Willie. I will give anything to have Berlin. Anything!'

The tension in the general's face had disappeared. As the flame had eaten away the candles and the warm wax had trickled on to the starched tablecloth, his mood had softened. Eisenhower was no longer a general on parade. The creases across his face dissolved and the muscles around his jaw stopped working overtime. 'Have I been too hard on the British?'

'We'll survive,' his companion responded, returning his smile.

'I didn't mean to be hard. Your Churchill's a great guy, really. Just wrong on this one, I guess. I'm sorry.' He looked coy as he tried to make amends. 'You know I like the British.'

'What, all of us?'

'Some more than others, I guess.'

'I'm glad to hear it.' There was a slight pause. 'Is there anything I can do?'

The general looked intently across the table at Kay Summersby, the woman who had been seconded early in the war to Eisenhower's headquarters as his driver and secretary, and who was now also his lover.

'Would you obey a direct order to come to bed, or shall I have you taken out at dawn and shot for disobedience?'

She threw her napkin playfully across the table at him, and thought how boyish he could still look with his blue eyes and explosive smile, even with his hair in rapid retreat.

'Well, if it would help further the cause of Anglo-American understanding . . .'

It was in their eyes that Hencke could see the change. Once they had been battle-hardened, men of steel, soldiers of the Wehrmacht who in the confines of the camp would gather together for the strength and support they could give each other. They would crowd around the numerous kindling fires in noisy groups, finding tasks to fill their days and maintain their spirits, beating tin cans into exotic cigarette cases, moulding and whittling jewellery from scraps of clear plastic salvaged from the cockpits of crashed planes, while those with less dexterity played chess, exchanged stories or simply shared photographs and experiences. Even in defeat they were defiant.

Now it had all gone. There was little conversation, only silent figures whiling away the hours huddled over the low flames, some using tin cans to cook the scraps of extra rations they had bribed out of the guards or wheedled from fellow prisoners through a crooked game of *Skat*, no longer sharing, gaunt faces blackened from squatting so close over the fires, heads bowed, eyes red rimmed and desperate peering out of sooty masks like clowns at a circus of the damned. As Hencke walked around the camp they would cast furtive glances to see who passed by before returning once more to stare into the flames, unable or unwilling to hold his gaze. Pilsudski had known what he was about, the bastard.

It wasn't just the finger. God, if that had been all it would have been over and done within a moment. Less pain than a boot camp hypodermic, one good heave and a cold shower and it would have been nothing more than unpleasant history. No, it was the feeling of utter worthlessness with which they were left. Pilsudski had reduced them to objects without value, with no rights, no feelings, no dignity, scarcely men at all. They had stood in the rain, raging inside at the injustice, sick with apprehension as the line of men shortened and their turn came ever closer. They were fighting men, yet in a minute Pilsudski's guards were going to reduce them to the impotence of castrated pigs, not physically, but inside, where the scars never heal. When it was over they had slunk around in their private worlds of shame, feeling dirty, guilty, more than two hundred individuals, detached and alone. And Hencke would need every one of them if he were to have any hope of success.

A lifetime ago he had been a teacher in a bustling provincial town where the children laughed and the trams ran on time. He had been happy, for a while, helping his wards enjoy a childhood he had never known. His mother had died in childbirth and he had been entrusted to the care of a maiden aunt. When his father failed to return from the gas-filled trenches of the First War she had regarded it as little short of personal betrayal. It confirmed her long-held view, gained one clumsy afternoon as a teenager in a hayrick, that all men were capable only of deception, and from that moment she never again spoke to another except when absolutely necessary. All her attention was lavished on the boy whom she would raise in her own image, the one man who would never descend into lust and betray her. It hadn't worked, of course.

She had kept him isolated and away from the corrupting influence of friends, ensuring that he grew up at first in awe and eventually in hate of her, until the self-righteous demands and accusations of ingratitude she cast at him had broken their bonds completely and he had been left on his own. So he had built himself a new life. He had lived his lost childhood through his young pupils, recapturing the dreams that had been stolen from him and devoting himself to the tasks of teaching with immense enthusiasm, combined with a degree of sensitivity and understanding that surprised those who knew nothing of his background. And few did, for outside school Hencke was intensely private, a man who insisted on the right to build his own world into which others were not invited until they had earned his trust, and he had convinced himself they would not infect the wounds left unhealed by his aunt. At last, in the small Sudeten town of Asch, he thought he had found happiness. Then the war forced its way across his doorstep and the world he had so painstakingly built for himself had been blasted away, leaving nothing but fragments. After that there had been nowhere left to hide. Pilsudski had tried to strip away his sense of personal security and hope, but he was too late. Others had got there first.

Yet he needed Pilsudski, with all his grotesque savagery. Hencke had stood in line, waiting his turn, feeling the harsh wind lash his back and the tightening of apprehension in his body as he drew closer to the table and its guards, but he had experienced neither fear nor outrage. Instead there was a sense of relief, of opportunity. The degradation itself left him empty, cold; he knew there were worse fates in war. Yet he also knew that stripping away their manhood had made the others malleable; it was precisely the effect Pilsudski wanted, but Hencke understood that he might turn it to his own advantage. Within each of the crouched and humbled figures around the prison camp burned a sense of outrage which, if harnessed, might turn them once more into a force of terrible retribution – his retribution. Hencke needed these men.

There was little enough chance with them, none at all without them.

As he looked across the flickering glow of a dozen tiny campfires and the hunched shoulders of those he wanted for his own personal cause, Hencke understood that the inevitable price of failure in war, even a war so near its end, would be death. But he knew he would have to risk it, risk everything, if his mission were to succeed. Even if it meant his being the last man to die . . .

TWO

Cazolet squeezed on to the narrow seat and tried to make himself comfortable. He knew he had no chance of succeeding. When the House of Commons had been hit by a stray Luftwaffe bomb in 1941, the team of firefighters, already sadly depleted by the firestorms blazing around London, had faced the choice of saving either the Commons or the more ancient and gracious construction of neighbouring Westminster Hall. The comfort of politicians was balanced in the scales against the preservation of an important part of the nation's Tudor heritage, and there was never any contest. The Commons had been left to burn until it was gutted.

For a while this had caused considerable disruption until the members of the House of Lords came to the rescue and gave over to their common-born colleagues the facilities of the undamaged Upper Chamber, a still more impressive Gothic edifice than the one left smouldering in ruins. Yet their hospitality had not stretched to the civil servants who accompany ministers, and so Cazolet and his kind were condemned to squashing on to a row of hard wooden stools tucked away in one corner. Not even the glories of uninhibited Victorian craftsmanship could do much to distract from the numbness that crept over Cazolet's body less than ten minutes after perching on one of those hideous stools. Still, today he had other distractions and for once had forgotten that he could feel little from his shirt tail down.

An air of expectation filled the Chamber. Members of Parliament, many of them in the uniforms of the armed forces in which they served, bustled to find themselves a

40

position on the red leather benches while others loitered around the extravagantly carved oak canopy covering the sovereign's throne. Something was up. The word had gone round that the Prime Minister was coming to the House to make an important statement, and everyone wanted to be in on it. Cazolet sat with a conspiratorial smile; these were the times he found his job so rewarding, when the whole world seemed to wait upon a prime ministerial statement, a statement which Cazolet himself had drafted. And this one was going to be a cracker.

The Prime Minister walked purposefully into the Chamber, conspicuous in full morning dress with flowing coat tails, a spotted and loosely secured bow tie at his throat and his father's gold watch fob stretched across the front of his waistcoat. The outfit was not new, indeed it gave the solid impression of having been made for him at least twenty years earlier, since it bulged and stretched in too many places. It should have been replaced long ago, but he felt comfortable in it. Anyway, Clemmie was always nagging him to be less extravagant.

No sooner had he found his place on the front bench than he was given the floor. 'Mr Speaker, I pray the House will forgive the exuberance of my attire,' he began, a thumb stuck firmly in his waistcoat pocket. The Old Man was teasing them, keeping them waiting, building up the atmosphere. 'I have not, as some Honourable Members might conclude, come straight from the racecourse' – there was a ripple of polite laughter. It wasn't a very good joke, but if he could begin with any form of joke the news must be exceptional – 'but from an audience with His Majesty the King. Just an hour or so ago I received news which I thought it only right to share with him and with the House at the first possible opportunity.'

'He's called an election,' someone shouted from the back benches. It was a Labour MP renowned for his ready heckle, and Churchill rose willingly to the bait as more laughter washed across the House.

'No, sir! The Honourable Gentleman must contain his impatience. He reminds me of a Black Widow spider, anxious for his date with destiny but who will undoubtedly discover that his love affair with the electorate will end only in his being brutally devoured.'

The Old Man was in good form, and there was general waving of Order Papers around the Chamber. The antagonisms of partisan politics had been laid to one side during the lifetime of the coalition government which Churchill led, but they were never far below the surface and were getting less restrained as it became apparent that an election and a return to normal parliamentary hostilities must be only weeks away.

'Mr Speaker, sir, the whole House will know that a few days ago the Allied armies reached the western bank of the Rhine, the historical border of Germany.' A low chorus of approval rose from the MPs, but Churchill quickly raised his hand to silence them. His tone had grown suddenly more serious. 'No one could have been in any doubt that the crossing of the Rhine would be a deeply hazardous enterprise, with all the bridges across that vast river destroyed and the Nazi armies fighting fanatically to protect the homeland with their own towns and villages at their backs.' He paused while he took a large linen handkerchief from the pocket of his trousers to clear his nose, and the habitual crease that ran down the centre of his forehead deepened into a frown. The Chamber was completely silent. Was it bad news after all? He had them all in his grasp – all, that is, except Cazolet, who was having ever more trouble containing his smile as he watched his master trifling with their emotions.

'The Rhine is the last great barrier standing between our armies and complete victory. I have to tell this House that late last night a junior officer, a lieutenant, of the United States First Army, succeeded in' – he hesitated slightly, toying with the words – 'walking across a bridge at a small town called Remagen. It appears that the Germans, in their anxiety, failed to blow the bridge properly. Mr Speaker, the Rhine has been crossed. We have a bridgehead on German soil!'

The announcement was greeted with an outpouring of relief and jubilation on all sides, many Members rising to their feet to applaud and others shaking the hands of opponents they would normally have difficulty addressing in a civil tone. Churchill stood, triumphant in their midst, yet wishing for all the world that he were young again and could exchange his role for that of the lowly American lieutenant.

Once he had resumed his seat, other MPs rose to offer their congratulations and thoughts, giving the Prime Minister fresh opportunity to bask in the sun of military success.

'What did you advise the King?' asked one.

The Prime Minister's demeanour was full of mischief. 'The House may not know that in the dark days of 1940 I gave His Majesty a carbine, for his own personal use in the event of invasion.' His eyes twinkled. 'I advised him that it was my firm opinion he would no longer need it.'

They loved it. Churchill's sole regret was that he couldn't hold the election instantly in the midst of such unqualified rejoicing. More questions, more praise. No one expected other than further fulsome accolades when Captain the Honourable Gerald Wickham-Browne, MC, DSM, caught the Speaker's attention. The captain, junior scion of minor aristocracy, had lost an eye during the retreat from Dunkirk yet still managed to regard military combat with the sort of unrestrained enthusiasm normally found only amongst schoolchildren at a cup final. He was on his feet, standing in military fashion, hands clasped behind his back and black eye-patch thrust proudly towards the distant ceiling. But he was not a happy man.

'Is the Prime Minister aware, as delighted as I am to hear the news, that the honour of being the first to cross the Rhine was to have been left to British troops under General Montgomery? While of course we are delighted at the Americans' good fortune in being able simply to walk across' – Cazolet marvelled at how Wickham-Browne man-

43

aged to make it sound as if a mongrel had run off with a string of prize sausages – 'what is now to be the role of British troops, who have been preparing for months for the storming of the Rhine and who by sheer bad luck have been denied their share of this triumph? Are we to get anything by way of . . .' He hesitated, unsure of the most appropriate word, before deciding it didn't matter a damn anyway. ' . . . compensation?'

Churchill rose to respond, his chin working up and down as he sought for the words of his reply, rubbing his thumbs in the palms of his hands in instinctive search for the cigar he wished he were smoking. 'Let us not quibble over the fortunes of war. It is enough that the Rhine has been crossed. But let us not forget what this event has proved to us. First, that German resistance is crumbling. And second, that if we can pursue the battle with speed and flexibility, and can grasp the opportunities which confusion and indiscipline amongst the enemy may present, then nothing can stop our march across Germany. I have no doubt that now is the moment of our greatest opportunity, and that British forces will be in the vanguard of the victory which is surely to come. I have already telegraphed my sincerest congratulations to General Eisenhower and told him that our troops stand ready for the next challenge. Onward! Nothing can stop us now!'

At times of great crisis, words can be more powerful than bullets. Churchill had proved that time and again during the days of the Blitz when he had precious few bullets and little else with which to resist the enemy and to maintain British morale. He was conscious of the effect his words could have, yet, as he resumed his seat to the congratulations of his parliamentary colleagues, he had not the slightest notion of the impact they were causing several hundred miles away, at the Supreme Headquarters of the Allied Expeditionary Forces, where his congratulatory telegram was bursting into fire like a grenade thrown through the window.

'What in God's name is this crap?' The message trembled in Eisenhower's hand.

44

British troops are ready ... Now is the moment to swarm across the bridgehead at Remagen ...

The flush of anger was spreading across his face as he read every new sentence. The adjutant who had delivered the telegram took another precautionary step backwards; the general was reputed to have an unreliable temper, and he didn't care to be around to suffer the uncertain consequences.

German resistance and morale may collapse if you strike before the enemy has time to regroup ...

Eisenhower continued to quote from Churchill's missive. 'Shit, doesn't he realize we've got less than two hundred men perched on that bridgehead and they could get blown away at any time? If we put so much as another pack of paperclips across that stinking bridge it'll collapse into the river. What'll happen then? Our guys on the bridgehead become sandwich meat, that's what!'

Suddenly he pounded his head as if to inflict punishment on himself. 'What a fool I am ... Losing my wits. Why didn't I realize straight away what that scheming old bastard was up to?' He read on.

The arguments for a direct drive on the German capital become irresistible. Let us drive down the autobahns which Hitler himself has built and not dare to stop until we have reached Berlin.

'Berlin! So that's still his game.'

He turned in his chair and screamed through the open door into the next office to his chief of staff. 'Beetle! Get in here and bring a stenographer. I want to send a reply.'

Lieutenant General Walter Bedell Smith and the stenographer scuttled in without a word and perched in front of Eisenhower. There they sat, with pencils poised, for several long moments while Eisenhower remained lost in thought.

45

Ice seemed to have taken the place of the fires within him. Eventually Bedell Smith could stand the uncertainty no longer.

'Changed your mind?'

Eisenhower raised his head from his thoughts and looked at him with piercing blue eyes.

'Beetle, how do I say "Fuck You" in British?'

The commander tapped his stick against the chair to demand silence. In the darkness of the night the entire prisoner complement of Transit Camp 174B huddled together on the exercise square in search of companionship and warmth, forming a human amphitheatre around the flames of an open fire. Their expectations were not high; they knew that whatever the commander had to say would bring little comfort. An *Ehrenrat* had been called, a 'Council of Elders', and that only happened when there was a real mess.

The commander was seated at their head, with his two senior officers on either side and several others standing behind. He was leaning on his stick even while seated, the flicker from the fire casting a lurid mask across his face like a player in a tragedy.

'My friends,' the commander began. They noticed that he had forsaken his customary formal greeting – 'Men of the Wehrmacht!'; there was no suggestion of command in his voice. 'My friends, I have gathered you all together to share with you the news I was given today. I can find no words to lessen the pain, and so I . . .' He lowered his head, struggling for composure and fresh strength. He cleared his throat, as if the words were sticking in his gullet like phlegm.

'The Russians are fighting on German soil. They are already well advanced into Pomerania, and have crossed the Oder. They are less than a hundred miles from the *Hauptstadt*, Berlin.'

The words carved like a razor through their midst as damp wood spat on the burning pyre, cremating their last hope of salvation. No one bothered to contest the news, to pretend

46

it was enemy propaganda. Such bravado belonged to the days when they had bombers in the air and food in their bellies, and those days were long since gone. They all understood what the news meant. Many of them had fought on the Russian Front, had seen the bestiality with which the Russian peasant soldiers treated captured Wehrmacht and civilians alike. They had found the mass graves of butchered officers, shot in the back of the head, of the women raped and mutilated, of the children slaughtered for no reason other than they had got in the way. The Russians knew only one way of fighting war, to the bitter end, and that end was now in sight. Cossacks were swarming into their homeland, penetrating their villages and their women, pillaging everything and everyone in their path. They, the soldiers of the Wehrmacht, had failed and their loved ones would pay the price.

'I'm so sorry,' was all the commander could find to say. He fell into silence until it became oppressive and he had to find something else to break it. 'My only satisfaction is that you have survived. You are brave men, I have fought and served with many of you. *We have survived.* Perhaps we may yet have the opportunity of rebuilding our country . . .'

He trailed off in a savage fit of coughing. There was shrapnel in his lungs and in other vital parts of his body, and to a man they knew that whatever might lie in store for the rest of them, the commander was fading fast. They had all seen the tell-tale translucence of the skin clinging to his skull and the bloodstains on his handkerchief. Only his pride and sense of duty had kept him going thus far. In sympathy and silent embarrassment they watched the commander bring up a little more of his fading life.

They stood around aimlessly, staring silently into the flames, dispirited and without hope, lost in contemplation of a homeland far away until they were distracted by the sight of one of their number stepping into the middle of the circle surrounding the fire. He wore the tattered uniform of an oberleutnant in some tank regiment – it was impossible to tell which; almost all the insignia were missing. Neverthe-

47

less he was a striking-looking figure, tall, lean to the point of gauntness, his cropped black hair parted near the middle so that it stood up in a defiant, almost disrespectful manner before flopping across the forehead of his long face. His features were finely carved as if sculpted from smooth clay, his cheekbones high – looks that suggested intelligence and sensitivity which seemed out of place in the middle of a band of warriors. Yet he had obviously seen combat, and sported a scar through the top of his lip which dragged one edge of his mouth downward, giving the impression of a perpetual sardonic smile. There was suffering in the face, and nowhere more clearly than in the eyes which were remarkably dark and deep-set as if trying to keep their distance from the world. They were careworn from more than just the numbing tiredness of past combat, yet as the commander gazed at him they became almost transparent. He felt he was peering right into the man's inner soul, and inside he could see the flicker of fire. There was passion and anger in this man. The prisoner snapped to attention.

'Permission to speak, sir?'

'You are . . . ?'

'My name is Hencke, sir.'

The commander nodded for him to continue.

'I have family in the east, in the Sudetenland. For all I know, the Russians are there already.' There were sympathetic nods from amongst the men. 'Your pardon, Commander, but I'm not content to sit idly back on my ass comforting myself in the thought that I am a survivor while those I love face the Russians. Sir!'

The reprimand implicit in his words and the rough language used to his commanding officer caused a stir of anger, but the commander waved it away. He was too tired to fight, particularly with one of his own men.

'I intended no sense of satisfaction in what I said, Hencke, but survival is all we have to look forward to. I fear there is little other choice.'

'I believe we always have a choice . . .' The sting of accusation in his voice had guaranteed him a hearing, but now he had their attention and his voice softened. 'Sir, it is the duty of German officers to resist. It is an oath of duty which we have all taken and which still, to us all, should be sacred.'

'An oath to generals and politicians who got us into this mess?' a voice interrupted from the darkness at the edge of the fire.

Hencke turned in the direction of the questioner. He had begun addressing the whole group, not just reporting to his senior officer, holding centre stage in the midst of an audience he could scarcely see in the night gloom. His gaze travelled around the group slowly, deliberately, piercing through the darkness, probing like a scalpel into their inner thoughts. 'I agree. What have our beloved generals and politicians done for me? I haven't even got buttons to do up my flies anymore, and my proudest possession is the piece of string I use for a belt. It's difficult marching unquestioningly behind your leaders with your trousers round your ankles – present commanders excepted, sir.'

A stirring of appreciation rustled through the prisoners.

'Whether our leaders have let us down or not, my oath of duty wasn't taken for their personal benefit but for my country and for those I left behind. It's them I'm interested in. They are the ones who deserve our help. And we're doing nothing to help them sitting round here scratching ourselves and gossiping about three "Fs".'

'Three "Fs"?' enquired the commander wearily.

'Er, "Food", "Freedom" and . . . "Females", sir,' one of his subordinates leaned over to advise him.

'Forget the females. I'd sell my mother for a tin of corned beef,' a voice volunteered from out of the shadows to general approval.

'Tell me, Hencke,' the commander continued. 'I share your frustration. But what on earth can we do? This is a prison camp, for God's sake.'

'We can roll over and let the guards kick us whenever they feel bored. We can continue to scrabble around in the mud for the scraps of food they choose to throw at us, hoping they'll get so tired of all this that one day they will simply throw open the gates and let us struggle back home. "One day. Some day. Never",' he mimicked the words of a song of lost love popular in Germany. 'In the meantime what are we left with? "Wag your tail" – "Lick my boots" – "Sit up and beg" – "*Bend over*".' He was moving around the circle, peering into the faces of the prisoners as he threw the guards' taunts at them. None returned his stare. 'Or we can remind our captors that we are still German soldiers, that simply because they wish to treat us like dogs there's no need for us to act like dogs. Show them that we're not garbage, that we're not here just for them to piss on whenever they feel like a bit of fun. OK, they may have captured us, but for God's sake don't allow them to crush us. Let's show that we're still men!'

'How? In Heaven's name, how can we resist in here?' The commander swung his cane around to indicate the barbed wire surrounding them.

'Not in here, sir. Out there.'

'What? You mean . . .'

'Escape.'

'But that's preposterous, Hencke. No German has managed to escape from Britain back to Germany through the course of this entire war. Not a single one! And you are willing to risk your life gambling against odds like that?'

'It's better than staying here to have a finger shoved up my ass. Sir.'

'I cannot allow you to escape, Hencke. It would be folly.'

'I'm not suggesting that I escape, sir. I'm suggesting we all do.'

His words hit the assembly like ice water, and the men began to shake themselves as if to get rid of an unwelcome drenching.

'Think about it, just for a second,' Hencke continued, anxious not to lose their attention as he walked, cat-like, around the circle. 'It's because no one's ever escaped that it

50

makes such sense. The guards are lazy and idle, and the last thing they expect is trouble. And if we all get out, the confusion will be huge, there'll be a far greater chance of at least one of us making it back.'

'It's worth a shot,' someone prompted.

'That's all you're likely to get – shot!' retorted the commander, wiping spittle from his lips. He had seen so much unnecessary death, his conscience couldn't take responsibility for permitting still more.

'Sir, when did you ever hear of a German POW being shot after trying to escape? These British are sticklers for the rules. Twenty-eight days solitary is the maximum they're allowed to throw at us.'

'Yes, but these Canadians don't play by the rule book . . .'

'This is the opportunity we've been waiting for to get our own back. What the hell are the Canadians going to do if they lose an entire campful of prisoners? More to the point, what are the British going to do to the Canadians? It's our chance to get our own back, to catch *them* with their trousers down!'

'Oh, yes. It'd screw the *verdammten* Canadians rigid,' a prisoner applauded. 'I'd just like to see Pilsudski's face the morning after. I'd risk anything for that.'

'But what purpose would it achieve?' the commander began, lacking the strength to join in the enthusiasm that was beginning to bloom around him.

'It would show our loved ones back home that, whatever they are about to go through, we have not forgotten them,' Hencke responded quietly, his words massaging away the doubts. 'Anyway, what's the alternative? Staying behind for more of this!' He stuck his middle finger in the air, imitating the gesture Pilsudski had thrown at the commander, and a shiver of fury cut through the assembly.

The commanding officer could sense the change of mood and motivation amongst his men. A chance to revenge the humiliation, to end the despair, no longer to be Pilsudski's catamites. To become whole men once again. It was his duty to stop it, of course; it was folly. But he no longer had the energy to resist. He sat, head resting in exhaustion on the top of his cane, unable to find any further protest while those around him chattered away with more animation and spirit than they had found since entering Camp 174B.

Hencke smiled grimly. The escape was on. His mission had begun.

Churchill attempted to wipe the dribble of rich gravy from his waistcoat with a crisp linen napkin, but all his effort served only to impregnate the grease more firmly into the fibre. He gave up the unequal struggle; the stain wouldn't be noticed, anyway, amongst all the rest. Perhaps he should have felt a prick of conscience surrounded by so much good food while most of the country were struggling on a weekly meat ration that looked no more appetizing than a Trafalgar Square pigeon, and eating breakfasts concocted from powdered egg that had the consistency of fast-drying concrete and much the same impact on the digestive system. Still, he could no more stand the pace on an empty stomach than he could run a war without shedding blood. Conscience often had to go into cold storage. So he would enjoy his food and his bathtime and continue to exhort others to use no more than five inches of water.

The Old Man was content. A few close friends, their wives glittering in all their pre-war finery, made an attentive audience. The ten diners had just finished demolishing a haunch of venison shot a few days previously on the Scottish estate of the host, Sir William Muirhead, and ferried down to London for the occasion. Runner beans from the hot-houses of Cornwall had also been served, bought off-ration but at lavish price, and washed down with a splendid claret. The war had played merry hell with current French vintages, but the best stock had been well preserved, stored deep in cellars, far out of reach of the Luftwaffe. All part of God's great plan, mused Churchill as he finished another glass.

'Seems that the flood of American soldiers through London

is playing havoc with prices in the West End,' chirped Sir William's wife. That afternoon she had come back from an expedition to Fortnum's, bemoaning the fact that not only had their prices for afternoon tea gone up but, far worse, she'd had to queue for more than ten minutes behind a group of GIs before getting a table. They had even left their tip, not discreetly under the plate but on top, right out for everyone to see. So vulgar.

'Makes a change from the Free French, I suppose,' Churchill pouted through a lopsided, indulgent grin.

Lady Muirhead failed to notice the glint in his eye. 'I'm sorry, Winston?'

'Prices in the West End. The Free French. Apparently every street-walker in London claims to belong to the Free French. Although scarcely any of them are French. And none of them, so I'm told, are free!'

There was general laughter as the PM relaxed amongst old friends, only the long-suffering Clemmie showing little appreciation. She'd heard it all before.

Another of the wives joined in. 'Do you know, I heard the other day that a bus full of schoolchildren had been brought into the West End to see the lights turned on, now the black-out has been lifted. Seems they were all terrified. Never seen anything like it before. Burst into tears and demanded to be taken back home.'

The laughter was less genuine, and Churchill chose not to join in. The comment had been silly and insensitive. What was there to laugh about with a generation of children brought up in a world of darkness and fear, where even the half-lights allowed by the new regulations caused confusion and misery? It was going to take a very long time to get back to normal after this war; indeed, it would take an effort as great as the war itself to rebuild what had been shattered. Did the country – did he – still have the fight for it? He thought of the forthcoming election once more, and that feeling of nervousness returned.

His host noticed the faraway look beginning to creep into

Churchill's eye and decided to intervene. 'Winston, I think it's time for a toast,' he said, refilling the Old Man's glass. 'I sometimes wondered whether we would ever reach this point, but at last it seems as if the war is almost over. We've won – no, *you've* won the war, Winston. I know those Yankee interlopers have come in for the finish, just like they did last time, and will no doubt claim much of the credit . . .'

'Just like they did last time!' someone added.

'But it wouldn't have happened, *couldn't* have happened without you and what you've done. I know there will be many more toasts in the weeks and months ahead, but as an old friend it would do me great honour if this could be the first.' He raised his glass. 'To you, Winston. With our thanks for winning the war.'

It was a genuine accolade, made all the more poignant because as an old friend there was no need for Muirhead to have made the gesture. There was a mutter of appreciation from around the table as the others joined in, and already Churchill's eyes were brimming with tears. He wiped the trickle away with the flat of his hand.

'Not quite over yet, you know. Still all to play for,' was the only response he seemed able to mount as Clemmie reached over to pat her own tribute.

'Still all to play for', Churchill heard the echo in his mind. Was it so? Eisenhower's response to his telegram, received that afternoon, had been blunt. 'Keeping all options open,' it had said. 'Review the situation on an ongoing basis . . . No rush to judgement.' All the cliches at which an American military mind could clutch. But in the event, Eisenhower's unwillingness to impair his authority over military matters had been clear and uncompromising. The hard facts were inescapable.

'I have not won this war, Bill,' Churchill continued, in a tone that dampened the reverie around the table. He waved down the polite protest of his host. 'Perhaps historians will be kind, and maybe it will be said that I prevented us from losing the war after Dunkirk. But look around us. Look not just at the West End of London, but across the battlefields of Europe. This war is now an American war, fought with American guns, American money and American lives. Today they have more troops engaged in combat than the whole of the British Empire. It is the Americans who will win this war, eventually. And, I fear, it is they who will be largely responsible for the peace.'

'Why do you fear it, Winston?'

'Because I am British, and would rather follow a British leader than an American. And because of the Americans' great generosity of spirit.'

'That's a fault?'

'Oh, like all things taken to excess, it can be.' He reflected into his champagne for a moment, then glanced towards his wife with a sheepish smile on his face. 'Clemmie, I have never told you this story, but we are too old to have secrets from each other.' She knew that to be a huge exaggeration, but chose not to contest the point. 'Many years ago when I was out of office, I was on a visit to the United States. I went to the Wall Street headquarters of a Mr Bernard Baruch, a Jewish financier who has become one of our dearest friends. And you will understand why . . . Barney showed me around his offices, and the new electronic equipment he had recently installed with which he was able to trade stocks and shares automatically. I was much taken by it and I asked to try my hand. It was like a wonderful new card game and, as my darling wife knows, I have a fondness for an occasional gamble.'

Clementine's eyebrows arched. Everyone around the table knew of the friction his gambling had caused. The Churchills had never been particularly wealthy, yet the Old Man's gaming spirit had always been intense. It was one of several vices he had inherited from his father.

'In those days I was inexperienced, less mature, and I admit that I was taken by the excitement of the chase as I tried to outwit the other traders. But no sooner had I begun to believe I had mastered the process than I discovered, to my horror, that it was too late. I had already lost. Not just a small sum of money but my entire fortune. One minute all that I had struggled to accumulate in the world was safe and the next, it was gone. I remember sitting at the desk looking out over the skyscape of Wall Street, contemplating the horror of returning to England to tell you, my darling, that I would have to sell Chartwell and everything else we possessed.'

There was a sense of embarrassment around the table, as if the others were intruding on the Churchills' private grief. Yet there had to be a point to the story.

'Then the door opened and in walked Baruch. How was I doing, he enquired, and I felt constrained to tell him. My entire fortune lost, my career inevitably at an end. He smiled, laughed! My plight seemed to him nothing more than a huge joke. Then he told me that was precisely what he expected would happen, that I was the Archangel rather than Mammon, and that I would never be a match for the likes of him. "Mr Baruch," I said, "my poor wife will have considerable difficulty agreeing with you about my heavenly qualities."' Churchill cast mournful eyes in the direction of Clementine, who was uncertain whether to smile dutifully or tear him limb from limb. 'So Baruch continued: "That is why I gave my office instructions that every time you bought, I would sell, and every time you sold, I would buy. Don't worry, your fortune is safe!"'

'Goodness me, Winston, you had us all quite terrified for a moment,' one of the ladies twittered. 'But I suppose it was a blessing in disguise.'

'Very effectively disguised at the time, I thought. It was the first occasion in my life that I realized I was neither omniscient nor immortal. That I had much which I could learn from our "Yankee interlopers". That they were generous to a fault. And how generously they are still giving.'

There were nods of approval around the table at the tribute, but even as he paid it Churchill could not but remember the words of Eisenhower's response. Far from pouring through the bridgehead at Remagen, the Supreme Allied Commander was being cautious, blaming the fragile state of the bridge, stating that it would take several days before it was clear whether the bridgehead would hold. So British troops in the north who were ready to advance on Berlin would have to continue sitting on their backsides while Eisenhower's penpushers dithered about whether US troops had enough prophylactics and nylons for the battle ahead. Damn the man! The war wasn't over yet and he wasn't ready to watch American generosity give away everything he had fought for. As he poured himself a brandy, Churchill made up his mind. He wasn't going to let go. He would have one more direct assault on Eisenhower. One way or another, they would get to Berlin first!

Dinner that night at Camp 174B had been a particularly quiet affair. Not that a mixture of sausage, canned herring and white bread eaten out of an empty corned beef tin and washed down with a mug of tea ever excited great enthusiasm, but the guards were grateful it had been finished rapidly. It left more time for a game of cards and a quiet cigarette.

It was shortly before dusk when one of the Canadian captors' attention had been attracted by a soldier beckoning in his direction from the shadows of a tent. As he approached he saw the prisoner held a watch in his hand; it was to be a trade. Another kraut who wanted extra rations or a dry pair of boots.

They moved behind the tent to put themselves away from the general body of prisoners. Illicit trading like this went on all the time, but it paid to be cautious. You didn't want the whole world to know that you were getting a genuine Swiss watch with twelve diamonds in the movement for the price of a couple of packs of cigarettes. But this deal was proving tricky. It was an excellent watch, one of the best the guard had seen in the camp, but the prisoner was demanding a ridiculous price.

It was as they were bent over in heated discussion, the guard wondering whether he should just confiscate the thing anyway, that he felt the cold touch of steel on the back of his neck.

'Don't try to be a hero. Just do as you're told, friend,' a voice said in heavily accented English. 'Put down your rifle slowly.'

He tried to turn round but the steel jabbed into his neck. 'I'll blow your head off if you try anything stupid.'

'You can't have got a gun – even if you had you wouldn't dare use it,' the Canadian protested, the uncertainty flooding through.

'You're going to gamble your life on it?'

'What do you want?'

'Your rifle laid on the ground, very slowly.'

'Or else?'

'Or else you die, my friend.'

Shit, why did it have to be him? The war nearly over, soon back to the farm outside Calgary with lots of silly stories to impress the girls about how he personally beat Hitler and won the war. And there would be no damn medals for getting his balls blown off in this God-forsaken part of Britain, a million miles from the front. Slowly, very slowly, he bent down and placed his rifle on the ground.

'Wise move, soldier.'

The guard didn't even have time to stand erect. No sooner was his hand away from the trigger than he was hit from behind with the heavy metal bracket that had been wrenched from a camp bed and held against his neck. It wasn't a very good imitation gun, but now it didn't matter. They had a real one, and a guard's uniform. All the tools they hoped they would need . . .

The brandy was flowing, and Churchill was once again in excellent humour. The women had withdrawn to another room, leaving the men to their own devices. In the absence of the ladies it had been confirmed that prices in the West End had indeed soared, and the only thing the whores were offering free was abuse.

'It was the same during the last war,' Muirhead confirmed, to the amusement of his guests. 'Nothing changes.'

'My dear sir, but it does,' Churchill interjected forcefully, wagging his cigar across the table and scattering ash everywhere. 'How well I remember, when I had returned from the Boer War, I received several very encouraging propositions from such ladies who made it abundantly clear that there would be no charge. I can only ascribe the present unhappy bout of inflation in the West End to a sad decline in values.' He chortled along with the rest, enjoying his own joke.

'That was rather special,' Muirhead chided. 'You had been chased across half of Africa by the entire Boer army.'

This was why the Old Man enjoyed Muirhead's dinners; the host always made a point of giving him plenty of scope for relating some of his favourite stories.

'Tell us about it,' one of the guests encouraged him and, hesitating only to give a perfunctory cough of modesty, the Old Man was off.

'The Boer' – he pronounced it 'Booa', as if to emphasize the race's reputation for thick-headed stubbornness – 'the Boer has so little imagination. There I was, a simple war correspondent doing my duty and armed with no more than a sharp pencil, when they apprehended me on manoeuvres, threw me into one of their wretched prison camps with the preposterous suggestion that I was some spy or saboteur. For all I knew I was going to be dragged off and shot. Anyway, I hated their diet of maize and dried beef, I would simply have faded away. So you see, my escape was not a matter of bravery. I had no choice in the matter. My stomach insisted.' He smiled, using his fingers to pop a little cube of cheese into his mouth which he chewed with relish. 'The only problem was that I was many hundreds of miles away from safety, and the Boers, alarmed at my impudence and the example I might set others, put a price on my head which grew with every passing day. "Winston Churchill: Dead or Alive". If only the British electorate had wanted me as passionately as

59

the Boers!' He paused to pour a little mountain of salt from the silver cellar on to some claret he had earlier spilled across the tablecloth, but it was already too late. The stain had dried.

'So how did you manage to make good your escape?'

'There is one great rule for an escapee on the run. Never do the predictable. Government authorities, and particularly Boer authorities, are slow-moving and ponderous. They think along narrow lines. So when they expected me to take the short, direct route to safety, I went the long way round. When they thought I would take a straight line, I took a crooked one. They cannot cope with the unexpected. Why, at one point when I was in Pretoria, hopelessly lost and confused about which road might lead to the railway station, I solved the problem very simply. I marched right up and asked a Boer policeman!'

While the other guests chuckled, Churchill paused to scratch his crotch with a total lack of self-consciousness. His table manners were atrocious. He had long ago ceased to bother about such trivial things, and when Clemmie had forcefully reprimanded him he had justified his behaviour as the self-indulgence of an old man. Anyway, he countered, it hadn't caused any slackening in the flood of dinner invitations.

'Seriously, Winston. If you had been captured you most certainly would have been shot, if only to discourage others. Why did you risk your life? Was it really that important?'

'I never realized how important until I returned home, where I found that my escape had been the focus of the newspapers' attention for weeks. Unwittingly I had become a hero of the nation and my escape had succeeded in bolstering the determination of the entire country to continue with the war until victory. It is a matter of morale, and you cannot fight a war without morale. As one editor kindly wrote, "One man, by his actions and example, can so inspire a nation that he will light a fire across a whole continent".'

A look of sheer wickedness crept into his eye. 'And, as I discovered, he can get a good discount into the bargain!'

The camp was in darkness. There were no lights along the perimeter fence and the only illumination came from within the old football changing rooms, which now served as a guard hut, and from the bright moon. But it was a blustery night with clouds scudding across the sky. Had any of the guards bothered to look they would have found shadowy figures flitting between the tents, playing hide-and-seek in the sporadic moonlight, but most of the Canadians were relaxing in the guard hut. There were just four guards on the main gate into the compound, and two patrolling the walkway between the double perimeter fence. Guard duty was a pain; there had never been any trouble and no prisoner in his right mind would want to escape back to the hell pit they'd just left in Europe. They were all, prisoners and guards alike, marking time till the fighting was over.

So when, from inside the shadowy compound, the pair patrolling the perimeter walkway saw one of their number beckoning to them, no suspicion was aroused. He had probably found two prisoners screwing each other or some other bit of fun to enliven the endless night hours of cold and boredom. They let themselves in the compound through a side gate in the wire; they didn't even think twice that the gateway was shielded from the main guard house across the compound by the prisoners' tents. After all, they hadn't put the tents there. Even after they darted between two of the tents and came face to face with their fellow guard pointing his Lee Enfield straight at them, they were still not concerned. It was only when they heard the familiar click of a round being forced into the chamber that they realized all was not well, and not until the moon had squeezed briefly between the clouds and fallen across Hencke's lean and determined face did they realize that this was not, after all, going to be their night.

'You're not . . .' one gasped in sudden understanding. But

it was too late. They had already raised their hands and were being relieved of their weapons.

'I . . . don't want to die,' the youngest guard blubbed as his wrists were tied behind him with a length of guy rope.

'Keep your miserable mouth shut and you won't have to,' a prisoner responded. The young guard was almost relieved when he felt the gag pushed firmly between his teeth.

The guards' legs were pinioned and they were bundled into the corner of one of the tents. It was only when the prisoners were leaving that one of them remembered. 'You're the miserable little bastard who held my head down on the table the other day, aren't you?' The youngster's eyes, all that could be seen above the gag, showed large and white. He was petrified. 'I'll never forget that. You were laughing your head off.' The prisoner swung back a leg as if to smash his testicles. None of the other prisoners did or said anything to stop him; the guard deserved everything he got. But as the German looked at the whimpering body on the ground in front of him, he seemed to change his mind. He spat in disgust and turned on his heel. Escape would be revenge enough.

A few minutes later a group of men moved towards the guard house, eight prisoners being marched sullenly along with three uniformed guards, rifles at the ready, escorting them from the rear.

'Open the gate!' one of the guards shouted. 'Got a bunch of troublemakers who need a little gentle reminding of who's in charge of this friggin' camp.'

The gates swung open and the prisoners marched through. The duty sergeant nodded as they approached, his rifle slung over his back as he took a drag from a cigarette. He waved a lazy torch in their direction. Hencke was standing directly in front of him before the beam fell across his face.

'Heil Hitler,' Hencke snapped.

'What . . . ?' was the only word the sergeant managed to expel before a rifle butt thumped him in the gut, putting him on the floor and rendering him incapable of any noise except a low gurgling retch. Around him the other guards were receiving similar treatment before being trussed and dragged off to join their companions in the tent.

The prisoners now had seven rifles. They also had surprise on their side and there was scarcely a protest when they burst into the guard hut and overpowered sixteen other guards. The seventeenth, the captain on duty, was taking a shower and thought the interruption was some prank by the other guards. He was not in good temper when he stepped from under the water to remonstrate, with nothing more than a sponge to maintain the dignity he thought due his senior rank. He was in even poorer temper after he had been bound and, minus even his sponge, dumped with the other captive guards.

'I'll freeze to death,' he complained.

'Be grateful that dying will take you so long,' came the response, after which the captain ceased protesting and saved his energy for trying to burrow as deeply as possible into the pile of warm bodies inside the tent.

The break-out had been conducted with ruthless German team work, but now it was every man for himself. They knew the prospects were not good; there had been no time for preparations. There was no civilian clothing, no maps, precious little food or money, what chance did they have? But they were free. Even an hour of freedom was enough. It would be a night to remember.

'Seeing the look on that stupid captain's face made it all worth while for me,' one of the prisoners smiled, pausing to shake Hencke's hand. 'The only pity is that Pilsudski's not around for a little of his own treatment. Still, maybe he'll get all that from his court martial. Thanks, Hencke. We owe you,' he said before turning to jog through the camp gates and into the unknown.

Then the commander was in front of him, bent over his stick. 'Good wishes, Hencke. It's madness, but lots of luck.'

Hencke looked into the other's exhausted face, then down at his stick.

'I'm not going anywhere, you know that,' the commander

said. 'Wouldn't make it past the gate and I'd only be a burden. I'm going to stay here, if you don't mind, and wait till the relief guard arrives in the morning. It will be enough for me to see what happens to Pilsudski when the British discover they've got the biggest prisoner escape of the war on their hands. Might stretch even their sense of humour . . .' He tried to smile but the effort was too much for him and he began coughing again. There was an air past caring about him and his eyes had taken on that distant, dull look of approaching death. He rested his weight against Hencke, trying to regain his breath. 'One thing, Hencke. I don't know who you are or where you come from, but you're special. I've seen the way you can lead men and the desire that drives you on. I don't mind admitting that you frighten me a little; such passion is extraordinary. It makes me wonder how, with such commitment, we managed to lose this wretched war . . .'

'It's not over yet. There's still plenty of dying to be done.'

'Plenty of dying to be done . . . You're right, of course.' The commander reflected on the words for a moment. 'I don't suppose anyone will make it back home but, if they do, it will be you. I want to ask you a favour. I'm not going to get back, not this time or ever. I don't have long, and you may be the last German I ever talk to.' The commander's hand reached out to grab Hencke with the force of desperation. 'My wife and children . . . they're in Stettin. If it's not already in Russian hands it soon will be. Please . . .' He scrabbled feverishly inside his uniform, producing a letter which he thrust at Hencke. 'Get this to them. It's my last chance, the last time I'll ever . . .' His breathing pattern was gone again and he struggled to find a little more energy, pulling in rasping lungfuls of air. 'If you've ever loved anyone you'll know how important this is to me. Do it for me, Hencke. Your word of honour, one German officer to another. Give this letter to them, with my love. If you get back.'

'When I get back.'

The commander nodded in agreement. 'How will you?'

'There's a motorbike around the back of the guard hut.'

'You're surely not going to use the main roads! They'll be bound to pick you up.'

'There are nearly two hundred and fifty escaping prisoners. None of them has the slightest idea what to do or where he's going. Most of them have only the vaguest idea even where they are. So they'll shy away from the towns and take to the countryside, moving by night. And the British will know that anything that moves through the woods at night for a hundred miles around this place will be either an escaped prisoner or a fox. In the mood they are likely to be in, chances are they'll shoot, just to be on the safe side.'

The commander shook his head in confusion at this blunt assessment, so much more callous than the one Hencke had offered around the camp fire. 'You talk about "them", as if you are quite separate, on your own.'

'The only chance anyone has is not to do what the rest of the crowd do. I've got four, maybe five hours to get well clear of this place before it starts swarming with troops. So I'm going to borrow the bike and take to the roads. All roads lead somewhere.' He began his preparations to depart, buttoning up the Canadian tunic which he was still wearing.

'Not in enemy uniform, for God's sake. They'll shoot you for sure!'

'They've got to catch me first,' Hencke shouted back over his shoulder.

Moments later the sound of an engine, a Norton 250, began throbbing through the night. 'They even left a map with it,' he smiled in triumph, revving the bike before letting out the clutch with a snap.

The commander gazed after the disappearing figure. 'You are a strange man, Hencke. But I chose the right man. You'll get back to wherever you came from, even if it's the other side of hell.'

He could neither see nor hear the motorbike by the time it pulled up sharply several hundred yards beyond the camp gates. Hencke reached into the pocket of his tunic where the commander had stuffed the precious envelope. 'My word of honour,' he whispered, 'one German officer to another.' He tore the letter into a hundred tiny fragments which scattered to the wind as he rode away.

THREE

The sun was rising and London was beginning to stir, but it made little difference within the Annexe. Daylight didn't penetrate here, and the only sign of the new day was the progress of the clocks and the arrival of those rostered for day duty. The duty secretary, Anthony Seizall, was rubbing the sleep from his eyes and staring at the telephone as if it had broken wind. Perplexed, he clamped it back to the side of his head.

'You're not pulling my leg, are you? Because if you are I shall have great pleasure in coming round with half a dozen of the local boys in blue and pulling the head off your bloody neck!' There was a pause while he listened to a heated voice on the other end of the phone, his head bent low over the bakelite mouthpiece and his straight hair falling over his eyes while he punctuated the conversation with references to a variety of spiritual saviours before descending into repeated low cursing. Seizall was chapel, practically teetotal. Something was clearly up.

Having listened for some time and taken voluminous pencil notes, at last he decided upon a course of action. 'What's your number? You won't object if I call you back, just to check this isn't complete cock-and-bull?' He did precisely that, confirming the authenticity of the caller, and replaced the phone with a grunt. At the moment it was about as much intelligent comment as he could offer.

He sat chewing the end of his pencil for several minutes, the tip of his rubbery nose twitching like a rabbit and dilating in time to the successive floods of indecision which swept over him. Eventually his gnawing broke the pencil clean in two; time was up, action was required. He proceeded down a maze of underground corridors, shaking his head from side to side as if trying one last time to disperse the fog of inadequacy that had settled upon him, until he came to the staff sleeping quarters. Hesitating only briefly for one final burst of indecision, he knocked on a door and entered.

'Sorry to wake you, Cazolet. Got a tricky one.'

Cazolet rolled over and waved his hands in front of his eyes, trying to ward off the light which was prying his lids apart. He spent a great deal of his time in the Annexe, and the result was a grey pallor across his face made worse by lack of sleep. He wasn't supposed to be on duty at the moment, but he knew the PM's mind so well that the other staff had taken to consulting him on many matters. What it meant, of course, was that they brought him all their problems, as if he didn't have several filing trays full of his own to deal with. But he didn't mind; consultation was the finest form of bureaucratic flattery.

'Seems there's been a break-out. Some POW transit camp in Yorkshire. Haven't got the final figures but it looks like — almost two hundred and fifty Jerry on the loose. I've double-checked, of course. No doubt about it, I'm afraid. Bit of a cock-up, really.' Seizall's sentences were clipped, giving but the barest detail, as if too much flavour might somehow involve him in it all, and every instinct in his civil service body told him to steer well clear of this one.

'I was just about to let the Old Man know,' Seizall continued. 'Trouble is he's fast asleep; got in dreadfully late last night from some boozy dinner party. And you know he's like a rhinoceros with piles when he's woken. So I thought I'd let him sleep on a little, but trouble is we've got to inform all the other necessary Departments ... What'll we do?'

'So all of a sudden it's *our* problem, is it?' Cazolet grumbled. One day, one day very soon, he prayed, they would let him get a full night's sleep. He poured cold water from a large jug into an enamel wash-basin – all that passed for facilities in the primitive subterranean accommodation – splashing urgent handfuls over his face to encourage a little more oxygen into his brain as Seizall stood uncomfortably in the doorway of the narrow room. The cold water seemed to have worked, for when Cazolet stood up from the wash-stand he was decisive.

'You tell all the other Departments, Seizall, and the news will be round Fleet Street before you've had time to finish breakfast. And once that's out, we'll never be able to put it back in the bag, wartime censorship or no. It'll be blaring out on Radio Berlin within five minutes. Two hundred and fifty of them? It's a disaster. And it's just what the Prime Minister's political opponents want. They'll pin the blame for slack security on him personally, try to make him look old and incompetent. So you go right ahead and inform everyone from the Labour Party to the Third Reich that we have one of the biggest security lash-ups of the war on our hands.' He dried his face vigorously with a towel while the import of his words sank in. 'Then you can go wake up the PM and tell him what you've done.'

The effect on Seizall was impressive. In twenty seconds his face had become even greyer than Cazolet's; he swallowed hard, his Adam's apple performing gyrations of distress.

'There is a better way,' Cazolet continued, his supremacy in the matter clearly established. 'We tell the minimum number of people – only those in the security services who need to know in order to get Jerry rounded up as quickly as possible. We make it clear to them that this is a matter of top national security, that any public discussion of the escape can only give comfort to the enemy. Be vague about the numbers. Then, when the Old Man's awake and in harness, we'll tell him what we've done. If he wants to let the whole world know, he can. But that's up to him, not you or me.'

Seizall was nodding, trying to look as if he were merely accepting endorsement of a course of action he had already made up his mind to pursue.

69

'There's a lot riding on this, Seizall. Perhaps the Old Man's entire political future. I think he'll be grateful you waited.'

For the first time that morning an impression of relief began to etch its way across the duty secretary's face and he paused to give silent thanks for the binding effect of powdered egg.

Dawn was beginning to paint lurid pictures in the sky, thin fingers of rain cloud stretching towards him like witches' claws, the fire-red tips making the heavens appear to drip with blood. Around Hencke the dark woods seemed to crowd in, the trees bending down as if trying to pluck him from the seat of his bike while the throbbing of the engine surrounded him in a cocoon of sound which carved out a little world of his own and detached him from reality. From the moment he had scattered the commander's letter to the wind he had kept his head low and the throttle stretched open, taking full advantage of the deserted roads. The wind snatched at his hair and froze his face and fingertips, all the while urging him onwards. He was free! But there was no elation in Hencke. As he looked at the fierce sky above him, the memories came crowding back. In the glow that brushed the clouds he saw only the embers he had found burning in the schoolhouse, consuming everything he loved. In the gloom of the trees bowing and sagging in the wind he found images of the veils pulled close around the mothers who had come to sorrow and mourn, weighed down by incomprehension at their loss. In the thumping noise of the engine there was no sound of freedom, only the tramp of boots as they had marched past smouldering wreckage. Hencke could not escape the memory of young bodies twisted and broken. Of books torn and burning, their ashes scattered in the growing winds of war. Of a pair of tiny shoes lying neatly at the entrance to the classroom, with no trace of the vibrant and joyful child who had been wearing them moments before. Of a love which should never have been and which could never be again. He clung on to the throttle like a drowning man clutches at a stick, charging recklessly onward, pursued by demons.

As the sky began to lose its lustre and take on the damp grey tones of March he found himself passing through more open countryside. The long avenues of haunted trees made way for the hedgerows of rural England; above the whistle of the wind he could hear the welcoming chorus of early morning, and the demons that had returned to haunt his mind faded in the daylight. They would be back, they always came back, yet for a moment the nightmare seemed to have drained from his soul. He was taking the first, deep breath of relief when he rounded a long bend between the hedgerows and stood hard on the brake pedal, sliding to a halt on the dewy surface. Before him, stretched full across the road and blocking his path, was a rusty farm tractor around which spilled a line of British soldiers, rifles raised, pointing directly at him.

It seemed as if his race was already over.

It was nearly eleven o'clock before Cazolet presented himself to the Marine guard stationed outside the Prime Minister's bedroom. As the sentry stepped smartly aside, Cazolet entered bearing a large cup of tea. Churchill stirred beneath the thick quilt. Typically he slept heavily and late, particularly after a good dinner, but five years of heartbreak and Hitler had conditioned him to come rapidly to full alert.

'William. To what do I owe this decidedly ambiguous pleasure?' He swept the dishevelled strands of greying russet hair back into place and reached out greedily for the tea, which he proceeded to slurp.

Cazolet related the events of the previous hours, with the Prime Minister concentrating hard on his tea cup and showing little sign of anxiety until he heard the numbers involved.

'Did I hear you correctly?'

'Nearly two hundred and fifty,' Cazolet confirmed. 'Several

thousand troops are being sent to the area, but as always they're in the wrong place. They are waiting on the south coast to embark for Europe, so it will take a little while for them to be redeployed to Yorkshire. In the meantime detachments of the local Home Guard have been activated and are manning road blocks around the camp. There's something else. I've instructed the Chief Constable in charge of co-ordinating the operation that news of the breakout must be treated on a strictly need-to-know basis, and that on no account must the numbers involved be released. He complained that this makes it very much more difficult for his men; not knowing the full facts ties their hands behind their backs.'

'Did you manage to persuade him?'

'Not until I reminded him that, with the war coming to an end, the next Honours List would be bound to include many civilians who had been particularly helpful on the home front. I think he saw the point.'

'But the news is bound to get out eventually,' Churchill mused, showing a distinct lack of enthusiasm, his tea momentarily forgotten, the cup stranded halfway between the saucer and his chin.

'Eventually, perhaps. But not before most of the escapees have been rounded up. By then it can be treated as a success story and not used by our enemies to undermine you.'

'My goodness, William. You have been busy guarding my back. Commendable!'

'Not really.' Cazolet's tone was impish. 'Pure self interest. Prime Ministers are not brought down without creating waves. In your case it would be a veritable tidal wave, which would quite swamp small boats such as mine . . .'

'Then may I wish you many long years of carefree sailing.'

There was an almost familial informality between the two. Cazolet had a supreme respect for Churchill. He had seen first-hand the pain borne by the Prime Minister when, alone and deserted by his allies, he had launched fierce public proclamations of defiance while in private shedding tears of

72

grief for the terrible cost and destruction which that defiance would impose. Cazolet had watched as the Old Man walked amongst hollow-eyed men and women standing forlornly in the rubble of their homes, families who were paying the full price of his stubbornness, while he encouraged – indeed, demanded – that they pick themselves up from the ruins to continue the resistance. To look a grieving mother in the eye and tell her that her sacrifice was still not enough took the courage of a Titan, and Cazolet had seen that Titan return to his official car, draw the curtains and sit quietly sobbing. Yet the Old Man had his faults, like all men. Cazolet had seen him vain, angry, rude, drunk and frequently disorderly, which served only to strengthen the bond of intellectual respect with that of affection. Anyway, it was difficult to be left in excessive awe of a man propped up in bed, swathed in three yards of pale pink pyjama silk and already puffing away at a huge cigar between mouthfuls of tea.

'The local police stations are being inundated with reports of suspicious characters; several have already been apprehended.' Cazolet glanced at his notebook. 'Two men were caught as they rode a stolen bicycle in full Luftwaffe uniform the wrong way down the village High Street. Apparently they would have been caught earlier, except for the misfortune that the bike they stole belonged to the local police constable.'

'Remind me of that when I call to congratulate the Chief Constable and thank him for his co-operation . . .'

'Four others were found early this morning, dead drunk behind the bar of a local pub. Seems they never had any intention of escaping further than the nearest drink. I suspect that most of them will be rounded up very quickly.'

'I'm sure you are right. But as we know, most of them don't matter; it's the one or two slipping through the net who carve their names in the history books.'

In silence Churchill contemplated what might lie ahead. Cazolet stood at the end of the bed, waiting. 'Any further instructions?'

The Old Man looked up, his expression serious. 'This may be a difficult day, William. I believe it calls for two eggs with my bacon and toast. And another cup of tea.'

Cazolet turned and left. For the first time in several days he was laughing out loud.

Hencke could count the barrels of eight Lee Enfields, all of which were pointing straight at him from a distance of less than ten feet. He could try to run them down, of course, but by the time he had slipped the clutch and moved no further than a few inches he reckoned that at least six of the eight bullets would have found him. Not much of an option, that. Neither was surrender, but what was the alternative? Already he could see the tips of the barrels waving nervously and could sense the fingers tightening around the triggers. As he throttled back and put the gears in neutral, Hencke's hand went to his throat, checking that the uniform he was wearing was properly buttoned. No surrender. Never that. There was too much at stake. He would try to bluff it out.

'Sergeant Cheval, Fourth Royal Quebec,' he snapped. God, could they really take his accent for a French Canadian? But don't wait and see – grab the initiative! 'Who's in charge?'

The rifles were still pointing at him, but some were beginning to waver in uncertainty. He began to study the men behind the muzzles; only two were in uniform, the rest were in an assortment of crumpled civilian clothing with nothing more than armbands for identification. Behind them, strewn amongst the hedgerows, lay several pedal cycles which apart from the battered tractor were their only apparent means of transportation. What luck! He had run into Dad's Army dragged out of their beds. Perhaps there was a chance, after all . . .

From behind the line of rifles stepped a man in his sixties armed with a Webley pistol, a fierce look in his eye and a carefully trimmed white moustache. He was the only one wearing a military cap. His uniform was smartly pressed and

74

his boots were immaculate. A veteran, and a man who wore his lieutenant's shoulder pips with pride, Hencke decided. Still astride the motorcycle, he came to a salute.

'Lieutenant, I am Sergeant Cheval of the Fourth Quebec,' he repeated the introduction. 'My regiment is guarding the camp.'

The Webley was still pointing straight at him and there was a bead of nervous perspiration across the bridge of the lieutenant's nose, but to the officer's rear Hencke could see the barrels of several rifles beginning to droop towards the ground.

'Less than two miles down the road there are thirty escaped Germans,' Hencke continued, waving behind him in the general direction of the north of England. The look of ferocity in the officer's eye had changed to one of suspicion and he was about to aim a flood of questions which Hencke knew he had no chance of withstanding. 'Many of them are armed. They've already killed several of my company!'

At this point the rifle barrels were raised once more in anxiety; this time they were pointing not at Hencke but back down the road. The lieutenant's lips were working away in agitation beneath his moustache. He was being overwhelmed by Hencke's news and the responsibility which had suddenly been thrust upon him after so many years of waiting, like the fishes, for an invasion which had never come. He had the rank but he couldn't match the experience suggested by Hencke's regular army uniform. He had a thousand questions to ask but could find the words for none of them.

'Lieutenant, the Germans are headed in this direction, they're not far behind. You must maintain your position here and be ready while I go and warn headquarters.' It was all so ludicrously makeshift. He hadn't the slightest idea where headquarters were located, but he supposed they must lie somewhere to the other side of the road block. That was enough. He began gently to rev the bike engine, testing the officer's resolve. 'And remember. They're dangerous!'

For the first time the lieutenant's eyes left him and began staring in the direction from which Hencke had appeared. The ferocity had gone; there was only anxiety left, and by the time he had dragged his attention back from the distant woodland the moment for making decisions was past. The Norton was already on the move.

'Good luck, Lieutenant,' Hencke shouted above the noise of the engine as he weaved around the tractor and the line of men. Their rifles were at shoulder level once more while their boots scratched nervously away at the pavement, trying to find a solid firing position. When Hencke looked behind him he could see a long row of backs. Only the officer was looking in his direction, the agonies of uncertainty twisting his face. But already it was too late . . .

Hencke waved and was gone.

The portrait of Louis XIV was nothing more than a cheap reproduction but there was no mistaking the profound look of disdain as it gazed down from the painted wooden walls. Eisenhower's daily briefing session with his military aides was coming to an end. The noise and bustle caused by the fifty or more advisers clattered around the dining room of the dingy red-brick secondary school in Reims which served as SHAEF's forward military headquarters.

'D'you know, Dwight, that old bastard wouldn't have bothered with all this.' General Omar Bradley, three-stars and Eisenhower's right hand, waved at the portrait. 'None of these briefing meetings, no listening to endless advice, no worries about whether the fuel was in the same place as the fighting. Just an order for the peasant army to pick up their pikes and start walking while he went back to his roast pig and mistress. What a way to fight a war.'

Eisenhower winced. Even with as good a friend as Bradley he wasn't in the mood to discuss mistresses. 'You're not suggesting I dress up in silk tights and a red wig like him?'

'Well, he ruled for something like seventy-odd years. Not bad for the times when you counted yourself lucky if the pox killed you off before the Black Death. And he was big in arts 'n stuff. They called him the Sun King. After all this is over, Ike, d'you think the sun's going to shine out from under your periwig?'

Eisenhower laughed. Bradley was always able to make him relax even when the going was particularly tough. As commander of the 12th Army Group which formed the backbone of the European command, Bradley shared the weight. While Eisenhower ordered and authorized, it was Bradley's job to implement. They shared both the successes and sacrifices of war, and it had built trust and affection.

'I wonder how that old bastard would have coped with the British, Brad?'

'What's dear old Monty been up to this time? Another press conference to let the world know how you and the Pope have got it all wrong? Or is he complaining again that he hasn't got a zipper big enough for his flies?' The disdain for General Bernard Montgomery was evident in both of them. A relationship which had always been difficult with their British colleague had become incandescent in recent months as Montgomery complained, cajoled, and claimed credit for other men's victories. He was Bradley's equivalent and Eisenhower's subordinate, but he rarely acted as such, particularly in the presence of the media when a poised pen or the pop of a flashbulb would send him off into grandiloquent summaries of the European battle scene which would have made even Louis feel uncomfortable.

'No, it's not Montgomery this time,' Eisenhower responded, blinking as the blinds were drawn back from the high windows to let in a flood of springtime light. 'It's the Old Man. Churchill. Didn't want to raise it in front of everyone, but I'm having real trouble getting the extra division out of him. Should have arrived days ago, but all

I get in its place is flannel and excuses. First he keeps complaining that the British forces in North Germany are left sitting idly on their backsides, then he won't give me the troops to do anything else. What does he expect me to do? Scare the Germans out of the North Sea ports by dropping my pants?'

'This isn't some screwball way of putting pressure on you to let him have Berlin, is it? You know, Berlin or nothing?'

'Could it really have come to that, Brad? Monty, yes, but surely not the Old Man. Sweet Jesus, I thought we were fighting this war together.' Eisenhower's square jaw began to work back and forth in exasperation. The allied command had worked so harmoniously right up until D-Day, the invasion of Europe, but once they had set foot on French soil the co-operation seemed to vanish in a political quagmire as deep and impassable as the trench mud of the first War. He cracked his knuckles as he recounted the times the British had got in the way, been stubbornly slow off the mark or had brazenly attempted to trip him up. Caen. Arnhem. Antwerp. The Ardennes. The Rhine . . . He had run out of knuckles, and of patience. 'I'll not let them make a damned fool of me any longer, Brad. I've taken about as much flak as I can stand. Hell, I wouldn't take this sort of crap even from the French! It's about time someone made our allies realize just who's in charge of this shooting match.'

There was an edge to his voice, uncharacteristic in a commander who was known for his equanimity and for seeing the other man's point of view. Bradley said nothing, gratified that at last his superior seemed determined to clamp down on the petulance of their colleagues. And not before time. Eisenhower dug deep into his pocket for the lucky pennies he always carried. 'Like worry beads,' he had once explained, 'except it scares the shit out of the men if the Supreme Commander is seen to worry. So I play with my pennies.' They were cascading from one hand to the other as he tried to pour away his frustration and

78

waited for an orderly to bring coffee. The orderly was pouring before Eisenhower returned to the point.

'It truly galls me to think of thousands of British troops sitting outside Dover doing nothing,' he muttered distractedly.

'I'm not sure where the general gets his information, but those troops sure as hell ain't there,' the orderly interrupted in a slow Texan drawl. He had been with Eisenhower a long time, not so much because of his valeting skills as his ability to read his master's moods, and to respond appropriately, usually with a humorous tale or a choice piece of gossip which otherwise would never have reached the Supreme Commander's ears. And Eisenhower loved a good gossip; it helped remind him there was still a real world out there.

'What d'you mean, Mickey?'

'Well, sir, you'll remember I've just been on leave in London?' he began. One of the perks of working for the boss was an almost limitless ability to contrive seats on transport planes flying away from the battle zone.

'Sure do,' Eisenhower responded. 'Only time for weeks I got a decent cup of coffee.'

'The general is so kind,' the orderly continued, completely unabashed. 'I got talking to some of our British friends. Strange little watering hole called the Ferret and Firkin. I never did figure out what the "firkin" bit was.'

'This story'd better be good, Mickey, or I'll have your balls on toast,' Eisenhower chuckled; the orderly's calculated impertinence was beginning to work its usual magic.

'There's these two Brit quartermasters ferretin' and firkin' and feeling pretty relaxed about the whole thing. Seems they were just about to join the fun here in Europe when most of their unit got orders to ship north, to York-Shire or wherever.' He managed to make it sound somewhere beyond the Arctic Circle. 'So this pair were left waging war with a mountain of supplies and equipment while the rest of their buddies were off opening a new battle front.'

79

'New front?' Bradley enquired.

'Well, General, I'm not supposed to breathe a word. Honest to God, they swore me to secrecy . . .' Mickey's eyes wandered theatrically around the room in search of eavesdroppers. 'But it seems like there's been a big breakout, a whole prison camp full of Germans on the loose with half the British army in hot pursuit. Sounded like the biggest round-up east of the Shenandoah, 'cept nobody's supposed to know a thing about it . . . Cream, General Bradley?'

But the two generals had lost interest in the coffee. 'Could it be, Brad? Could it really be so cretinous?'

Bradley sucked thoughtfully at his teeth. 'What would we do in the same circumstances? I guess we'd want to keep it quiet. Hell, if we'd lost a whole campful of prisoners, Montgomery would be on every radio broadcast braying like a jackass and offering to help sweep up the mess.'

'But to withhold an entire division from Europe at a time when Churchill is screaming for more action, just to cover up their own blunder . . . ?'

'Politics, Dwight. Capital "P". This whole damn war is growing to be all about politics.'

Eisenhower's easy mood had vanished, steel re-entered his voice. 'That's no excuse for incompetence and duplicity, not when the lives of my men are at stake. Check this story out for me, Brad, see if it's true.'

'And if it is?'

'Fight fire with fire. Take on the politicians at their own game.' The lucky pennies jangled into the palm of his hand, where he gripped them tightly in a clenched fist. A tight smile of determination and of decision broke on his face. 'You know, Brad, maybe Mr Churchill could do with some help rounding up his strays . . .'

Why on earth had they been painted red? Some Bolshy bloody painter, he supposed. Maybe he should have them repainted blue, a good Tory colour, and ignore the bleatings

80

he would get from the two Labour members of his War Cabinet. Still, it scarcely mattered any more. The war in Europe would be finished with soon, the bombardment of London by Hitler's rockets finished with even sooner as their launch sites were over-run, and then he wouldn't have to use this subterranean rathole any more. Oh, to be in fresh air once again . . . He leaned back in his chair and blew a cloud of smoke towards the low ceiling and its huge steel girders, painted as red as traffic lights, which had captured his attention. According to the engineers they were strong enough to bear the collapsed weight of the entire building underneath which the wartime Cabinet complex had been built. 'Has anyone told Goering?' he once enquired sceptically. He always felt uneasy under here. It was not that he was afraid to die, his contempt for his personal safety had been proven on battlegrounds throughout the British Empire during his younger years as a soldier, but that had been in the mountains of India's North West Frontier, on the Sudanese plains or the open veldt in Southern Africa. Not cooped up in a sewer. He felt claustrophobic, uneasy, and the damp wormed its way into his bones to insist that he was an old man – with a great past perhaps, but certainly with an ever-shortening future. His bad shoulder was playing up again and he tried unsuccessfully to massage the ache from it. Not much longer, he sighed, as he watched the cigar smoke being caught in the draught of a wall fan and dispersed to the far corners of the small room amongst the fifteen other people attending Cabinet.

Churchill was distracted. The First Lord of the Admiralty was droning on about shipping figures, a matter which had ceased to interest Churchill since Admiral Doenitz's U-boats had lost control of the Atlantic and stopped sinking merchantmen by the score. At that time it had been a matter of finding enough food to eat and oil to fuel the Spitfires and Hurricanes. Now it was all about tonnages of this and tonnages of that and how the fishermen were demanding the return of their boats requisitioned for war duty. Statistics.

81

Bloody statistics. He had no mind for them any more. Some people wanted to fight the entire war with statistics, but war wasn't about desiccated figures; it was about men, real-life flesh and blood men, and hopefully more of the other side's flesh and blood than your own. He dragged his thoughts back down from between the bright red rafters as the First Sea Lord came to a close.

'Well, gentlemen, I think that concludes the business on today's Cabinet agenda. Thank you for your . . .'

Before he could finish there was a waving of a hand somewhere on his left side. Churchill turned to peer over the circular frames of his spectacles and spotted Ernest Bevin gesticulating for his attention. No interruption from Bevin was ever welcome. The Minister for Labour and National Service had done a grand job cajoling every last effort out of the workers and had succeeded in heading off any serious strike activity, no one could deny that. But he was a died-in-the-wool, red-blooded, black-hearted, callous-handed Socialist, and the sooner Churchill could dispense with this wartime coalition and throw the Socialists out of the Cabinet, the better.

'Prime Minister, not yet if you please,' Bevin insisted, a quizzical, lopsided expression stretched across his leathery face which gave the impression of his being slow and dogged, like a rumpled bloodhound searching for a lost trail. Every syllable betrayed his origins as a London van driver, but that hadn't stopped him climbing out of the gutter and ascending very far – as far as Churchill's left hand. 'I've 'ad some disturbing news this morning. I was called up at 'ome by a journalist from America's CBS . . .'

Churchill frowned disparagingly, making no attempt to hide his view of anybody who made himself available to journalists at home in the morning.

'Talked of reports about a great prisoner of war escape in Yorkshire last week. The details were very sketchy; something like three hundred Germans escaped, 'e said.' There

82

was a slight pause while he considered how to frame the question before deciding, as he normally did, that bluntness was better than politeness. 'What about it? What's going on, Prime Minister? Is it true? What 'ave you been 'iding from us?'

It was too much for Churchill. He was tired, very tired, and despite his ministrations the pain in his shoulder was getting worse. He'd been looking for someone to lose his temper with all morning since Clemmie had started up again with her endless nagging about his 'extravagance' and worrying about how they were going to pay for everything from his cigars to the new drains at Chartwell. With his wife he had a lifetime's practice of closing his ears and gritting his teeth; with Bevin he could find no cause for restraint. Partly it was a deep unease that this bloody man now sitting at his left might soon have the opportunity to move closer still, thanks to the electorate, perhaps even to centre stage and Churchill's own place. Mostly, it was sheer rage at having been caught, but he didn't stop to bother with the logic; he was simply in the mood for it. With alarming abruptness the PM's fists beat upon the makeshift Cabinet table. His pen flew up from the blotter and performed a full somersault, while the lid of the red despatch box in front of him came down with a crash.

'How on earth are we expected to run a war when we are bombarded with questions like that? Whose side is your reporter friend on, for God's sake? Hasn't Hitler made our lives difficult enough without half the American press corps snapping at our heels?' Churchill's shoulders were hunched and rounded, his solid forehead thrust forward like a bull about to charge, an impression made all the more acute as in the surge of excitement his glasses slid to the end of his nose to reveal furious red eyes.

There was not a sound from within the room beyond the exertions of the Old Man's breathing. The Cabinet Secretary had stopped taking notes while most of the others in the room found things at the edges of their blotting pads which required their close attention. Only Bevin seemed unperturbed.

'For the record, Prime Minister, the man's a journalist, not the Gestapo. And I'd like an answer to my question. Seems simple enough to me. If any of what 'e 'ad to say is true I think the Cabinet 'as a right to know.' He returned Churchill's glare. He'd been on too many picket lines and threatened by too many brutish employers during his trade union activities to be put off the scent by verbal intimidation. He'd lost strikes, of course, but only when they'd been starved into submission, and this smelled like a juicy bone which might keep him going for some time.

Churchill needed to play for time to recover his composure. It was all very well losing his temper, but only if it had a point and gave him an advantage. There was none in this.

'Has anybody else picked up this sort of gossip?' He made it sound as if he were making enquiries about a venereal disease. He glowered around the room, finding little response until he lit upon Beaverbrook, his close friend and Minister for Production, who was clearly agitated. Beaverbrook had tried urgently and unsuccessfully to catch him before Cabinet but, as usual, Churchill had been late and in a rush – delayed by Clemmie's damned nagging. Had Beaverbrook been trying to warn him? Beaverbrook knew all the gossip that was running around Fleet Street – hell, he owned half of it – and now he was nodding his head as if to confirm what Bevin had said. He looked forlorn, biting his bottom lip, implying that even with his immense grip on the media there was little chance of bottling this one up. But he remained silent and Churchill was grateful for that, at least; it helped give him a means of escape.

The Prime Minister coughed to break the awkward hush. 'Very well,' he said. 'I'm glad such inaccurate reports have not yet been widely circulated, because it gives me the opportunity to tell you the facts. This is a serious security matter, which is why it has not been included explicitly on the Cabinet agenda, although it had always been my intention to raise it today under "Any Other Business".' He shot a venomous glance at Bevin, daring him to challenge the lie, but all he got back was an inscrutable stare from behind pebble glasses. In the many years they had done combat with each other Churchill had never been able to penetrate through those thick glasses to find the man beneath. Damn him! He was from a different world, a creature from another planet who had only the meanest of connections with the Britain for which Churchill had fought all his life. Churchill would never understand him.

'There was indeed a large escape last week from a camp in Yorkshire,' Churchill continued, the flush slowly disappearing from his cheeks, 'not, I hasten to add, as large as the wild rumours we have just heard might indicate.' He took from within his ministerial box the note which Cazolet had prepared for him on a daily basis since the break-out. Statistics. More damned statistics, but he was grateful for them now. 'Ten days ago there was a mass escape from Camp 174B in Yorkshire. The camp was guarded by Canadians.' A nice point that; colonials were to blame. 'A total of two hundred and forty-seven Germans were involved.'

There was a gasp of astonishment from around the table as the scale of the fiasco sank in.

'The Cabinet will appreciate, I am sure, what impact news of the event might have had in the wrong hands. It might have caused panic amongst the public and could have given succour only to the enemy. As it is' – he scanned the note – 'two hundred and thirty-two of the prisoners had been recaptured by seven o'clock this morning. This biggest POW break-out of the war has been contained, almost snuffed out, and the damage it might have done has been avoided. It is a glowing tribute to our security forces that the escapees have been rounded up so quickly. In spite of the initial misfortunes of our Canadian cousins, the incident has proved a testament

85

to the success of the police, the armed services and, of course, this government in coping with these unique and unforeseen circumstances.'

'Hear, hear,' Beaverbrook growled, setting aside the temporary embarrassment of his Canadian birth.

'So I was right,' Bevin snapped, sniffing the air as if trying to scent the weakness in Churchill's explanation. 'Why didn't you tell us right off about this? Why did we 'ave to smoke you out?'

'It was merely a tactical security matter, nothing more, and offered no fundamental question of policy for the Cabinet to deal with. We've had escapes before which haven't been discussed at Cabinet. This matter was being handled competently and safely and there was no point in indulging in premature discussion of it.'

'You call the largest POW escape of the war a "tactical security matter"?'

'To the extent that there were any security implications involved I, as both Prime Minister and Minister of Defence, was kept constantly informed. The constitutional requirements have been fully satisfied.'

Churchill felt more relaxed, he was regaining control. Once it was out in the open it wasn't half as bad as he had feared. And Bevin had lost the floor; someone else was raising a question.

'But what of the remaining fifteen prisoners? And are we to allow the country to hear about this through CBS?'

Churchill smacked his hand decisively on the dark blue velvet of the Cabinet table. 'I think you will all agree, gentlemen, that we have reached an entirely appropriate stage at which to seek the public's assistance in rounding up the fifteen strays and stragglers.'

'So we'll no longer 'ide it, we'll make a full public announcement?' Bevin pressed.

'I agree with the Minister. It's time the people heard about this most recent British success.'

There was a snort of ridicule from Bevin, but no more. It

86

had been a close-run thing and Churchill would dearly love to have the individual who leaked the news dangling by his balls from a bomb bay at 30,000 feet but, for the moment, it would do. It would have to. He had no other choice.

The tip of the sun began to peer above the cliff face away to the east, sending a shimmer of silver light across the sea and stirring life and colour into the small boats which had been sleeping on the Mediterranean swell. Already the daybreak had hit the island of Sainte Marguerite which lay in the bay beyond Cannes and soon the light would begin to take on a soft, golden-red hue as the dawn claimed control of the sky. It was not unusually warm for late March in the French Riviera, but after the winter rigours of Northern France it seemed like mid-summer to Eisenhower, who in any conditions insisted on sleeping with the window open. The lace curtains billowed as the first morning breeze rustled into the master bedroom at Sous le Vent, the private villa which had been loaned to him for a few days and, as was his intention, the war seemed a million miles away. Even Supreme Commanders need their breaks.

The point had been brought firmly home when he discovered a rat in one of the classrooms serving as his office at Reims HQ. He had taken out his revolver and, from a distance of no more than a few feet, shot at it. He missed. Carefully he had put on his glasses and shot again. And missed again. The third shot succeeded only in blowing off its tail, and a sergeant had used a chair to put both the rat and the Supreme Commander out of their misery. Eisenhower was tired, he had been losing weight and the patchwork quilt of lines beneath his eyes had sagged into whirlpools of fatigue. He needed to steady his hand and to get his mind off the war.

WAC First Lieutenant Kay Summersby stirred from her sleep as the breeze hit her. She was naked, and rolled over to bury herself in the sandy-silver hair on Eisenhower's chest. He was already awake, reading one of his favourite Wild West novels, *Cartridge Carnival*. Nice thing about Westerns, the good guys always won. Her fingers traced the line from his chin down to his navel. He was ticklish, always had been, and he wriggled to free himself from her attentions. He was just getting to the good bit, and he had his priorities, particularly before breakfast. Damn him. She had to accept that she took her place in a long line behind his family and his war and the huge demands which both imposed upon him – but a cheap bloody novel?

She put both arms around him and squeezed him generously. 'I wish this could go on for ever,' she said, nuzzling his belly.

'Yeah. This is a great place,' he responded. He didn't look up from the book. He knew she hadn't been talking about the villa, and she knew that as always he was avoiding the subject, but now was not the time to get into any deeper conversation about their relationship. Perhaps there never would be a time. She withdrew her arms and rolled out of bed, stretching the sleep out of her body before putting on his general's shirt and sitting down on the edge of the bed to brush her hair. He always said she looked great in khaki, particularly his khaki, and last night had been no exception. She noticed that another button was hanging from a thread. She would have to sew it on herself, since she refused to give his orderly Mickey the satisfaction of a licentious leer when he took away yet another of the general's rumpled shirts for repair. They had been so careful, tried so hard to be discreet, but inevitably the number of people who knew of their affair had grown and would continue to grow. It made it still more important for them to discuss their future, even while it made Eisenhower steadily more reluctant to face up to the problem. He had so many other challenges to contend with; it was so easy to justify putting off any discussion or consideration until later. Always later. In the meantime they snatched whatever time and pleasure they could, and for the moment at least that was all she could expect.

'Be patient, Kay. I know it's difficult, but the war will be over soon. Then we can sort ourselves out.' Eisenhower had glanced up from his book to notice the sad, pensive look on her face. He didn't have the answers, but it didn't mean he was totally insensitive to the problem.

'And then what, Dwight? What does a Supreme Commander do after there's no more war to fight?'

'Damned if I know,' he responded. He snapped the book shut, and she knew she had hit the target. 'But I suppose it won't be long before we find out. I'm meeting with that wily old bastard Churchill in a couple of days to inspect our operations for crossing the Rhine. Once we're driving into the heart of Germany we'll soon discover just how hard Hitler's going to struggle before he goes down. So long as we cut off his escape route to the Alps, it can't be more than a few weeks.' He reached over and gently took her hand. 'And once we've sorted out Europe, then maybe we'll have time to sort out ourselves.'

'And have you sorted out Mr Churchill?'

A broad grin erupted across his unshaven face and he clapped his hands together in delight. 'Want to know what I did? Shall I tell you?' But he had already made up his mind to share it with her. 'The Old Man got himself in a real pickle. A huge POW escape from somewhere in the north just at the time he was supposed to be sending a division of new troops to the front. So instead of fighting in Europe he had them scurrying round the British countryside like demented drovers in a thunderstorm while he tried to hush the whole thing up.'

'So . . . ?'

'So I put a couple of mountain cats into the herd. Got some American press boys chasing the story. A few hours later it was all over the newspapers, which means in a few days' time I should get my goddamn troops!' He was chuckling loudly. 'You know, Kay, there's the Old Man, the greatest politician in Europe who lives, breathes and belches politics, and I beat him at his own game. It was so easy!'

'Politics? You've always said that politics only got in the way, that politicians should concentrate on supplying you with the men and *matériel* and leave the rest up to you,' she responded. It was more than just a playful jest; she sensed that he had changed, in his views about war, and perhaps about himself.

'Dammit, it was Churchill who told me that war was too important to be left to the fighting men. As we get nearer to the end of the war, he said, politics will become more important in the way the war is fought. Like Clausewitz. That war is only a continuation of politics by more violent means. I always thought that was crap . . .'

'And now, Dwight?'

'Well, I guess even military commanders have to use a little politics on occasion if they want to get their own way. And you know what else, Kay?' He was grinning with that schoolboy charm of his. 'I enjoyed it. I really enjoyed it! Maybe after this is all over I'll go back to Abilene and run for dog-catcher. As you say, I'm going to need something to do after this shooting match is over.'

She saw him beginning to toy with some idea in his mind, ill-formed, incomplete, but vibrant, an idea in which she sensed she would have no place. He was slipping away from her. But she had never really had him. 'See only today, forget tomorrow,' she had told herself when they had first started. He had promised her love and was as sincere as he could be, but she knew, or was getting to know, that love came some way down his list of priorities. If necessary, she would become simply another of the innumerable sacrifices a Supreme Commander has to make. 'Help him. Help his war.' That's all she could expect. And don't spoil today by pining for tomorrow because, some day, tomorrow will never come.

She gritted her teeth in submission to the inevitable. As soon as this holiday was over there would be countless thousands of people demanding their share of Eisenhower, claiming his attention, getting in her way. But today, at least,

90

he belonged to her. Exclusively. 'OK, Mr President. There's one question I have for you.' She slid her hand provocatively up his leg and high on to his thigh. 'What're your views on the emancipation of women . . . ?'

FOUR

London had become hell. When Hencke first arrived, by fortune he had found himself immersed and anonymous in a sea of humanity. The capital was teeming – with soldiers on leave, with homeless persons bombed on to the streets and scratching around for a place to shelter, with refugees from occupied Europe. None of them seemed to belong anywhere, none could be easily traced by the authorities and, most helpful of all, many of them were foreign. Hencke could slip between the folds, unnoticed. It had kept him going for several days while he recovered from the exertions of the escape and the race through the back roads of England, and while he tried to focus on what he should do next. He'd slept on the platform of Swiss Cottage underground station, crowded with others who had nowhere else to go or who were simply unwilling to risk the attentions of a V-1 or V-2 while sleeping in their own, unprotected beds. It had been like a tower of Babel built beside railway lines with a cocktail of foreign tongues stirred vigorously by European Jews, Poles, Greeks, Hungarians, even a sprinkling of Yugoslavs, alongside resident Londoners and itinerant Scots and Irish. He got little sleep in the fetid atmosphere but it had been warm and even welcoming; his strong accent was unlikely to arouse suspicion amongst the cosmopolitan crowd. There had also been food, queued for at the soup kitchens or begged off American GIs, all of whom seemed to have a pocket stuffed full with oranges, chocolate and cigarettes and who were constantly surrounded by groups of youngsters clamouring for gum. As the war moved closer towards its end there were too many people wandering the streets of London with no background and no permanent residence for one more dishevelled foreigner to arouse much suspicion, and anyway people were tired of suspicion. It had worn them out over all these years, and it was a relief to be able to relax, to let the guard down, to smile once more.

Then news of the escape had broken. On every street corner a newspaper billboard proclaimed it, in every soup kitchen queue people discussed it. Fifteen still free! Within three days only seven left at large! Hencke could feel eyes everywhere, probing, questioning, demanding to know who he was and why he had no money to buy food. It was his imagination, of course; there was no evidence to suggest that the authorities were concentrating their attention on London in particular, but the sea of humanity in which he had been able to swim seemed to have become angry and full of menace, threatening to swallow him at any moment. He knew it was only a matter of time before his luck disappeared, before he was caught out, when someone asked an impossible question or his nerve broke and he gave himself away.

The day had come when the billboards screamed 'One More To Go!' He was the last one, on his own. He had no more time. For the previous three days he had been keeping watch on the Spanish Embassy early in the morning, around lunchtime and again in the late afternoon, always from a different position, constantly on the move to avoid rousing the suspicions of the police guard, but studying everyone who entered and left. He was looking for the diplomatic staff, trying to recognize those who passed through every day, and trying to guess which of them could be trusted and might help. Spain was nominally neutral yet had been friendly towards the Axis ever since the fledgling Luftwaffe had helped Franco bomb Guernica and the Republican movement into rubble. In spite of their neutrality someone might remember, and might repay the debt. But which one? How to tell a man's motivation from the way he dresses, from the turn of his collar or the crook of his nose? To distinguish a brave man from a coward, or a potential friend from somebody

93

who wanted simply to play it by the rules? Hencke had to try.

It had to be today. He had begun to take chances. His nerves were frayed and his hunger was beginning to burn in spite of the hand-outs, and the previous night he had fallen into conversation on the underground station with a married couple who had offered to share their thermos of coffee with him. What did he do? How long had he been in England? He reminded them of their son, whom they hadn't seen in six months while he had been battling his way up the backbone of Italy. Why had Hencke been exempted from military service? Why wasn't he out there fighting? Within five minutes he had contradicted himself twice and their generosity had turned to resentment. They thought he was a draft dodger, and it wouldn't be long before someone came to the correct conclusion. So it had to be today.

The embassy was a square-built Victorian affair, solid rather than pretentious, tucked away in the corner of Belgrave Square. It had a large portico which seemed to be the only entrance and through which every visitor and staff member had to pass. Immediately outside stood the police guard, checking credentials. It had been doubled since news of the escape had leaked. So Hencke walked around the square, sat on a park bench, read a newspaper and did his best not to look suspicious, all the time feeling as conspicuous as a boy scout in a convent. The man in the trilby and trenchcoat had entered the embassy shortly before eight o'clock and, if he followed the pattern of the previous two days, would be out for a stroll through nearby Hyde Park at twelve-thirty precisely. But what if he changed his plans? If he decided to take an early break? If he weren't a diplomat after all? To curb his anxiety Hencke was back waiting on the corner near the embassy shortly after eleven a.m. He had to dispense with the newspaper; it was shaking too much in his unsteady hands. His impatience meant he risked the attentions of the duty policemen, but it was time for taking risks.

94

The man appeared precisely on time. His collar was up and the trilby pulled down firmly over his head against the squallish wind, but there was no mistake. Hencke hurried on ahead, taking the opposite route around the square and relieved to see the other man pacing along his accustomed route, his briefcase tucked under his left arm. By habit he would stop by a bench overlooking the lake in the park and produce sandwiches from the briefcase, munching through them before throwing any remnants of crumbs and crust to the sparrows. He liked birds, perhaps that was why Hencke had decided to trust him. His own father had been an avid ornithologist, so his aunt had told him. That's all he had of his father, a scrap of information about his hobbies and an even scrappier but greatly treasured photograph, taken a few days before he left for the trenches and which had been lost in the charred ruins of the schoolhouse. So the Spaniard liked birds, too; perhaps it was an omen.

While the first sandwich was being extracted from the briefcase and consumed, Hencke took the opportunity to scout around the area of the park bench, checking whether there were any watchers hidden behind the bright spring foliage of the trees or bushes, trying to control his anxiety. By the time the second and final sandwich had appeared he knew he had to make his move.

'Please, do you have a cigarette?' Hencke enquired after he had sat down at the opposite end of the bench.

The Spaniard turned towards him. He was in his early thirties with dark skin and a long face from which protruded a sharp, aquiline nose. The expression behind it was not friendly. Hencke was by this time peculiarly dishevelled. He hadn't shaved for four days, his once-glossy black hair was matted and the suit of clothes he had stolen after dumping the motorcycle had become grubby and unkempt. There was an unhealthy flush across his lean face and a wild look in his eyes; Hencke thought he was developing a fever, contracted by too much nervous sweating in the damp March air. He probably smelled, too. The Spaniard stared, examined the

95

crumpled man who had accosted him and, without offering a word, returned to his sandwich.

Hencke clenched his fists. Perhaps he had made a dreadful mistake after all. The diplomat proceeded to scatter crumbs on the ground and attract the attentions of sparrows and pigeons. Even the ducks on the lake were beginning to honk their appreciation and clamber out of the water towards him. Within seconds he was festooned with birds and in the distance Hencke could see two nannies with their broods of children advancing towards them with the intention of joining in the fun. Soon he would be surrounded.

'You're from the Spanish Embassy, aren't you? I must speak with you.'

The man turned to stare once again. 'Who are you? What do you want?' he demanded aggressively.

Hencke drew a deep breath. The nannies were only yards away. It was now or never. 'I'm German. The escaped prisoner of war. I need your help.'

The Spaniard turned pale beneath his olive skin and shot to his feet, standing erect as the last of the breadcrumbs were scattered on the ground. Feeding time was over and the birds fled; at least it had the advantage of deflecting the two advancing nannies.

'You must be mad! Why on earth do you think I should help you? What on earth can I do?' The diplomat looked around him anxiously, whether to guard against approaching danger or to summon the nearest policeman Hencke could only guess. 'The whole country is looking for you. You're the most wanted man in Britain. In God's name why pick on me?'

At least he was not screaming at the top of his lungs for help, thought Hencke. He was just plain scared. 'I picked on you because I have nowhere else to go. I must have your help.'

'Don't you realize there's nothing I can do? Spain is neutral, it doesn't get involved in this war.'

'Germany got involved in your war. Or have you forgotten that already?'

'That was nearly ten years ago. This is preposterous . . . I must be off.' The Spaniard began to brush the final crumbs from his raincoat in order to depart. It was almost over for Hencke.

'But you must help . . .'

'No. I can do no such thing. Neutral. Don't you understand!' He glanced around him once more. 'If you continue to pester me I shall call for the police. Look . . . I'm sorry, but you don't realize.' His tone softened slightly. The initial shock and panic had gone, but the deep unease remained. 'You are the hottest target in the whole of London. You must understand. Every embassy is being watched, our telephones are being tapped, everyone is on the lookout for you. It's impossible for anyone to help you and it would be madness for anyone to try.' He reached into his pockets and pulled out a couple of crumpled notes and a handful of coins. 'Here. Take some money; you look as if you could do with something to eat. But that's all. There's nothing more I can do.'

'Wish me luck, eh . . . ?' Hencke muttered bitterly, glancing derisively at the few pounds in his hand. It was all going wrong.

'Not even that. NEUTRAL. Don't you understand?' The Spaniard was becoming agitated again, wondering whether he had already gone too far. He began striding away, wishing to put as much distance as possible between himself and this nightmare that had been thrust towards him.

Hencke made after him, but all he could see was the man's back. 'One other thing you can do for me? It won't hurt . . .' He began to raise his voice as the diplomat's figure receded into the distance. 'You have the means. Get a message back to Berlin for me. From Peter Hencke.' He had to shout now. 'Tell them I'm coming back!'

The diplomat didn't falter in his stride. In a moment he was gone.

Hencke was left alone, defeated. His fever was getting

97

worse, he was cold to his core and disheartened. He looked ravenously at the complaining ducks.

They were overhead again tonight, as they had been for nights innumerable and ceaseless, wave after wave of them on their way to Leipzig, perhaps, or Hanover, or most likely Berlin. Down in the tiny cellar it was impossible to tell if they were British Lancasters or American B-17s, since the throbbing of heavy bombers sounded much the same when you had buried yourself as deep beneath the ground as you could go, but the two elderly women held each other's hands for comfort and hoped the planes were British. The Americans were more trigger-happy and careless – or was it just plain skittish? – and liable to unload their bombs anywhere. The small town of Friesenheim had for centuries nestled comfortably in the security of the valley carved through Westphalia by the head-waters of the Ruhr river, but the valley ran west to east from what was left of the industrial complexes concentrated along the Rhine and acted as a highway for Bomber Command right into the heart of Germany. Friesenheim was on no one's list of priority targets, but that hadn't prevented it from being hit several times in the last month as bomber crews got into trouble, got into a panic, or simply got it wrong. In places like Friesenheim there was no such thing as the skill or the art of survival, it was nothing more than a matter of fortune. You crept into your shelters and stayed there for days on end until the weather was bad enough to keep the bombers away, not knowing how long your meagre food supplies were likely to last, sharing everything with the rats, your nerves shot to hell as the walls closed in and praying that you would be one of the lucky ones who wouldn't die in this hole, or be buried alive, or be drowned as the sewers burst and flooded into your hiding place.

You spent a lot of time praying, because prayer was all you had to defend yourself, yet frequently even prayer was not enough. A few nights previously a rogue 10,000-pound bomb which had become stuck in its rack was dislodged and dropped over Friesenheim by a USAF crew on its way home. The townsfolk were well sheltered and 133 of them, mostly women and children, had been packed into the ancient crypt which acted as an air raid shelter underneath the Evangelical church. The pastor had been conducting, encouraging all present to sing at the top of their voices in the hope that it would drown the noise of battle overhead. His wife scurried around serving ersatz coffee and comforting a baby born four days previously.

No one heard the bomb. The walls of the church were thick and the crypt deep, as was the fashion in the *Mittelalter* days during the long and glorious reign of Charlemagne when the first foundations had been laid. But there was a grille set in the ground at the back of the nave which was used to facilitate the passage of heavy objects such as coffins or casks of wine in and out of the crypt. It was only a small grille but the bomb had struck the grating at an angle, bouncing down the chute and into the crypt, where it exploded in the middle of the pastor's choir practice. A fluke, a million to one chance, but in the confined space the devastation was appalling. Only twenty-three had been pulled alive from underneath the collapsed church and several of those had died in the days since, the local hospital long ago having run out of anaesthetics, of antibiotics, of trained doctors, and of hope. Of the pastor, his wife and the baby there had been nothing left but a memory.

The two elderly women found it hard to change the habits of a lifetime so, in spite of the evidence of the crypt, they huddled in their cellar and continued praying and hoping, smoking cigarettes made out of dandelions and listening to the radio. They found the radio of most comfort. It was their link with sanity, letting them know in the middle of the darkest night that life still went on somewhere outside their tiny, fear-filled world. Otherwise it would be easy to imagine that they were the only people left alive, that the rest of humanity had killed itself and they were left in the darkness as the last survivors of a mad, suicidal world.

Only the radio and the next wave of bombers brought them back to reality. And reality tonight was another interminable broadcast by Goebbels. As always it brought news from the war front and a call for still further sacrifice to resist the criminals threatening the homeland, larded with vituperative attacks on the nameless Jewish conspirators who had promoted the war and sought the extinction of the German race – although it was clear to most listeners that in recent weeks the emphasis of the news had changed, with reports from the battle fronts becoming briefer and more vague, while the denunciation of those responsible for the growing calamity grew ever more fantastic. Yet tonight there was something different, a new element in the formula. News of a massive break-out by German prisoners-of-war in England, 'a powerful illustration that the spirit of our fighting men is not broken and clear proof of how vulnerable our enemies still are, even in their homeland. The British Tommies scurry around after escaped prisoners when the whisky-sodden war criminal Churchill would have them butchering German women and children. Even without their weapons, the unquenchable determination of our German soldiers is continuing to resist the onslaught of our enemies and helping to defend the Fatherland. Resistance, in all manners, at all times, must be our watchword!'

One of the women held a piece of bread and hard cheese in her hand, all they had left until the bombing stopped and they could forage for new provisions. Tears were trickling down her cheek and falling on to the stale, dark bread, but she seemed not to notice. She was staring into another world that she remembered from long ago, one which had long since been destroyed and which she knew she would never see rebuilt.

'The British are sparing no effort to recapture our escaped German soldiers, but even after many days they have not succeeded. The entire country is on alert, looking out for one brave German whom all the might of the British cannot seem to apprehend. My friends, a new German hero has been born, a man who singlehandedly is defying thousands of British security men and tweaking the bulbous nose of Churchill. Even when thrown into of one of the British torture camps he refused to submit. He continued to fight. His courage and devotion to duty never wavered. His resolution should be an example to us all. The whole of Germany salutes one of our bravest men. Peter Hencke!'

The woman wiped her nose with a small embroidered handkerchief she took from her sleeve, but the tears continued to flow. 'What's the use? Why run? Why resist any more? Haven't we done enough already?' The words were soft, scarcely audible, directed more to herself than the other woman.

'Frau Deichsfischer,' the other muttered, 'you mustn't give up hope.'

'I've given up everything else . . . A husband. My sons. Two brothers. How much more do they want from me? What else do I have to give?'

They lapsed into silence as the crackling voice across the radio continued its address.

'Peter Hencke has set the historic example demanded of us all by the Fuehrer. Resist! To the bitter end! Knowing that the National Socialist spirit will survive and outsmart our enemies. Even now our Fuehrer is working in Berlin on plans which will bring new victories to our German armies and exhaust the Allies' will to continue the fight. Even in these dark hours we must not forget that victory can still be ours, so long as we remain determined to keep the faith and never to give in. Long live the German *Volk*. Long live our beloved Fuehrer, Adolf Hitler! Death to the Jewish conspirators! My friends, keep up the good fight!'

The strains of the national anthem blared out across the cellar and Frau Deichsfischer reached out to lower the volume. As she did so the bread, by now thoroughly soaked with her tears, crumbled in her hand and fell to the floor. She looked at the crumbs in despair. 'In God's name, why do they want us to go on? What can be worse than this?' she sobbed.

'The Russians, Frau Deichsfischer,' the other whispered. 'The Russians.'

The transcript of Goebbels' broadcast lay on Cazolet's desk. As was the custom with Goebbels' lengthy ramblings, the important sections had been highlighted in pen and he scanned them quickly. He arrived at the references to Hencke and rubbed his tired eyes in a futile attempt to persuade them they had made a mistake. How on earth had Goebbels discovered the identity of the one remaining escapee? Without a name, he was just a statistic, a single digit in the vast lists of war. With it he became human, could be touched and sensed, and Goebbels was transforming him into the torch carrier for the entire German war effort. 'Bloody hell,' was all Cazolet managed to say before placing the transcript on top of the Prime Minister's despatch box. The Old Man wasn't going to like this.

'The Fuehrer will not permit it, Erich, because I will not permit it. I hope I make myself clear?'

There was no response, only a look of defiance on the other man's face.

'Erich, your son's there, isn't he?' Dr Josef Goebbels, Reichsminister for Public Enlightenment and Propaganda, held up his hand to stifle the other man's protests. 'Look, I know you're not arguing for a withdrawal on personal grounds, but since your son *is* there let me explain why it's imperative we hang on to Prague as long as we can. No matter what the cost.'

From an immaculate silver case he offered a cigarette to Major Erich Hirschfeldt, one of the longest-serving members of the FBK – *Fuehrerbegleit-kommando* – the hand-picked SS detachment which acted as the Fuehrer's personal bodyguard. The major's hand trembled slightly as he took the cigarette. His hand hadn't shaken, Goebbels reflected, at any other time during all the years in which Goebbels had known him, when Hirschfeldt had led the street gangs which had split so many heads in the early days and had suffered so many casualties themselves, when he had personally executed dozens of men at Hitler's order after Stauffenberg's failed assassination plot, or even a few weeks ago when he had clawed his way out from under the collapsed roof of the Reich Chancellery's east wing after being buried for almost five hours. Yet that was all gone. He was no longer a fearless defender of the cause but a simple German father, scared about his son, needing a shoulder to cry on.

'He's . . . the only son I have left, Herr Reichsminister,' Hirschfeldt stammered as he tried to light the cigarette.

'I can understand how you feel, Erich. Remember, I have a son and five daughters myself.' Goebbels smiled reassuringly. He hated playing agony aunt but he couldn't afford to have Hirschfeldt falling to pieces. The impact on the others would be appalling. It was bad enough that day by day they were being forced to retreat out of the sunlight and magnificent edifices of the Reich's *Hauptstadt* into the underground cellars with their bare concrete walls and atmosphere of catacomb decay; they couldn't survive the collapse of discipline too. Goebbels had to hold on to them all, everyone in Berlin from the Fuehrer and Hirschfeldt all the way down to the telephone operators and drivers because, if they fell apart, everyone in what was left of the Third Reich would know about it within hours and it would all be finished within days. He must get them to hold on, for just a little longer.

'I know things look grim but all is not lost. Think, Erich, think of what might still be salvaged. This coalition between capitalists and Stalinists – how long can it last? Every day as their armies draw closer across the battlefields it becomes more likely that this bastard alliance will be torn apart and they will fall upon each other. Churchill hates Stalin, Stalin loathes Churchill and that sick old man Roosevelt understands and trusts neither. We only have to hang on a little longer, Erich. Give the damned alliance time to disintegrate, that's all we need.' His voice was soft and encouraging, full of confidence; it was confidence not yet shared.

103

'But do we have time? Will there be anything left to save?' The agony was chiselled into Hirschfeldt's face. Once he'd had a faith built of steel which could withstand any number of blows, but Hirschfeldt had watched incredulously as his own faith had rotted and rusted away beneath the tears he had shed for his son. He would have condemned other men for it – *had* condemned many for much lesser offences in the earlier years of glory, but now it had taken over his entire being and he felt unable to resist.

'This unholy partnership will burst apart – believe me,' Goebbels said with passion. 'But the Reich must still be intact to take advantage of that historic moment, don't you see? That's why your son and Schoerner's army must hang on to defend Prague as long as possible; they cannot be allowed to withdraw or surrender. Will your grandchildren forgive us, Erich, if we surrender our armies on foreign soil without a fight? Did we forgive our fathers' generation for the humiliation of 1918? I have no intention of surrendering our armies intact so they can be dragged off to prison camps while our enemies march across our undefended frontiers to pillage their way through our womenfolk. Think of your wife, Erich. Is that what you want for her? Schoerner must hold on in Czechoslovakia as long as possible. If it means more sacrifice, it is a price we must willingly bear.'

He studied the major closely – the drooping head, the hunched shoulders, the once-immaculate black uniform become dusty and tarnished, the boots unpolished, the dark rings around the eyes supported by a two-day growth of stubble. Goebbels was a master with words, but he also realized that words alone were not always enough. They hadn't worked with Hirschfeldt.

'Look, Erich, perhaps you need a change. This scurrying around like troglodytes is enough to depress anyone. If you really feel it's so important, I could get you transferred to Prague, to be with your son. How better to take care of him . . . ?' And how better to take care of you, you miserable bastard, whose long face and doubting eyes are in danger of

104

infecting everyone around the Fuehrer? As if the Fuehrer didn't have enough doubts himself. So off to the eastern front with you, Fritzi, and a chance to die usefully for your country instead of living miserable and contagious here in Berlin. And by your death allow Goebbels the chance to create another heroic myth, of a man at the right hand of the Fuehrer who insisted on defending the Reich to his last breath. Hirschfeldt had been a good servant, up till now. He deserved the opportunity to die a hero.

Hirschfeldt looked up with exhausted eyes. He had been around the silver tongue of Goebbels long enough to know what he really meant. 'I'm sorry, Herr Reichsminister. I love my country . . .' He took a long pull on the cigarette and tried to muster a smile, but it didn't carry much conviction. He nodded in resignation and acceptance of his fate.

'You'll be all right, Erich. Trust me,' Goebbels said, gazing at the wreck of a once-mighty man in front of him. The spectacle started him worrying. He began to wonder whether Peter Hencke had a family . . .

A special observation post had been erected overlooking the river on a hill above Xanten, complete with camouflage netting, mobile caravan and a host of junior liaison officers who hung around chatting in the background. From their vantage point they could see the broad sweep of the Rhine as it unfolded in front of them, a great ribbon of water disappearing northwards like a winding road into the early morning haze which still clung to its edges. To their left lay the ruins of Xanten, the spire of its church savagely torn off, the town emasculated, while above them scurried squadrons of fighters like swarming bees on a ceaseless mission through skies which were beginning to turn crystal blue as the sun burnt off the mist. It was a good day for dying, and there would be plenty of it before nightfall.

Churchill, in a bulging uniform of the 4th Hussars which he chose to wear on his visits to the front, clapped his hands in excitement as he turned to Eisenhower. 'My God, but this makes the blood run thicker through the veins!' There was strong colour in his cheeks for the first time in weeks, and the sparkle had returned to his eyes. 'How I envy you fighting men. In my lifetime, General, I have seen war grow steadily more murderous and awesome, and perhaps I should be condemned for finding any glory in such a deadly clash of wills, but this' – he waved a gloved paw across the panorama in front of them – 'this is so exhilarating! You know, the easiest way of telling the true character of a man is to study his response to the call of the bugle – does it fill his guts with fire or render them liquid with fear? That's when you know his real worth.'

Eisenhower, who hadn't heard a bugle sounded in anger since reveille at boot camp, nodded and said nothing. He hadn't wanted the Old Man here at the battle front, but Churchill had insisted – and Eisenhower knew that as usual he would try to interfere, throwing off an abundance of home-spun military theories and anecdotes with all the energy and subtlety of an exploding catherine wheel. As if launching the major Allied crossing of the Rhine wasn't going to present him with enough difficulties . . . For a short while, however, Eisenhower would have no reason to worry, since further conversation was made impossible as the massed guns below commenced their barrage of the German positions on the opposite bank, filling clear skies with the menace and anger of thunder. They watched, mesmerized by the pinpricks of fire from nearly 2000 artillery barrels and the great plumes of smoke and destruction that erupted seconds later on the far bank. In response there were but a few tiny flickers of resistance from the positions facing them.

As instantly as it had begun the shelling ceased, as though the film they were watching had been pulled from its projector. There was silence, more deafening in its way than the sound of the guns, a stillness which surrounded them like a cloak, making the moments seem like hours and sending a shiver of anticipation through the tiny group. Eisenhower consulted his watch. 'Time for the drop.'

106

Yet they were not to have it all their own way. No sooner had he spoken than, away in the great distance, a thin white trail of smoke or condensation began to climb slowly into the sky.

'Hell fire,' Eisenhower muttered, the satisfaction gone from his voice. 'A V-2, on its way to London, I'd guess.'

'No, General. Remember your bible, when Moses led his tribes across the Red Sea. There was a pillar of smoke then, too. We have God's blessing this day.'

'Unfortunately, in my experience the Germans are very bad at reading smoke signals,' Eisenhower responded caustically. It was all very well for the Old Man to come and make speeches from the hill top, like a new Sermon on the Mount, proclaiming his belief in God, but they were Eisenhower's men down there about to die, and after all these years of war he found death a more concrete concept than the Hereafter.

Then the Dakotas came, wave after wave of them, flying low and in tight formation with their fuselage doors open and men standing in the doorway, ready to jump. They had all but disappeared into the mists across the Rhine when the group on the hilltop began to see the parachutes open, falling gently as seed might be scattered on the ground. And there was reaping along with the sowing; soon the Dakotas returned, many in trouble and some on fire. The far bank was not going to be vacated by the enemy without a struggle. And the German guns seemed to have gained strength, pouring a hail of shells across the river and into the Allied positions. Soon a salvo of enemy shells began to creep towards the hilltop, gouging out a crater of earth and destruction as each shell stretched ever closer. Junior officers rushed forward to hustle the Prime Minister and the Supreme Commander back towards safety, but Churchill ignored them, stepping forward as if to meet the challenge head-on, oblivious of the danger, seeming to show supreme faith that this was not his time to die. Eisenhower, embarrassed by the older man's bravado, brushed aside the protests of his staff and stayed out

107

in the open. He was damned if he was going to be shown up by a seventy-year-old civilian.

Soon the moment had passed, the shells were gone, and Eisenhower was left with a feeling of deep irritation at the stupidity of it all. He didn't share the Old Man's direct line to God and the moment of danger had left his mouth dry. It would have been a pathetic way to go, the Supreme Commander and the Prime Minister swept away just when the victory was theirs to claim, all for a moment of petty play-acting. Heaven rid him of meddlesome politicians!

Churchill's face was glowing when eventually he turned away from the view. 'Marvellous! Marvellous!' was all he could say. As he stepped closer to Eisenhower, however, his face took on a more considered expression, a scowl of concentration seeming to split his forehead in two. Something was bothering him.

'My dear General, you have done a magnificent job today. I have no doubt that by nightfall we shall have achieved our objectives and another great step will have been taken towards final victory.'

The old bastard's buttering me up, Eisenhower said to himself. What does he want?

'Seeing the valour of our troops and the selfless way they are willing to lay down their lives for that victory, it makes me more certain than ever that we have no option, in honour, but to ensure that their courage and sacrifice are not offered in vain.'

So that's it! He never gives up . . .

'We cannot afford to win the war yet see the peace we have worked so hard to build thrown away. We must push as far east as possible – surely you must see the sense in that?'

'As far as Berlin, Mr Prime Minister?'

'At least as far as Berlin . . .'

The American shook his head, slowly and deliberately. He had guessed this would come, they had told him Churchill was as hard to shift as a mule in mud, but now he felt almost relieved that he had taken so badly to Churchill's vainglorious defiance of the German shelling. It made him more determined than ever to get this over and done with, and if it meant some plain speaking to the Old Man without any of the diplomatic niceties, well – sure as hell he was in the mood for it.

'It's too late. Over. Done with. Berlin isn't going to happen, Mr Churchill.'

The Prime Minister was taken aback. He wasn't used to such outspoken defiance. 'No' is not a word used between allies, not baldly and up front like this. 'But surely that is mistaken . . .' He bit his lip. His lisp became much more pronounced when he was off guard, and his choice of words was clumsy. 'General, we could be in Berlin inside a fortnight. You cannot possibly pretend it's too late . . .'

'Mr Churchill, believe me, it's too late. I've already been in contact with Marshal Stalin. We need to co-ordinate our efforts as our troops advance towards each other across Germany. And we've agreed. Berlin is his.'

Churchill's lips pouted incredulously like a hooked fish, then his jaw dropped, until it sagged on to his chest. The exhilaration drained from his face and he began to search for his words with uncharacteristic diffidence. 'You . . . have taken it upon yourself . . . to communicate directly with the Russians? Without any reference to me? Or President Roosevelt?' Churchill could scarcely believe the words, even as he found them. 'In God's name, General, what the devil do you think you're playing at?' he shouted, loudly enough for the aides to wander discreetly a few steps further away. 'You can't go round making deals with the bloody Russians!' He thrust his walking stick into the soft ground, like a medieval knight showing his colours.

Eisenhower did not flinch. 'On military matters, indeed I can.'

'This isn't military. This is high politics. And to my mind, high bloody treason!'

'Prime Minister, politics may be your game but the military conduct of this war and the defeat of the German armies is *my* responsibility as Supreme Allied Commander. My conversations with Moscow have been entirely non-political.'

'With Stalin?'

'With Marshal Stalin as Supreme Commander of the Red Army. Yes.'

The aides of both men had begun to shuffle closer once again, anxious not to be completely out of earshot. This was going to be one for the grandchildren.

'You have stabbed me in the back. Ruined everything which I and my country have fought for all these years.'

'That's rot. Berlin's of no military consequence. It has no great defence industries, no strategic significance. Only piles of smashed coffee shops and hordes of civilians, many of whom are going to be slaughtered no matter who takes Berlin.'

'It is of supreme political importance, General Eisenhower . . .'

'That's one for the politicians, sir. Not for me. I'm concerned solely with the military aspects of this war which I want to finish with as little loss of Allied life as I can manage. For that it's essential I come to tactical battlefield agreements with the Russians. That's all I've done.' There was a small, insincere smile playing around Eisenhower's lips. He had the argument rehearsed word perfect, including all that crap about it having nothing to do with politics. He was a military man but he was beginning to learn about politics. Fast.

The two men stood on the bare hillside, silhouetted against the panorama of the Rhine and its military activity, with all the passion and hostility of the thousands of men below seemingly concentrated in the few feet between them. One aide later said it was like watching an old-fashioned duel, the weapons being words instead of cocked pistols.

'Be in no doubt, General, that I shall contact the President. Immediately. This decision must and will be overturned. And if it means your removal or even court martial, then so be it!' Churchill pushed one foot forward towards his adversary, as if preparing to fire.

In contrast the American seemed to relax, shrugging his shoulders, already confident that the threat would miss its target. 'Think, sir. Think very carefully before you rush into that. You know just how sick the President is. Frankly, he's been incapable of handling any serious paperwork for several weeks. He's dying, that's the view of those around him. And he's certainly not fit enough to handle matters like this. Any decision will simply be shunted back down the line. Probably right back to me. And it's inevitable there will be some considerable delay, by which time' – he shrugged – 'it will all be history.'

Churchill began to feel he was being outmanoeuvred. He waved his hands as if to imply that the issues were much broader than Eisenhower could possibly contemplate, his voice booming in an attempt to bully the American into submission. 'War should be a building block, not just a mindless system of destruction! Politics must have its place in the way a war is fought.'

'Like the sort of politics you've been playing with my reinforcements?'

'What on earth do you mean?' Churchill was startled.

'The several thousand troops who should be out there now, winning the war' – he jerked his thumb in the direction of the great river behind him – 'instead of scurrying around Britain searching for one escaped prisoner. What is the world going to think, Mr Churchill, of a leader who publicly urges a bloody advance towards Berlin while at the same time privately denying that effort its necessary reinforcements? People might conclude that you've been playing politics with the military effort and with the lives of tens of thousands of innocent soldiers. Seems to me it's not just my job that's at risk here . . .'

Churchill's complexion had become suffused with the heat of anger and indignation. 'You are threatening me, General!'

Eisenhower returned the challenge with steady, ice-cool

111

eyes. 'Oh, no, Mr Churchill,' he said softly. 'I'm just calling your bluff.'

Goebbels watched the broken figure of Hirschfeldt shuffle out the door. The condemnation of a friend who had served the cause faithfully for so many years left no trace of emotion in his face. It was just another sacrifice required by war. He had long ago learned to compartmentalize his emotions, not to allow them to get in the way of doing his job. And he was very good at his job.

Almost before the sagging back of Hirschfeldt had disappeared the doorway was filled with the figure of Captain Otto Misch, also a member of the FBK, immaculately suited in his Waffen SS uniform complete with death's head insignia and slashing shoulder flashes. Misch was tall, blond, sinewy, every inch as if he had stepped straight out of a recruiting poster, but the three fingers missing on his left hand and the Iron Cross pinned at his neck declared that he was no paper hero. He had seen action, and revelled in it. That was why he had been selected for the élite. Although a veteran, Misch was young, still in his early twenties, and beneath the veneer of the uniform and medals he was still callow with little experience or confidence outside his military life. Ruthless, unquestioning, indefatigable, dedicated to ensuring that his leader's will was done, but immature and in complete awe of Goebbels – in the Reichsminister's mind it was an exemplary combination of qualities which was why he had chosen Misch as his ADC. It had the added advantage, Goebbels mused, that the captain would not dare to respond to the advances which his wife Magda offered so freely to any good-looking young man who came within her orbit, particularly a specimen who, like Misch, made up for his intellectual and social inadequacies with the physical frame of a stallion. The cow always chose someone as different from himself as possible . . .

And the choice was enormous. It was a deep sadness to Goebbels that National Socialism had attracted over the

112

years so few people of intellectual quality. That hurt. But there had been no time for persuasion and argument, to employ the tools of discussion and debate in the rush to build the Reich. Perhaps if they had been able to give themselves a breathing space, if they hadn't invaded Russia so soon . . .

The click of Misch's polished heels interrupted Goebbels' reflections. 'You called, Herr Reichsminister.'

'Hirschfeldt. He's being posted to Prague. Effective immediately. I want that son-of-a-bitch out of here within an hour. See to it.'

'*Zu Befehl!*' Misch responded, but made no move to leave as Goebbels indicated he had something else on his mind.

The Reichsminister rose from his chair and began to pace the small room, trailing one foot behind him. He had been born with a club foot which he had dragged after him all his life. He had always taken care not to be forced to march swiftly in public, to ensure that the cinema newsreels hid the impediment and made him look as whole and as manly as the others. It was why he could never be a leader in his own right, and perhaps why he had been attracted to Hitler from the first. The Fuehrer never marched briskly but always adopted a strolling swagger; it made it easy for Goebbels to keep up without embarrassment. Yet the days spent in claustrophobic underground shelters, with the excursions outside becoming increasingly less frequent, had aggravated his leg. The fuggy atmosphere seemed to stick in the lungs, the blood circulated less freely, the damp seemed to worm its way inside his foot and the dull ache stretched from his toes to every other part of his body and soul. He rubbed his thigh, trying to force the blood to circulate some warmth, but it was no good.

'Let's get out of this sewer, Misch. Christ, I need some fresh air.'

Without a word the captain followed him through the door, where they turned right and immediately began ascending a long flight of bare concrete stairs. They proceeded slowly, one step at a time since the brace on Goebbels' leg made using stairs difficult. There were lifts, at least when the power supplies were operating, but a few evenings before he had been stuck in a lift after one of the first bombs of the nightly raid had fractured a main power system. He had been forced to wait for more than two hours in a lightless, tiny steel box which at any moment threatened to become his coffin. He had needed all his considerable mental powers to control his mind let alone his bladder as he waited, powerless and trapped, in the dark to die. It had given him nightmares, a hatred of being stuck underground in these wretched bunkers and an overwhelming, animalistic desire to die out in the open, not in a hole in the ground. So Goebbels didn't use lifts anymore.

Soon he and Misch were in the gardens of the Reich Chancellery. He stood for a while, allowing the daylight to replenish his energies, breathing in air which bore no taint of the gas filters and oily air-conditioning. The Allied raids had reduced much of the ornate gardens to a rubbish heap, yet the daffodils were in bloom and he plucked one, savouring its faint scent and admiring its lustre and bright colour. The flowers would be blooming in the Alps by now, he thought. The narcissi, the alyssum, the whole mountainside would be bursting with life, and hope.

'Before the daffodils fade, Misch. We must be ready before the daffodils fade,' he muttered after several minutes.

'Yes, sir!' Misch responded, with as little comprehension as if the Reichsminister had been discussing the finer points of Nietzsche.

'I must buy time!' He would trade half his remaining panzer divisions for the few more weeks required to prepare for the Alps. 'Misch, what does the twentieth of April mean to you?'

'The Fuehrer's birthday, sir.'

'Exactly. Less than a month. We must be ready by then. We won't have another chance. When they all gather to honour the Fuehrer I want the occasion to be a celebration, not a damned wake. We need something special, an omen, a symbol, something which will turn the gathering into a

114

revival of the German fighting spirit and give us the time we need.' His eyes burned and his scrawny neck strained like a greyhound in the slips. His thin fingers with their finely manicured nails closed claw-like around the daffodil until it disappeared.

'Misch. We need Peter Hencke!'

The bloom fell to the ground, crushed.

'I will not submit to your blackmail, General!' Churchill clenched both his fists, as if he were ready to take a swing at Eisenhower should he come a few inches closer.

'No blackmail, Prime Minister. Only facts. Hard and cruel, perhaps, but facts you can't avoid.' Eisenhower had taken out a cigarette and was lighting it carefully. He needed one, to be sure, but more importantly he wanted Churchill to see his steady hand, how much in control he was.

'What *facts* are these?'.

'The fact, Prime Minister, that after this shooting match is over, there's going to be only two great powers in Europe. The Americans and the Russians. Germany and France are defeated. Britain is exhausted. Don't get me wrong, I take no pleasure in it. But my admiration for what you and your countryfolk have done can't change the fact that you're on your knees.'

Churchill was flexing his bottom lip as if chewing Eisenhower's words in preparation for spitting them out, but for the moment he held his silence.

'You can't duck it, you can only pick sides. American or Russian. It may not be fair, but Britain has no other choice.'

'What sort of choice is that?'

'Not much of a choice, I admit. A power from half-way round the world which left Europe to rot after the last war, or a bunch of Communists led by a ruthless son-of-a-bitch who'd slit his grandmother's belly just for the practice.'

'Then why, oh why, give him Berlin?' The tone was almost pleading.

115

'Because Berlin is of less military importance than cutting Hitler off from his hideaway in the Alps. And because it's my duty to see that the piles of dead which get left behind in the rubble are Russian rather than American!' He drew long and thoughtfully on his cigarette. 'Time to choose, Mr Churchill.'

There was a long silence. Less than a mile away, a Dakota returning from the dropping zone came down in flames, the explosion as it hit the ground emitting a deep roar and sending a ball of fire and black smoke many hundreds of feet up in the air, but neither of the men noticed. They were busy deciding the future of post-war Europe, two elderly and overweight men stuffed uncomfortably into khaki uniforms.

Eventually Churchill broke the silence. 'What is it that you want of me?'

'I want you to stop fighting over Berlin. Not another word, a sigh, no raised eyebrow or even an impatient puff of cigar smoke. For me it has become an article of faith that you accept my judgement on this matter and we put it behind us. You raised the stakes, now it's time to pay. I want an end to the little games you've been playing. And above all I want those troops you've been keeping from me.' Eisenhower's tone was matter-of-fact, as if he were reciting a shopping list.

Churchill swallowed deep. It was sticking in his gullet. 'But I need the troops to prevent Hencke from getting back to Germany. That could be an even bigger disaster for you.'

'Then there's only one solution. Do your job. Get Hencke!'

In the garden of the Chancellery, the crumpled daffodil lay at Goebbels' feet. 'So that's your task, Misch. Hencke is our talisman, our good luck charm, the one who can rekindle the German will to resist and buy us time. This may be our last chance, the only thing standing between us and total annihilation. Find him, whoever he is, wherever he is, before

116

the Allies do, and bring him to Berlin. If it's the last thing you do, you must bring me Hencke!'

Churchill stood on the hilltop, his Golgotha as he later came to call it, where Eisenhower and his aides had left him alone with his misery. It was a long time before Cazolet dared disturb him.

'It's over, Willie. We've lost. He wants Hencke's head on a plate and the troops back in the front line. We shall never get to Berlin now.' He wiped his damp eyes with a huge linen handkerchief. 'To win the war, Willie. To win after all the toil and bloody tribulation, yet to lose the peace, to have it thrown away at the last gasp. Will they ever forgive us?'

'Defeat is but a state of mind, Prime Minister.'

'Who said that?'

'You did. Back in 1941.'

'The whole of the world is turning on its head, Willie. We went to war to prevent Germany moving east; now the East is about to come to us.' He blew his nose in one final, huge, tempestuous fashion. 'Ironic, isn't it? Hencke and I. On the same side! But you must get him for me, Willie. Eisenhower demands it. It's all gone awry and Hencke has become the most devilish and dangerous man in Europe. We must reel him in before he does us any more harm.'

Part Two

FIVE

Hencke shivered uncontrollably, feeling more wretched and forsaken than a fox before hounds. Even on a bad day a fox has some chance, he mused. Hiding in a copse, doubling back to confuse the pack, taking advantage of sudden bad weather which might deter his pursuers and take the sting out of their efforts before the light fades and they eventually tire or get bored and go home. But he would get no such chance. He had become the most wanted man in Europe. Every hour of every day, in any hiding place he chose, he would be hunted. They would never tire.

He was hungry, soaked by the incessant London rain and sheltering in a doorway of a back-street in Cricklewood. He didn't know where to turn; he was on the verge of despair. Prompted by the couple who thought he was a draft-dodger, many pairs of eyes had been turned to him in the Underground, eventually forcing him out of his shelter. The money thrust at him by the Spanish diplomat had largely gone in buying a hot meal and a fresh set of clothes to make him look less conspicuous, but now the second-hand suit was little more than sodden rags clinging to his back and his boots were full of water. Thoughts of giving up were beginning to bombard his mind. It was the easy course and the more wretched his physical condition the more attractive it seemed. Just to let go, to sink gently back into the relative warmth and comfort of captivity, to stop running.

But he wasn't going to stop; he owed too many people, had too many memories to do that. His aunt had always said he could never make it on his own, that without her he was nothing. She'd been wrong then and he wasn't going to prove her right now, not after all this time. He'd drown in this damned English rain first.

He huddled in the recesses of the doorway, flinching every time someone passed by, wondering how soon it would be before a policeman found this vagrant and demanded to see the identity papers which didn't exist and realized that he had stumbled upon the most important prize of his career. Hencke had discovered during the last few days of wretched weather that doorways were not all the same. Some gave better protection, deeper shadows, warmer corners. Others gave easy access to a maze of back-streets into which he could disappear, given half a head start. This doorway was different; it gave him a view. Across the street there was a pub, with a fresh supply of beer and with the noise and jostle of ordinary people enjoying themselves. Somewhere inside a piano was being played, not very well but with a captivating enthusiasm. At that moment Hencke needed the sight and sound of people more than a four-course meal, to be reminded that there was a world outside his life of fear and flight, and to cling to the hope that some day he might be allowed to return to it.

Cricklewood was the Irish quarter, poor, run-down, dirty, like all immigrant quarters. Yet perhaps because of the deprivation the moments of relaxation were embraced with more vigour and genuine relish than in less grubby areas of London, particularly on a Friday night. And although Hencke was losing track of time and didn't know it, tonight was Friday. The piano beat out song after Irish song, the laughter was as coarse and disrespectful as the conversation, and Hencke longed to be part of it. He dug into his pocket and pulled out the few coins he had left. Eight pence. Enough for a small glass of beer. He hauled himself out of the doorway and stepped towards the pub.

Inside the lights were bright after the darkness of the street, and it made him conscious of the bedraggled state of his clothes. He needn't have worried; most of the men were still in their working clothes and, judging by the amount of paint and cement dust on their trousers and mud on their boots, they had arrived straight from a building site. The cursory glances thrown at him through the smoky atmosphere were warm and friendly; fate had chosen his pub with care. He bought his small glass of beer at the brightly polished bar without problem; in spite of indications around the pub that the English – or Irish, at least – had a seemingly infinite variety of beers from which to choose, there was only one on offer this evening. He settled into a corner and soaked up the warmth.

He didn't rush his beer; he wanted time to relax and, in any case, the beer tasted awful with a sharp, bitter tang. He put it down to wartime shortages. All around the conversation was of home, of Ireland, conducted in broad accents difficult for him to follow. Most people seemed to wish themselves in a different place, 'across' as he heard them refer to it; he identified with their longing and understood. It was a different world, like the one he could remember from many years ago, before the time when all conversation became dominated by the war, when men still joked about tomorrow and complained about their work and their wives. There seemed to be little talk about the war, and in their tales and reminiscences he could detect no sympathy for the British. At the next table two young women were talking about 'the boys' and 'the struggle' but it was clear they were not referring to the battle with Germany. He sat back and let their conversation drift over him.

He soon realized he had made a dreadful mistake. While the chatter washed around him and he listened to nostalgic talk of times past and a homeland far away, his own memories came flooding back. Of the happiness he once enjoyed in a homeland he had loved, of the bright faces that used to smile at him before they were riven with pain and death, of the love that he had shared and which had been shattered by shrapnel and taken from him by the men he would hate for ever. Normally such memories made him hard and determined, but he was weak from exposure and hunger and the mouthfuls of beer were beginning to have a soporific, sentimentalizing effect. He felt the resistance ebbing away from him; he wanted to curl up into a ball, to cast the world aside, to forget and to sleep for ever.

But the world had other ideas. As he felt himself floating off and the atmosphere of the pub stripping away his defences layer by layer, he picked up the conversation of the young women at the next table. Of Patrick, who would be out in another eight months. 'And never any chance of parole. Mind you, there was never much chance of his giving them any good behaviour.' Of the different ways in which a coat might be refashioned. Of the longing to be back home, with a job and a husband. Of the bitterness at having been forced by poverty to exchange the empty rolling pastures of Donegal for a flea-bitten bed in Cricklewood which three people used in shifts. Of the offal which could be bought off-ration and disguised as food. And of 'that little German bastard who's got the bloody Tommies on the run. Mother preserve him!'

It wasn't a choice, more an instinct grown mighty with desperation. He had no one else to trust and nowhere else to go. He'd run out of ideas, money and strength. As the piano struck up a new tune and the men in the bar began to sing in deep, sorrowful voices the words of a republican battle hymn, Hencke reached across and touched one of the women on the arm.

'Excuse me. I'm that little German bastard. Would you help me, please?'

They looked at him in a mixture of astonishment and alarm, unable to utter a word, their world stopped. He wondered what they would do when they recovered – cry in alarm? – yet in his exhaustion his worries had a distant, almost academic air. Base reality came rushing back as the door of the pub burst open to reveal eight London policemen with drawn truncheons. They stood blocking the entrance, staring around, while silence and resentment descended between walls which a moment before had been ringing with

124

gaiety. For one interminable moment nothing moved except for the eyes of the policemen as they roved around the pub. Hencke felt his mouth run dry. One of the bobbies was looking straight at him.

She could find no fear in his expression, it was all too sudden for that, but she couldn't fail to see desperation and defiance. It was a look she knew well. She had seen it in Paddy's face when the army came for him, and again when the judge had sent him down. She'd seen it in her mother's face when they told her that her husband wouldn't be coming home again, ever, not with all those bullets in him. In the depths of Hencke's steady, dark eyes she could see memories of pain and anger, and she knew about those, too. She had little time for the Germans and their violence, but she had no time at all for the British and she would do almost anything to get her own back. Yet hadn't she troubles enough without walking into new ones in the pub?

She sat wrestling with the contradictions, not knowing if she wanted or would be able to help, until one of the policemen began beating his truncheon up and down in the palm of his hand, slowly thumping out a message of menace and hate. It was enough. She leaned across to two men on a neighbouring table and whispered urgently between their lowered heads. Just a few words, but there was a nod of understanding, the briefest pause, before the two men stood. It was the first sign of any response to the unwanted invasion, and all eyes were upon them. Without a word one clenched his fist and struck the other full on the chin, sending him sprawling across a table and knocking glasses everywhere. A neighbour retaliated on behalf of his fallen friend and in an instant a volcano of commotion had erupted in front of Hencke. The pub became filled with a pandemonium of shouts, curses, waving arms, smashing glass, women's screams and breaking furniture. Then the truncheons started flying. He scarcely had time to see one of the policemen succumbing to an assault by two elderly and determined

125

women armed with heavy handbags before he felt an insistent tugging at his arm. It was the girl.

'Come on, Adolf. Time we left.' She clasped his hand and dragged him, stumbling and uncomprehending, towards the rear of the pub. As they passed the bar he heard her shout, 'Turn off the bloody lights, Harry!' and he ducked as a glass crashed off the panelled wall above his head and shattered into a hundred fragments. He was still shaking the shards from his hair when he was dragged through a door and into the women's toilet, a dim and squalid little place with a cracked and badly stained basin but, to his relief, another door. He ran after her into a dark yard surrounded by a high wall, but piled up against the wall forming stepping places were several crates and already the girl was scrambling up them. She peered cautiously over the wall before urging him on. 'It's clear!' she shouted, disappearing over the other side.

Hencke followed. Behind him the noise of battle inside the pub was beginning to subside; even the most determined of opponents were having trouble sustaining a good fight in total darkness. He threw himself over the wall. His jacket caught on something, there was a tearing sound and he felt a burning sensation across his forearm, but before he knew any more he was in a cobbled back-street with the girl urging him to run. He had landed heavily and was winded, and it could be only moments before the police found the back door and were upon them. Stumbling through the puddles of rain, he followed her flapping raincoat into the night.

They ran until they were both exhausted, through dark streets, avoiding the lights, alert for the sound of pursuit, until they could run no longer. Their lungs rasped from the effort, the rain trickled down their foreheads to mix with the sweat, their energy gone.

'I think we've done it, Adolf,' she panted, looking up at him through strands of russet hair which had hung in long tresses before the rain turned them into a soaking mat.

126

'My name . . .' he muttered doggedly between great gulps of air, 'is not Adolf. It is Hencke. Peter Hencke.'

'OK, Peter Hencke. Any ideas what we do for an encore?'

She wrapped her raincoat around her, tying the belt tightly. Her efforts served to outline her slender waist and hips, while beneath the clutter of damp clothing her struggle for breath emphasized the shape of her breasts. She was young, less than twenty, he guessed, on the verge of full womanhood, with a handsome oval face and healthy skin which shone translucent in the rain. What the hell was she doing here, he began to wonder, before deciding that he was too weary even to speculate.

As a fresh squall of rain hit them they heard the bells. A jangling alarm began to sound on all sides, approaching, growing louder, bells of warning, bells – so the sudden look of fear on her face told him – of authority. They were near, just around the corner, accompanied by much shouting and noise of commotion. His mind recognized peril, demanded action, but his body was confused with exhaustion; the louder the bells grew, the more distant and infirm his legs seemed to become. Hencke glanced desperately down the street, searching for some source of salvation, but all he could see was the unmistakable sight of a police car rushing through the night towards them. He might have run but it would have served no purpose. He couldn't outpace a car and, anyway, he had no reserves left. He leaned back against the wall, his eyes closed, waiting for the inevitable.

When he opened his eyes, he was staring into the face of a policeman who was studying him intently. Hencke's coat was torn to ribbons by his leap over the wall, the burning sensation on his forearm had turned out to be a throbbing pain from a deep cut with blood trickling down his fingertips, and the look on his face told its own story of agony. The policeman was reaching out for him.

'You all right, sir? Had a close shave by the looks of you. Still, quite a number of others not so lucky, I'm afraid.

You and the lady come with me, we'll get you fixed up . . .'

Uncomprehending, speechless, Hencke was led around the corner. The spectacle that confronted him was so overwhelming that he all but stumbled in alarm before the policeman caught and steadied him. They were in a street, more brightly lit than the one they had just left, with tall rows of houses stretching on either side. The street was residential, not very salubrious, with the worn-down air of a shoe which has had too much use. The buildings were tenements, normally crowded with people, many of whom were at this moment spilled along the street. Immediately in front of Hencke there should have been a solid frontage of brick; instead there was a hole some forty yards across, filled with rubble, smoke, smashed wooden beams, splinters of steel and teams of men clawing away with their hands at the ruins.

'You live there, did you?' the policeman enquired solicitously.

Hencke shook his head.

'Oh, passing by, were you? Bloody V-2s. Can't hear them coming, not like the doodle-bugs. First thing you know is when it's hit. Too late by then, usually. You're lucky, really lucky, believe me. Still, you and the lady must be badly shocked. Come on, let's get that arm seen to and find you both a cuppa . . .'

They were led along a street full of fire tenders, dust, ambulances, air raid wardens, rescue squads, housewives dispensing blankets and sympathy, doctors and nurses tending the injured, and policemen. Lots of policemen. And bodies. In a quiet corner there were already a dozen corpses covered by blankets. A woman's feet stuck out from under one blanket, a child's hand from beneath another, tightly clutching a teddy bear with one arm torn off. And the memories came flooding back . . .

Neither he nor the girl said anything while his arm was tended, the Red Cross nurse used to dealing with patients in shock and happy to do all the chattering herself. It appeared the rocket had fallen some fifteen minutes earlier, about the

128

time the pub fight started. Perhaps that was what had masked the sound of the explosion. The section of the street which had disappeared into the crater normally housed over a hundred people, the nurse said. She hoped that most of them had been out enjoying their Friday evening, but many clearly had not and the row of bodies being assembled under the blankets grew longer with every passing minute. She would like Hitler and all the rest to be brought back to London and a German hanged on every site in the city where a bomb had fallen. Her fiancé had been captured in Singapore and was still, she believed, a prisoner of the Japanese, and the same went for that lot too. She wanted Hencke to go to hospital for stitches, the wound was deep, but he refused, so she disinfected it and bandaged it tightly.

'Just keep it quiet for a couple of days and don't do too much running around, love,' she advised. 'You'll be as right as rain.'

With that they were packed off for a cup of tea from the mobile canteen.

The girl had wanted to forgo the tea and sidle out while they could, but Hencke shook his head. 'Wait. We're all right for the moment. Take the tea.' He was trembling from the shock and the cold, and he needed time to recover.

But there was something else. In the shadows behind the canteen the line of bodies was still growing. Distraught men and women would occasionally walk over to turn back the covering blankets and search for a loved one. No one interfered; death like this had long been routine in London.

It was after their second cup of tea, drunk without a word, that he took her firmly by the hand and led her towards the line of blankets. He avoided those which obviously covered women or children, but the others he began to turn back, staring at the dead, holding on to his companion's hand as if they were a couple seeking mutual comfort. He found what he was looking for underneath the eighth blanket. A man's body, you could tell that by the trousers and the hair on his chest. But of the face there was nothing other than a mass of angry bone and flesh in no recognizable human pattern. The girl drew back in horror, but Hencke knelt down close, as if grieving. Another couple passed by giving them a wide and sympathetic berth, leaving them alone in their sorrow. The Irish girl watched transfixed as Hencke removed an oval dog-tag from his own neck and placed it around the neck of the corpse, before standing up in apparent distress.

'It might confuse them for a while,' he whispered, 'buy us a little time.'

'Now can we get out of here? Or do you fancy hanging around a little longer, just in case the Prime Minister decides to pay a visit?'

She grabbed his hand and was dragging him away when they passed by the body of the girl clutching the mutilated teddy bear. Hencke stopped and stared. Tears filled his eyes and his lips moved in agitation, whispering silent words of anguish, remembering. He fell to his knees and began to pray.

'Holy Mother of God,' the girl snapped in exasperation, looking around for the posse of policemen she expected would descend on them at any moment. 'Can't we do our praying later?'

But he would not be hurried. He finished, oblivious to the bustle of the street, before leaning down and taking the child's tiny hand. With great tenderness he prised the armless toy away from her. 'For luck, Little One,' he whispered, and gently covered her hand with the blanket.

When he rose he stood tall, shoulders braced, and for the first time she saw what a powerful frame he had. The shocked and crumpled man of moments earlier was gone. In his eyes burned the glow of a bitterness and a determination which she understood well.

'Let's go,' he said grimly, tucking the bear inside his shirt. 'There's still much I have to do.'

The Old Man was sitting on his own, in the gloom, with just a small table lamp to cast light. Had he been paying attention to the box of papers at his side he would undoubtedly have suffered severe eye strain, but the papers lay untouched. Churchill was alone with the thoughts that had preoccupied him ever since his return from Germany. He might have expected to be exhilarated, being the first Allied political leader to set foot on enemy soil, but there was no zest in him. He had been brooding, sulking some were saying, and had neglected not only his official duties but also the normal civilities that attend governmental life. Even Clemmie had taken umbrage, deciding on the spur of the moment to visit relatives in the country for a few days rather than indulge in yet another heated and utterly pointless exchange with her husband. She was used to his moods and tempers, but she could see no reason for this bout of petulance. It was not as though he had lost a battle – or so she thought.

Only Cazolet had shown any inclination to be with him, and the rest of the Private Office had been more than content for him to shoulder the burden. Cazolet had sat for many hours, ignoring the barbs and the criticism, showing indifference to Churchill's irascible accusations of disloyalty aimed at those around him, even offering a rebuke when the Old Man had gone inexcusably far. Cazolet considered he was over-reacting, and told him so. Yet self-inflicted or not, the pain was real. He resembled a great old oak, now dying, ancient limbs sagging under their own weight, the sap no longer rising. Instead of thrusting for the sky he seemed to be slowly falling apart.

As Cazolet entered the Old Man looked up. There was no friendly rustle of leaves, no welcome in his eyes. He was swathed in his favourite silk dressing-gown whose rich brilliance he usually outshone, but tonight his garb seemed oddly out of place.

'They've got him,' Cazolet said. 'Or at least they're pretty sure it's him. Ironic. It was a V-2 the other night. They pulled him out from under the rubble.'

'What do you mean – "they're pretty sure"? Is it him or isn't it, for God's sake? Or does someone want me to

131

come down to the mortuary to make a personal identification?'

Cazolet ignored the sarcasm. 'There's not much to identify, that's the problem. Just a man's body with its head blown off and a German identity disc around the neck.'

'Prison camp records? Size? Weight? Hair colour? Isn't there something else?'

'That will all take a little time, I'm afraid. The state of the camps, particularly for transit prisoners, is pretty awful. The whole system's been swamped and the records are all over the place. It'll probably take a couple of days before they're sure . . . But how else could Hencke's ID end up on a body underneath tons of rubble?'

'I don't know. I really don't know . . .'

Churchill's eyes were closed, as if in prayer. For several minutes he scarcely moved, he might have been asleep, but Cazolet could see the occasional agitated shaking of his head, the only sign of some inner turmoil. When at last Churchill looked up, Cazolet saw the change in the eyes. The emptiness had gone, in its place was a spark of emotion – not joy, certainly, more grim resolution, but a spark nonetheless.

'Great turning points in history are usually marked by death, William. I never guessed it would be Hencke's.'

'We don't know for certain.'

'He's dead. He must be dead, don't you see? It's as if he has been holding up the onward march of history, and history cannot wait. There is a great war out there which must be finished, one way or the other. Events have moved beyond our control and we must follow in their wake, whether we like it or not.' He took a deep mouthful of brandy. When he spoke again there was resignation in his voice. 'Get me General Eisenhower on the phone.'

'But we can't be sure . . .'

'The war isn't going to wait around for your doubts, Willie!' he snapped, unwilling to brook any delay now that his mind was made up. 'I need to get hold of Eisenhower and tell him that one more brave man is dead and he can have his damned troops. There's nothing to be gained by holding on to them any longer.'

'It's nearly midnight, two in the morning at the general's HQ,' Cazolet protested. All of a sudden he didn't understand, and he could no longer be certain whether the Old Man was thinking straight. 'To be honest, I'm a little confused . . .'

'I, too, am confused, William. Last time I enquired I was His Majesty's First Minister and Secretary of State for War. I don't recall having laid down either of those heavy burdens. Which gives me the right and you the duty to get the good general on that bloody phone without further prancing around. Or would it make it easier if in future I gave you orders in Swahili, as the King's English seems to be something of a problem?'

Swallowing his doubts and his irritation, Cazolet picked up the telephone and tapped to attract the operator's attention. 'See if General Eisenhower's in the land of the living, would you, Grace? The Prime Minister would like a word . . .'

It was damned uncomfortable and the smell appalling. That's what made it such a good hiding place.

After they escaped from the bomb site she had dragged him through the shadows of yet more anonymous back-streets, pausing only to make a hasty telephone call before arriving at an unkempt boarding-house set back from the road behind a bushy, secluding hedge. Their reception lacked any trace of enthusiasm. Behind the front door hovered a small and wiry man who appeared greatly agitated and whose polished bald head was flushed and sweating profusely in spite of the cold. He wore an unironed shirt and an unwelcoming glower, closing the door quickly before rushing them into a back room with curtains tightly drawn. Hencke was instructed to wait in the sparsely furnished bed-sit with its squeaky floorboards and dusty sheets while she busied herself with the proprietor. They obviously knew each other well, but that didn't prevent her frequent disappearances from the

133

room to consult with him turning into a running battle conducted in voices which became increasingly heated. He didn't seem pleased to see Hencke.

'Don't worry about Uncle Billy. He's a miserable sod with a nervous disposition, but he'll do as he's told.' She said it with such authority that Hencke never doubted her. It was during a pause in the ongoing argument held just outside the door that Hencke first learned her name. Sinead. No other name. He also discovered her secret. 'You'll guess this much anyway before this is over, so I'll tell you now and you'll get very little else. So don't go asking bloody stupid questions which I can't answer.' She lit a cigarette and offered him a whiskey, but he declined. He remembered how quickly the half pint of beer had begun to affect him after so long without a drink.

'We're Irish Nationalists. Don't believe everything you've heard about us,' she hastened to add with a nervous smile. 'We're nice people really.'

Hencke declined to mention he'd scarcely heard anything about Irish Nationalists, although what little he had heard was none too complimentary. War makes strange companions.

'The British occupy half our country. We want it back,' she continued. 'And we're willing to fight for it, if necessary. Fortunately for you, it's meant getting our boys in and out of London without the police knowing, and that's what we'll have to try with you. Get you to Ireland. There you'll be safe – and half way home.'

Hencke sat quietly, saying nothing, trying to figure her out. She had an open, honest face, a natural smile and full lips which belied the uncompromising tone of her words. The scattering of freckles across the bridge of her ski-slope nose and the healthy bloom in her cheeks gave her an aura of innocence, yet once she had taken off her raincoat there was no denying her womanhood. As she felt the pressure of his steady gaze she lost her sense of authority and began to feel awkward and girlish. She lit another cigarette, her lips

134

closing nervously around the tip like a young girl at a village dance waiting for her first date. She had poise beyond her years in dealing with Hencke, yet a touching naivety about herself. Her large hazel eyes bubbled with enthusiasm, but already there were the first crinkles of maturity appearing at their downcast corners. Something in them suggested a sadness which tinged her ebullience, marking her while not yet scarring. Her initial appearance, he decided, was misleading. This was no ordinary Friday-night girl in a pub. He had already learned not to make the mistake of patronizing her.

'So, how will you . . .'

'No questions, Peter Hencke. This could all go wrong and they might get their hands back on you. I don't want you giving away our whole game. So keep your eyes closed and your mouth shut and we'll get along just fine.'

'One thing I must know, Sin . . . Sinead.' He was unused to the name, and had to wrap his Middle European lips carefully around it. 'One question. Why did you decide to help me?'

She smiled softly. 'The most difficult question of all. That's just what Uncle Billy's been bellyaching about. And I can't say I've got much of an answer.' Self-consciously she twisted the bracelet on her wrist. 'You looked so pathetic in the pub, starving and wet, and that always appeals to an Irish girl's heart. Then I had to make my mind up – you or those bloody bobbies. Not much of a choice, really. You could be Attila the Hun for all I care, you'd still be preferable to those black-hearted bastards. Anyway, you have lovely eyes. They sort of glow. Like my brother's.'

'Patrick?'

'How do you know?' she shot back, suspicion creeping into her voice.

'The pub. You were talking about him in the pub. And Donegal. And home.'

'We thought you were asleep. So you were eavesdropping?'

135

'No. Just identifying with someone who wanted so much to be home.'

There was an uneasy silence. The conversation had become very personal, and here she was sitting on a bed swapping intimacies with a stranger.

'How long will it be before we can get to Ireland?' he asked.

'Depends. Our group's been in hibernation since the war began; for some while your lot was doing a much better job of getting at the British than we could ever hope to do. So it may take us a few days to get hold of the right people. With luck less than a week.'

'How?'

'I can't tell you.'

'Secret?'

'Not really. It just depends who we can find at a moment's notice after five years. We'll have to blow away a few cobwebs.'

'I don't get it. Five years . . . you must have been still in school.'

A flush of embarrassment came to her cheeks.

'How many men have you smuggled out?' he demanded, but her only answer was downcast eyes. 'Don't tell me I'm your first?' He couldn't disguise his incredulity.

'My family's been part of the struggle all my life,' she said fiercely, fighting against her own awkwardness. 'I was there when they arrested my brother and locked him away. I sat holding my father's hand on the night before they killed him. Three Orangemen who found him in an alleyway, called him the father of a Republican pig and shot him where he stood. Not even executed him. They blew his kneecaps away first, then put two into his guts so that he would die, but not too quickly. They made sure he'd suffer first. And made sure my mother would suffer, every day and every night for the rest of her life. Mr Hencke, I know as much about this business as I need to!'

There were no tears but she was shaking all over. Hencke reached out and held her hand to stop it trembling. 'I've

136

already seen what you can do, Sinead No-Name. Believe me, I've got no reason to complain. I know. I was there, remember?' His words thawed through her blushes. Anyway, where else did he have to go? 'Do your best, that's all I ask.'

Her best, two nights later, proved to be a dilapidated truck carrying sacks of vegetables and empty fish crates to Liverpool. The sacks gave reasonable cover behind which to hide from prying eyes, the sour smell of fish offering added discouragement to anyone venturing too far into the entrails of the load. But for Sinead and Hencke, hiding in a small compartment crafted out of crates and sacks deep inside the lorry, it meant a night of bone-bruising discomfort. Their hiding place was claustrophobic and dark, and every jolt of the old axles seemed to transmit itself directly through the hard wooden floorboards in spite of the small mattress thrown on the floor. They lay on the mattress, trying to brace themselves against the incessant jarring as they drove through the outskirts of London on to the main Liverpool road. The noise and discomfort made conversation difficult and the enforced intimacy left them both feeling awkward, so they settled back as best they could, bathed in the glow of a flashlight which gave their faces a ghoulish, melodramatic cast.

They were making steady progress north on the A5 through the suburbs of Birmingham when they hit the potholes. They were driving along a stretch of road which had received attention from a Focke Wolf's bomb load in the early part of the war. The surface damage had long since been repaired, but underneath, the Victorian sewers had leaked and grumbled and groaned, until finally they had collapsed. The lorry's front wheel crashed into a deep hole, the steering wheel spun from the driver's hands and the vehicle was sent skidding across the road before coming to rest, front wing buckled, against a brick wall. From their hiding place they heard one burst of profanity from the driver before other voices crowded round. This was not the first vehicle to come to grief that night on this stretch of road, and

137

with the wartime spirit of camaraderie abounding there were plenty of voices to offer consolation and many hands to help. The tyre had punctured; it would have to be replaced and the crumpled front wing bent out. 'Should only take us twenty minutes,' they heard one cheerful voice saying.

They were still feeling their bruises when someone climbed into the back, flashing a torch around in search of the spare wheel. 'I'll do it!' the driver exclaimed, an edge of panic in his words, but already it was too late. While Hencke froze, the girl wriggled as close to him as possible, trying to burrow into his overcoat and make their profile as anonymous as one of the sacks of vegetables. Moments later the beam of a powerful torch began to probe around them, licking like a lizard's tongue into the corners, bouncing off sacks and trying to peek through the gaps between the fish crates. She squeezed ever more tightly into his body as the light swam around and above them, her body taut, holding her breath, feeling her heart beating like a tattoo against his chest. Then the light disappeared. The tyre had been located; their hiding place had worked.

The repairs, as the helpful stranger had predicted, did not take long. Soon the lorry was ready to proceed, but there were new agonies as they heard the muffled sound of not one but three men climbing back into the cab. God, surely the driver wasn't offering lifts! They didn't discover until much later that two soldiers on leave had asked to be taken on to Liverpool and the driver, anxious not to create suspicion by refusing, had been forced to agree.

As the lorry was drawing away they realized their predicament. The load had shifted. Only a little, but as they relaxed their grip on each other and tried to regain their original positions on the mattress they discovered there was no room left. They were stuck, face to face, unable to move because of the load and unable to talk or call for help because of the presence of strangers just feet away. Even the flashlight was too great a risk, so they continued on in darkness, every

138

muscle tensed, their only means of communication being through the touch of their bodies. They were so close she could feel every part of him – the bristles on his chin and neck, the muscles on his sinewy shoulders, the heaving of his chest as he breathed, even the sharpness of his buttons and the bulge of the child's toy stuffed inside his shirt. Their enforced intimacy had caused his legs to entwine involuntarily with hers, his breath wafted through her hair and down the back of her neck. Every move of their bodies, every bounce of the truck, brought them into fresh contact, and she knew there was no part of her own body which he couldn't feel or sense. They were close enough to smell each other. She might have expected him to be frozen with embarrassment; she wouldn't have been astonished had he become aroused and immensely masculine, but all she could sense was diffidence. His body was there, beside her and upon her with a muscular thigh stuck between her own, but it was as if he were merely an observer, treating her body with the curiosity characteristic of a surgeon, or a sommelier examining a wine with a sense of professional detachment without any intention of drinking. She tried to wriggle to get herself more comfortable, to let him know she didn't mind. Several of the boys she knew would have given anything – and had frequently promised to do so – for the chance of being in contact with her like this. But Hencke, as she already knew, was different from other men. He offered no response. He seemed to have built a protective shell around himself and he wasn't going to break it open for any young girl in the back of a lorry.

They lay like this for another hour, he silent, she lost in the tingling of her senses, before the lorry stopped again to disgorge its unwanted guests. A few minutes later they reached their destination in a quiet siding where the driver was able to remove the press of sacks and crates to release them. As Sinead clambered down she was trembling. From stiffness. From the excitement which the warmth and pressure of his body had aroused within her, and the feelings of

139

guilt which that had caused. From curiosity about this strange man. And, even more, from curiosity about herself.

'Say, Beetle! Where's the place we liberated, the one with all those salt mines stuffed full of booty?'

Lieutenant General Bedell Smith entered Eisenhower's room with as much haste as the dignity of his rank would allow. 'D'you mean the place near Merkers? The Third Reich seems to have been using it as a bank vault. Not only crates of gold and silver plate but there's also a collection of art looted from all over Europe. Half the Louvre seems to be there in wooden packing cases; we're already getting telegrams by the hour from de Gaulle claiming most of it. Then there's at least two huge halls full of nothing but bank notes. Don't know yet whether they're duds or the real McCoy . . .'

'Yeah, but wasn't there a mountain of wine crates – claret, brandy, that sort of thing?'

Bedell Smith checked his list. 'Right. Historic vintages mostly, intended for Goering, so the locals are saying. We also found a whole batch of papers which we thought might be vital to the war effort. Just got the translations in. You want to hear? – "The delicate smell of the fruit is just slightly obscured by the nutty transformation of the oak tannins . . . the length and elegance of these delicious cognacs compare so favourably with the pretty Parisian girls . . ." Turns out the friggin' things were some vintner's tasting notes.'

'OK, OK. Get a crate of the brandy. Send it to Mr Churchill with my compliments and some sort of message about it being from one Napoleon to another. You know the kind of thing. To get back on track with him.'

'Good idea. There's lots of it. One crate enough?'

'I want to show there are no hard feelings, Beetle. Not suggest I'm in love with him. For Chrissake the idea's to keep him quiet, not to give him any encouragement. Anyway, the old bastard drinks too much as it is. Wouldn't want him

140

getting carried away and coming up with any more of his bright ideas. Would we?'

The lieutenant general winked mischievously, offered a smart salute and hurried on his way.

SIX

Liverpool tasted different. Instead of London's choking fog there was the sharp tang of salt air, with many fewer military vehicles roaring down the streets throwing diesel fumes at him. People on the streets hurried along, keeping their heads low, bending into the breeze that blew off the Irish Sea, the distant echo of a railway station ringing in their ears. A cinema was turning out its patrons after the last show, nearly catching Hencke and the girl in the rush. 'Trampled to death by Noël Coward. My father would never forgive me!' Sinead had joked, before she remembered that she probably shouldn't joke about her father, her mother would not approve.

It was a long walk before they entered a cul-de-sac, at the head of which stood a tall, imposing house of four floors, in darkness except for a porch lamp making circles of light in the stiff breeze. They stopped under a tree, like any courting couple not in a hurry to find their way home, while Sinead made a careful inspection of the house and its surrounds. She was uneasy, something was not right and they moved on, back to the streets, taking a cup of tea at a late-night canteen near the docks, never lingering too long in one place, anxious to avoid enquiring eyes, shivering as the damp sea air turned colder with the night, tripping over dustbins and piles of rubbish in dark alleyways which served as homes to bad-tempered cats. Hencke was exhausted from the ceaseless walking after the inactivity of the prison camp but it was not until the first hint of dawn that they were back in the cul-de-sac facing the tall house. This time, after a brief inspection, Sinead seemed to have found what she was looking for and hurried him towards the door. Someone opened it without her knocking.

The someone turned out to be a tall and exceedingly handsome woman in her late forties, perhaps past her prime but with much femininity still and great, possibly excessive care taken about her appearance. She closed the door quickly behind them while Hencke blinked in the blaze of light which lit the interior. As he looked around he could not hide his astonishment. There were other, younger women standing to the sides of the large hallway. He blinked again to make certain but there was no mistake. He hadn't been told, and in a thousand lifetimes would never have guessed.

'Well, I'll be . . .'

'Later, dearie. Anything's possible if you behave yourself, but for the moment let's get you safely tucked up out of the way,' the woman responded.

'A brothel . . . ?'

'Where else would a good Catholic girl take a man like you,' Sinead chuckled mischievously. 'But there's no time for gawking. Come on with you.'

The house was quiet but not asleep, as if pausing to catch its breath before the night shift clocked off. Sinead led him past a broad, gilded staircase which swept to the upper floors, past chaise-longues tastefully covered with brightly patterned upholstery and adorned with women in even more brightly patterned costumes which decorated without denying what lay underneath. None of them looked up or appeared to take any notice, burying themselves in magazines or cigarettes which protruded from extravagant holders. Everything glittered without being truly gaudy, was orderly, in its carefully chosen place, and there was little room for doubt that the madame ruled with an iron fist inside her elbow-length satin gloves.

He was hustled through a down-to-earth kitchen where a pot of coffee bubbled away on the stove and one counter stood crammed with bottles of varied colours and kicks, then up bare wooden stairs which in earlier times servants had used to clamber from the scullery to their attic rooms without disturbing the family, until eventually he was led through a brightly lit corridor and into a room where the door was locked securely behind them.

Sinead waved her hand to pre-empt the inevitable flood of questions. 'Before you start, you've got to believe me. This is the safest place in Liverpool for you.'

'A brothel?'

'This is a high-class establishment, the best there is. And the finest safe house on the road back to Ireland. The British would never raid it; they'd be terrified of how many chief inspectors and judges they'd unearth.'

A look of amusement crinkled the edges of his eyes and for the first time since they had met she thought he was smiling, although it was difficult to tell. The scar on his upper lip twitched occasionally, yet she could never be sure.

'And a wonderful place, no doubt, for picking up all kinds of useful information across the pillows,' he suggested.

'But you catch on fast, Peter Hencke. And, my God, you seem to recover fast, too!'

Hencke had walked over to a small table laden with two plates, food and drink, and was already ripping and chewing his way through a cold pork chop. In a stride she was beside him, snatching hungrily at her own meal. The food was like nothing either of them had eaten for months. Pork chop, cheese, chicken, butter, even fresh fruit, nothing which could be found off-ration, a feast which could only have been obtained at considerable expense under the counters and behind the curtains of the black market. They tore at it.

'They seem to like you here,' he spluttered through a slice of chocolate cake.

'The woman at the door, she's my father's second cousin,' she replied with a mouth equally full. 'I told you. This is a family affair.'

They were smiling at each other across the mouthfuls of food. They couldn't easily sit down – there was only the

144

large brass bed – so they stood and stuffed until, overcome by the delight of rare indulgence, they had entered a race to see which of them could finish first. She won, by a short biscuit.

'You bastard. You let me win,' she accused him gaily.

'Nothing so gallant,' he shook his head. 'Do you realize I've just eaten the equivalent of a month's rations in the prison camp? I think I may be sick.' As if to give weight to his words, he stretched out unsteadily and sank on to the bed. For the first time since their departure from London she looked at him closely. He was exhausted. The lean face had grown gaunt, the cheeks hollowed, the scar about his mouth carved more deeply into his skin. His eyes had sunk into dark pockets, yet they still held that glow of defiance which so intrigued her. Once again she wondered what drove him onwards while so many others had given in.

'Here. For medicinal purposes.' She uncorked a bottle of scotch and handed him a large slug in a tall tumbler, but even as she reached across to him she saw he was already asleep. 'The first friendly bed you've slept in for a long time, Peter Hencke. Enjoy it.' She sat on the end of the bed, looking at him.

When he awoke it was dark still – no, that couldn't be, it had been dawn when they arrived. Had he slept the entire day? The only door in the room apart from the entrance had been left open, leading to an extravagantly decorated bathroom full of mirrors and tiles and polished brass, with a pile of fresh cotton towels at the foot of an ornate cast-iron bath. The water was hot, and soon he was soaking up to his neck, having laced the water with scented salts he found in a glass jar. He tried to remember the last time he'd had a bath. He couldn't. Then he felt a cool draught across his chest and arms as the outer door opened and someone entered the bedroom.

'By the sounds of all that splashing I suppose it's a silly question to ask if you're dressed yet? Do you know that war-time regulations allow us only a couple of bucketfuls of

water in the bath? You'd best be careful. Be pathetic if someone turned you in for a criminal waste of water.'

'At the moment they would certainly find me unable to
put up a great deal of resistance.'

'Then you'd better make yourself presentable. There's a
robe hanging from the back of the door. Throw me your
clothes; I'll get them cleaned.'

In a minute he was out, towelling his hair until it was
again dark and sleek, trying to make himself look respectable
in a cotton robe which was pink and too short and which
exposed the smooth, hairless skin of his chest. She tried hard
not to stare.

'Good morning. Or is it?' he enquired.

'It's eight p.m. You've been asleep fourteen hours.'

'Tell me, how much longer will I be here? I hate to complain, I suppose it's every man's dream to be locked inside a
brothel, but after the prison camp I feel nervous locked up
anywhere.'

'Can't tell, maybe not long. But Aunt Mary . . .' She
twiddled her fingers nervously, not wishing to look at him.
'She said she'd like to help. Not personally, of course, but . . .'
The young girl inside her was babbling a little. 'She said she'd
be happy – you know – to send along one of the girls. On the
house, so to speak.'

At last it was blurted out and he began to laugh. 'That's
. . . very nice of your Aunt Mary but . . .' He shook his head.
'I don't think so.'

She blushed. 'A man of principle, Peter Hencke?'

'No, Sinead. Don't make me what I'm not.'

He could sense her relief and thought he understood. He
was hers. This was a great adventure for her and he, or at
least his safety, was her prize. The stories that would be told
by her friends and family for a long time to come would be
her stories, no one else's. She didn't want some tarted-up
part-time hooker spoiling it with tales about him she
couldn't possibly hope to match. He smiled at her secret,
happy to play along.

'Don't you know that Nazis are supposed to drink babies' blood and screw nothing but young virgins?'

'What! And go to bed only with teddy bears?' she chuckled. 'What sort of Nazi are you, Peter Hencke, sat here wearing a fluffy pink dressing-gown and nothing else beyond a smile?'

They both began to laugh, from relief, from the bond of growing friendship and shared secrets, from the fact that neither had found much to laugh about for so long, until they both collapsed on the bed, sobbing with the effort.

They were still laughing when they heard the commotion downstairs. The banging of doors. The raised voices. Feminine screams of surprise mixed with male shouts of authority.

'Holy Mother, it can't be a raid!' she gasped.

'I thought you said the British . . .'

'They never have . . .'

The door was flung open. One of the girls stood panting, her ample chest heaving beneath a flimsy covering of lace. 'American MPs! Looking for one of their sodding sergeants,' she shouted before disappearing to warn others.

Hencke's eyes searched desperately around the room, for a way out, a means of escape. He didn't need to say anything.

She shook her head, her face pale. 'There's nowhere to run, Peter.'

'Then I am lost.'

She bit into her lower lip. 'I won't have it. No!' In one action she kicked off her shoes and scrabbled at her sweater, tugging at it until she popped out. 'We've maybe one chance.' The zip was undone, the skirt already falling to the floor, with the petticoat following. 'You're not American. You're a civilian having some fun in a brothel.' Stockings, suspenders. 'If they believe that, maybe they'll leave us alone.' She tore at the straps of her bra with a ferocity which caused something to give. Then it was her knickers and she was standing there naked, glowing. 'So pull your bloody finger out and get into bed!'

She had rushed across and was leaning over him, pulling

147

at the robe, when the door burst open once again. The form of a young military policeman filled the doorway, all metal helmet, armband, white webbing, razor-sharp creases and polished boots. He had a night-stick in his hands and a nervous tic around his left eye, which was trained on Sinead and had to be torn away before finally settling on Hencke. The soldier took one step into the room.

'So, what's going on here?' His voice was youthful, light on the authority of age and experience and lacking totally in any sense of occasion.

Before he could move further than a pace Sinead was in front of him, blocking his path, hands on the curve of her naked hips, her full breasts wobbling with indignation as she faced up to him.

'What's the matter with you stupid Yanks? Never seen a woman getting laid before? If you're here for lessons you'll have to wait your turn like all the rest. In the meantime just bugger off and let a girl get on with a night's work!'

The tic around the MP's eye seemed to double in intensity and he made no attempt to move further into the room, which he could only have done by touching Sinead. He seemed embarrassed to be confronted by a woman, stark naked and a good twelve inches shorter than himself. It hadn't ever happened to him before. Not a completely naked woman, not under any circumstances. Never.

'Christ, Peterson,' a voice called from down the corridor. 'What the devil are you up to? Is he goddamned there or not?'

The soldier looked up nervously from his inspection of her bright red nipples and glanced again towards Hencke, studying him for a fraction of a second before looking back down at Sinead and her nakedness.

'Er . . . no, Sarge! Not in here.'

'Are you certain, asshole?'

The MP was looking distinctly uneasy and beginning to sweat. Sinead, confusing him by switching her tactics, had

148

hold of his night-stick and was stroking it tantalisingly between her breasts.

'Come back later, soldier, when I'm through with this one. Let's have some fun,' she whispered.

He shot another nervous glance in Hencke's direction, comparing his profile to the description of the errant soldier they were seeking. There was real anguish in his eyes. He was mortified while he looked at Sinead, yet he couldn't bear to take his eyes off her. 'No, definitely not here, Sergeant,' he croaked.

'Then what are you waiting for? Get your butt up to the next floor,' the disembodied voice of authority came back down the corridor, just as Sinead's fingers reached in the direction of the soldier's shirt buttons.

'Yes, Sergeant,' he whimpered, and was gone.

Sinead closed the door quietly before she turned round. She had a brave half-smile on her face which she tried desperately to turn into a convincing look of triumph, but the lower lip began to wobble and in a moment the resistance was gone and tears were flooding down her face. She threw herself into Hencke's arms and sobbed great tears of tension and relief. She was still crying when she lifted her head and began kissing him passionately, her salty tongue probing between his lips.

He did not respond, just as he had failed to do in the lorry, but she was making all the running. Her body was warm from the nervous energy, her nipples burning against his own body, her tears turning to sighs of passion.

'Peter, in this world it may be our last time. Please!'

Something told him that for her it was also the first time. She was so young, scarcely older than some of his pupils. He was confused, uncertain, the self-righteous moralizing of his aunt ringing in his ears, but his indecision was overwhelmed by Sinead's insistence. In the end he had little real choice but to join in and, if not exactly enjoy it, at least to take comfort in her gratification. She knew what she wanted, instinctively, even if she wasn't totally clear how she wanted it. The raw energy more than compensated for her youthful ignorance. It wasn't great sex, but for her it would always be special.

She lay back to catch her breath, coming down to earth, her whole body tingling, feeling places within for the first time. She knew it was a moment she would never be able to forget, or to repeat, no matter how many years she might live. Not even with Hencke. It was a long time before either of them spoke.

'You have someone back home?' Perhaps it wasn't the most tactful question but she couldn't help herself; she didn't have much experience at this. She had to ask. She felt now she had the right.

'No. Not any more.' His words were clipped, without any trace of self-pity, as if all emotion had already been wrung out of him. But in the gaze which held her she could once again see the fire inside, and there was pain.

'You lost someone, too?'

He didn't respond, simply nodded.

'But if they're gone, why are you so impatient to get back home?' She made it sound like a rebuke.

'Wouldn't you be?'

She propped herself on an elbow. 'I'm not sure, Peter. Back to Germany? I don't want to take sides in your war, but over here we don't hear pleasant things about Germany.'

'It's like many places. Some good parts and fine people. Many bad. Like most places. Like Ireland, I suspect.' He was deflecting her questions, throwing the challenge back at her. 'Why did they arrest your brother?'

She didn't reply immediately. 'They claimed he left a bomb. There was a warning. But a policeman got hurt . . .'

'Did he do it?'

'I . . .' She pulled away from him and her face flushed with anger that he should dare raise the question, but his eyes were searching around inside her. He already knew. 'I . . . don't know. In all honesty I truly don't know.' There was great misery about her. 'And I don't know why, Peter Hencke, but that's the first time I've ever said as much to anybody.

150

Even to myself.' He had penetrated more than her body, and with the admission, a little bubble of faith which had survived all previous doubts and assaults quietly burst within her.

'So he might be guilty?'

'The policeman didn't die,' she began in mitigation, but she wasn't convincing even herself. Her head fell forward to hide her confusion, her long auburn curls falling about the pale skin of her breasts. 'He was crippled. He won't ever walk again.'

'He had family? Children?'

She could do no more than nod.

'And friends, who were so filled with revenge that they shot your father. This is your "family affair"?'

'I didn't start our troubles, Peter.'

'You may not have started it. But who's going to finish it? That's always the difficult part.'

Suddenly she resented the assault upon her integrity and ideals, and the way he was ripping her world apart. 'I suppose you're going to tell me that it wasn't Hitler but Poland which started World War Bloody Two. And that you're going home to finish it!'

'I'm sorry, Sinead. I have no right. I didn't mean to insult you.' He reached out to touch her hand, to re-establish contact. She didn't respond, but neither did she move away. 'I have my own "family affairs" to see to,' he continued.

'But why, Peter? You said you had no family left.'

'I have memories. Sometimes all you have left are memories.'

'And can you live just for memories?'

She studied him closely, following the profile from his high forehead down his long nose to the scarred lip and sharp, determined chin. He didn't reply straight away. It seemed a lifetime since anyone had got close enough to ask such questions.

'I've tried. Yet . . . you spend your life looking back, and the farther you have to look back the more you die each day,

151

little by little. No, I can't live for memories, no one can. You mustn't try.'

'But you are prepared to die for them?'

She waited, but there was no answer. For all their adventure and talk together she still knew little more than his name. He was a man who kept his secrets wrapped tightly around him, a man with fire in his veins and steel in his bones, yet who could still cry over a little girl and her teddy bear.

'Why are you going back?'

He remained silent, unwilling or unable to say, staring blankly at the ceiling.

'Peter Hencke, I don't want you to be the last man to die in this bloody war!'

A wry smile began to play around his lips – or was it the scar? 'No one wants to be the last man to die. Not in this war, not in any war.'

'Does . . . that mean you'll be coming back?'

He turned to face her until she could see his eyes. He didn't want any misunderstanding.

'You mustn't hope for me to be something I cannot be. No, Sinead, don't think of it.' He shook his head. 'I won't be coming back.'

SEVEN

'Not too hot for you, sir?'

The only reply was a grunt.

At least he's not complaining, not yet, thought the barber. Doesn't mind me scalding my fingers raw, but let him feel the slightest discomfort from the hot towels and he'd let the entire bloody street know. After which he'd moan about his shave not being close enough. And he never left a tip, not even at Christmas.

'Did you see they got Hencke at last?'

'What, you mean that bloody German? Thought they'd picked him up a long time ago.'

It was not an uncommon assumption. With so many stories queuing up to demand space in the news columns as the war drew to its climax, the coverage of Hencke's escape had rapidly disappeared from the pages. Even today's report had been restrained, wrapping up what editors decided was an old story.

'No. They found the blighter in Cricklewood – or what was left of him. Seems he'd been leading the police a right merry chase, then a couple of nights ago he got caught underneath one of their V-2s. Poor sod. Seems unfair some-how.'

With victory within their grasp the British sense of fair play was beginning to flourish once more. And since Hencke had a name he was no longer simply another bloody Kraut but a real character, even an underdog, and the barber held a sporting regard for any underdog, particularly since he had done the decent thing and thrown himself under one of his own rockets.

153

'Serves the miserable Hun right,' the customer barked from underneath the towels. 'Should have shot him if they'd caught him alive. Probably a damned war criminal anyway; most of them are.'

'Well, I don't suppose we shall be able to shoot them all.'

'Damn it, but I'd like to try,' the voice came back from within the fog of steam, as the barber tried to remember from behind which desk the customer had fought his war. 'Particularly this one.'

'Why him?'

'Most dangerous type of Hun. Doesn't know when he's beaten. Too stupid and arrogant to know when he's lost the bloody war.' But it was more than that. It was his example, one lonely man – even a German – running around the country sticking his fingers in the face of Authority, an example which all too many seemed willing to follow. It couldn't be tolerated. These were difficult and unsettled times, when people needed to be reminded about their proper place and duties. There was more than one way to lose an empire. 'And be damned careful how you trim the moustache!'

The barber stopped the razor and examined the customer's throat. One day, he promised himself. One day . . .

In Berlin the news that Hencke's body had been discovered was heard widely, even though it was carried only by the BBC and listening to enemy radio was an offence punishable by summary execution on the street corner. The populace took comfort in the fact that the law was unenforceable; there simply weren't enough lamp posts. But in the Bunker the news became available to very few; Goebbels saw to that. Hencke had been his prize. Great hopes had been raised upon the prospect – which many took as a promise – of a triumphant return to Germany, and he didn't like to disappoint the Fuehrer. Indeed, it was Goebbels' full-time task to keep the spirits of the Fuehrer high, to persuade him that salvation was still at hand, to find every omen, helpful horoscope or shred of encouraging news and cling to it like a climber to an ice face.

Above all, however, Goebbels was a realist. That's why he was so useful to the Fuehrer. He wasn't a carpet-widdling spaniel like so many of the others. He told the Fuehrer what he wanted to hear, of course, but not to ingratiate himself and flatter, only to encourage and strengthen. If they were to salvage anything from the heap of scrap into which Germany was being bombed, they needed time and the undisputed leadership which only the Fuehrer could provide.

And they needed luck. It was ironic how, after all their planning and preparation and *putsch*-ing, all the great victories and still greater reverses, everything came down to a matter of luck. If only they'd invaded Russia a year later, after an armistice on the Western front. Or reached Moscow a month earlier, before the snows. If only that oaf Goering had continued bombing the British airfields a few weeks longer when the enemy had only a handful of aircraft left, instead of turning his snout towards the blitzing of London. If only the Japanese hadn't bombed Pearl Harbor and brought the Americans rushing into the war. If only . . . It all came down to luck and fickle fortune in the end. That's where Hencke came in. Goebbels wanted him as his lucky charm, to dangle round the neck of the Fuehrer, to ward off the doubters and defeatists who undermined the leader's morale and to give him back the resolve to continue for the few vital weeks they needed. With Hencke and a little luck anything would still be possible. Yet suddenly the luck seemed to have run out.

Hencke was beginning to feel that death might, after all, be a soft option. They hadn't been long in the rusty fishing smack, only a few hours, but the seas were rough and growing fiercer, and he was a rotten sailor.

She noticed the sudden sallowness in his complexion and the grimness about his mouth, the scar tugging at his lip.

155

'Think positive. The weather makes it more difficult for the coast-guard, too. Anyway, we've not long now,' she encouraged.

No sooner had she spoken than through the low-hanging storm clouds on the horizon appeared the outlines of a rocky coast.

'What is this place?'

'Man. The Isle of Man, they call it.'

'I thought we were going to Ireland?'

'One step at a time. The Isle of Man is in the middle of the Irish Sea, halfway there. All the direct routes to Ireland are carefully guarded. We're going to try to slip through the back door.'

'As long as it's dry land I don't think I care any more . . .'

'You should feel at home. The island is full of Germans and Italians sitting out the end of the war.'

'What?'

'It's one of the main internment points for enemy aliens and prisoners.'

'You're taking me to an island the British use as one vast prison camp?' he groaned, trying to find the strength to raise an eyebrow.

'It's the Irish in me,' she said, mocking him. 'But don't worry. They're so busy trying to stop people getting out that no one expects anybody to try to get *in*.'

Hencke had held out, against seemingly overwhelming odds, until they were approaching the relative calm of a small west-facing harbour called Peel, over which towered the crumbling red stonework of a ruined castle. He and Sinead had no opportunity to admire the view; they had been ordered into the hold to hide them from prying eyes. So Hencke had lost sight of the horizon, the only immovable and unheaving object to which his fragile senses had been able to cling, at precisely the moment his stomach was assailed by the overpowering stench of fish. His resistance came to a sudden end.

'And this is the secret weapon with which Germany is

156

going to win the war?' Sinead taunted as he sat hunched over a bucket.

'If you have any mercy, shoot me.'

'Too late,' interrupted the skipper, clattering down wooden stairs which led from the deck. 'Apparently the British government have just announced that you are lying on a slab in a mortuary somewhere in London. Officially you're dead already!'

Hencke thought for a moment about attempting a smile, but decided that triumphs could never be celebrated on a retching stomach. He reached for the bucket.

Any depression that Josef Goebbels might have allowed himself on hearing that his talisman had been found crushed under a pile of German-induced rubble quickly disappeared when he received the top-secret cable from the German Embassy in Dublin. *Hencke . . . Alive . . . Free . . . In Dublin. Halfway Home!*

It was 10 April. Russians less than eighty miles east of Berlin, their advance troops already ripping through the outskirts of Vienna. To the west the Americans, Canadians and British, swarming across their bridgeheads on the Rhine, their vanguard almost as close to Berlin as the Red Army and making faster headway. The great Reich which had once stretched from the edges of Moscow to the Atlantic and from the northern tip of Norway as far as Africa, now reduced to a narrow ribbon a few dozen miles across as the vast armies of their enemies pressed in on all sides. For a man whose task it was to manufacture propaganda, all that recent weeks had given him by way of raw material were bricks of straw.

But now! A saga of German courage, of triumph against seemingly insuperable odds, an epic example of endurance which showed that all was not lost, that victory could still be theirs! All they needed was time, a little more sacrifice from the German people, another burst of national resistance. If only Germany could hold on a few weeks longer, Stalin would go too far as he had always done, the West would begin to understand how wrong they had been to trust him, and how much greater was the menace of Bolshevism than any posed by Nazism. Then, perhaps, they could come down from their Alpine fastness . . .

If only Germany could hold on a little longer. If only the Fuehrer could hold on. And with the inspiration of Hencke's example, they both might.

He brushed aside the fine layer of dust that had already settled on the cable, savouring once more the most encouraging news he had received in months. More dust began instantly to fall. The Americans and British were bombing the capital around the clock, the last hope of German resistance in the air had already been blasted from the sky or reduced to matchwood on pulverized airfields, and even the bits of Berlin that had not suffered direct hits were being slowly shaken to pieces. It was April, yet scarcely a tree in the city bore any leaf, as if a Valkyrian whirlwind had stripped them bare. The skies above the capital were beginning to fill with the yellow, acrid smoke of cordite, soot and dust which turned day into night and the eternal hope of spring into darkest autumn. Goebbels fanned the flames of hope amongst all who would listen, but he knew the odds lay heavily against him.

And all because of one man. Winston Bloody Churchill! The evil old drunkard who, if only he hadn't been so monumentally stubborn and shortsighted, could have brought the war to an end less than a year after it started with Britain and its empire still intact, and Germany straddled across Europe. They could have shared the world between them. But in his whisky-sodden blindness he had thrown away the historical destiny of their two great nations, had bled them both dry, Winston Bloody Churchill, who had been biting their backsides for years. Well, perhaps it was time for him to take some of his own medicine. And the poison was here, in Goebbels' hand.

He knew he couldn't wait until Hencke was back. Hencke

158

might never get back or, if he did, it might all be too late. Goebbels needed something now, not next week. So he would announce Hencke's survival and escape to Ireland, and humiliate Churchill in his bare-faced lie, and hope to cause so much confusion that the world would never again believe a thing that the British leader told them, even if he had Hencke, his grandmother and his entire fornicating family on public display in London Zoo.

The lights flickered and dimmed as the blast from a nearby explosion momentarily disturbed the smooth running of the generator. Another cloud of dust descended from the ceiling and fell around Goebbels. But in the half light, he didn't seem to mind. For the first time in days, he was smiling.

'I did warn you.'

'Puff, Willie! Don't whine, man,' Churchill responded angrily. 'You don't win wars by sitting on your rear end behind cosy wooden desks and filing damn paper all day. You have to take risks. We took a risk. So we lost. It's not the first time, for God's sake.'

'But Berlin Radio has accused you of blatantly lying . . .'

'Willie, the great British public expect politicians to lie. They would be astonished if we didn't.'

'Then what. . . ?'

'The thing to worry about,' Churchill said, continuing Cazolet's lesson while chewing the end off a cigar, 'is not lying. It's getting so obviously caught. Looks incompetent. As if we are losing our touch. Can't afford that in a run-up to an election, Willie. We simply cannot afford that.'

Cazolet didn't care for the way in which Churchill seemed to ascribe all the decisions that had been taken – or, at least, all the mistakes that had been made – to them both jointly. This had been a cock-up, in which he was deeply involved, of course, but he had warned the Old Man most meticulously and he had little enthusiasm for sharing equally in the consequences, particularly when it was as yet unclear precisely what those consequences might be.

159

'Willie, it's not over yet, you know.' Churchill shook his head sorrowfully, his fleshy jowls quivering in agitation. 'It all sounded so simple when it started. Hencke was but another soldier, of little consequence in the overall balance of affairs, no more than the merest flicker of a candle in the darkening night of German defeat. But . . .' Churchill sighed deeply. 'He is no longer just another anonymous soldier. Eisenhower chose to turn him into a token of his victory over me; now Goebbels has embraced him as a symbol of resistance. He will try to destroy me through Hencke.'

'Surely not . . .' Cazolet began, thinking that Churchill was going too far in personalizing events, but the Old Man raised his voice to shout him down.

'They are trying to turn him into an agent of my defeat and destruction! And if Goebbels ever gets his hands on Hencke, he will humiliate me, Willie. For every day Goebbels lasts, in every broadcast Radio Berlin makes, the lie will come to life. We shall never hear the end of it.' Churchill waved away the smoke that was clinging around his head so that he could see Cazolet clearly, and his assistant could see him. 'Hencke must not get to Berlin. Under any circumstances, Willie. Do you hear me? Not back to Berlin. Not into the clutches of Goebbels.'

'But he's not even in Britain any more . . .'

'He is not yet back in Germany, either! And Goebbels needs him there in a hurry.'

'So . . .?'

'In order to use him as a weapon against me, Goebbels has given us the means of our salvation. He has made a grievous error. He should never have told us he was in Ireland.'

'But we can't touch him in Ireland. Can we?'

'If I could get to him in Ireland, neutral or no, I would. But they would never be so stupid as to allow us to find him. Already he will have been smuggled out of Dublin, to somewhere safe, somewhere beyond us. But!' The cigar stabbed the air, leaving a smoky exclamation mark hovering between them. 'To accommodate his disastrous timetable Goebbels

160

has to get him from Ireland back to Germany in a fearful hurry. He cannot be smuggled through Spain or some third country – too long. He cannot be flown there, for we have total mastery of the skies. They have no ships left afloat which could make the journey. No. There is only one way. By submarine!'

Cazolet was nodding slowly as he digested and confirmed the Old Man's reasoning.

'And there is only one route, Willie! To run the gauntlet of the English Channel, so full as it is of our frigates and patrol boats, would be suicide. A twenty-mile stretch of water without so much as a friendly rock behind which to hide. He couldn't escape detection if he tried to swim through! No, Willie, no. He must go the long way round, beyond Scotland and down through the North Sea. There he might hope to hide in the depths, to escape our attentions. Nearly two hundred thousand square miles of dark water. There he might stand a chance.' Churchill seemed caught up in the challenge himself. 'And it is *there* we must stop him. We must move everything we have and throw a gate across the North Sea so solid that even the fishes will have trouble penetrating it.' The voice became less full of enthusiasm. 'We must leave nothing to chance, Willie. We must stop him there.'

After many years spent so close to the Old Man, Cazolet was accustomed to the sharply swinging emotions, his sudden tempers too, but never had he seen his mood change so quickly. One moment Churchill had been lost in self pity, the next caught up in the thrill of trying to outwit Goebbels and even his own sea defences, yet now he was shedding tears.

'Goebbels has sacrificed him, to get at me. He could have waited, got Hencke back home before making his wretched announcement, keep us unawares. But he couldn't wait to humiliate me. Goebbels has betrayed him with the kiss of Judas. And so we must betray him also and nail him to a hard cross on which only brave men perish.' His bottom lip quivered with anguish, the head fell forward, the tears began to fall into his lap, tears of sorrow, of pity, and of guilt. 'We move great armies around the chessboard of war, knowing the battle will result in tens of thousands of deaths. When I went to thank the troops on the night before they left for the Normandy beaches, they cheered, even with the knowledge that many of them were shortly to die as a result of my orders. There will be death warrants to be issued even after this war is over, and I shall not shrink from signing them. The game of war brings death, and the devil has ensured that this has been a hellishly long game. But to order the destruction of this one brave man, whose only crime has been to love his country and to show the most peculiar courage, to order him cast over like a pawn, is almost more than I can bear. For he is no ordinary man. The whole world has betrayed him, poor, poor man. And now it is our turn. But I have to – you do understand, don't you? – it's him or me.'

Churchill reached over to grab the knee of his young companion, beseeching his understanding. The tears flowed copiously. 'Willie, there is something I have to tell you about Hencke . . .'

The sun was setting, a vivid cusp on the horizon, by the time they reached their destination. They had been travelling since morning, just the two of them in a battered Bedford farm truck, for the last three hours bumping along unmade tracks as they scurried as rapidly as the conditions would allow beside the bleak coastline of western Ireland. They had passed barely a dozen cottages and several of those had stood abandoned and roofless, their bare chimney stacks like memorials to a better, past life. The way of life in this part of Ireland had scarcely changed since the Famine, she had explained, except to get worse. The scenery was green yet barren, and the rugged basalt coastline stood out like the craters of the moon as it was caught by the embers of the dying sun.

She parked the truck on the cliffs above a broad bay; there

was no cover to hide the vehicle, no tree, no bush, only bare grassy slopes. Out to sea the final rays of the sun kissed the tops of low islands that guarded the entrance to the bay and kept its waters calm and smooth. All was still, the only sound the lapping of the tide and the mewing of gulls as they cartwheeled overhead and plunged into the sea in search of sprats. They trod carefully down a rocky path which he would never have spotted had he not been walking on it. They held each other's hands tightly. She led the way, while he acted as a great anchor to guard against the boulders and stones trying to trip them and send them stumbling, until they had clambered down to the narrow shingle beach below. The tide lapped gently across the stones.

'What do we do now?' he asked.

She checked her watch. 'We wait.'

They were the only words exchanged. They knew these would be their last moments yet neither could find the things to say. They stood side by side looking out to sea, still holding hands, losing themselves in colours which in the final struggle of day were swirling turbulently above the horizon. She felt the elements mimicking the turmoil inside her, happy that he was almost safe, while feeling desolate that his salvation would make her miserable for the rest of her life. She thought once more of that night in Liverpool when, for a fleeting moment, she felt she had got close to him. But the feeling had never returned.

Then it began. The sea before them which had been peaceful and at rest started to lift and part, a fermenting brew of waves and foam which rippled out and filled the bay.

'Your lift,' she said simply.

They watched as through the clinging beds of kelp rose the profile of a conning tower, its U-boat insignia still identifiable in the last light of day, and already there were men scuttling across the upper deck, manning the anti-aircraft guns and launching a small collapsible rowing boat. It was soon approaching the shore, its crew alert and wary. Hencke and Sinead had only moments left together.

163

'Thanks,' he whispered. He was still looking out to sea rather than at her.

'No thanks needed. I love you.'

'Please, don't. Don't love me.'

'But I do, Peter Hencke.'

'You mustn't, Sinead. There's no future for us.' Still he could not look at her.

The rowing boat was already beginning to scrape its way onto the beach, with two armed sailors jumping out and taking guard against unforeseen danger.

'Kill hope, Peter, and you kill the heart. Don't take that from me.'

'I know what you mean. Believe me. But I'm not coming back.'

'The war will be over eventually. . .'

'Not even then. Not for me. I'm sorry.'

She wanted to scream at him, to demand that he open the doors inside which he kept so tightly bolted, that he owed her more than 'I'm sorry' after all she'd done, that the least he could give her was an explanation, but an officer was scrambling up the shingle towards them and was almost upon them.

'Captain Eling,' he introduced himself with a salute. 'My compliments! Please come with me.'

She tried once more but the captain was glancing around anxiously.

'Please. We must leave. Immediately.'

Only then did Hencke look directly at her, with that light in his eyes turned from defiance to a soft glow of comfort. 'I shall remember you, always.'

'Pity we can't live on memories.'

'But at least we can live *with* them, which is more than many will be able to say after this madness is over.'

'What will you remember?'

He smiled, and perhaps for the first time she felt the doors inside opening a little. 'Someone who took my despair and gave me hope. Someone with whom I shared a special kind of love. Someone who, in a different world, could have become my dearest friend. And who knows, perhaps in the next world it might be.'

'Then there's no need to be sorry, is there.'

'No regrets?'

Hesitantly, reluctantly almost, she shook her head.

'I'm very glad to have met you, Sinead No-Name.' And with that his hands slipped from hers and he was gone.

He didn't look back all the time the boat slapped through the water on its way out to the waiting submarine. As they approached, in the gathering dusk, he could see the crew lined up along the hull, watching him. He heard no one give an order but as they drew near the men and officers raised their arms in salute. The final red and purple glow was fading into a dark sky and the submarine stood in silhouette, the last rays of day glinting off the conning tower and bringing an edge of fire to the dull and battered metalwork, making him feel as though he were in the midst of a timeless ceremony of champions, like a warrior being greeted on arrival in Valhalla.

He turned to the captain in puzzlement. 'Why?'

The captain paused to consider his answer. He had several weeks' growth of beard, his white officer's cap was crumpled and the eyes beneath appeared haunted and exhausted. His face bore the marks of many missions. 'Because we understand the meaning of duty, and know what it's like to risk everything to get home. A submariner is never captured, he never has the option like so many others nowadays of sitting safely on his ass and waiting in comfort for the end of the war. A submariner knows only one thing – to fight or to die. In our book, Hencke, you're one of us.' The captain's hand came to touch the peak of his cap and offer his own respectful salute, one fighting man to another.

'They sent an entire submarine crew – just for one man?'

'Three crews of three submarines. Out there are two more U-boats. Me to take you. The other two to act as decoys. We have to assume that the whole British anti-submarine effort

165

is waiting for us out there. It's going to be one hell of a ride.'

'Decoys? You mean like decoy ducks?'

The captain gave a thin, humourless grin. 'Something like that. Decoys who will fly off in opposite directions and hope to drag the British after them. Disperse their effort, create a hole in their defences through which we might sneak undetected.'

'But that's no better than . . .'

'War is a dangerous profession. We're used to it. At least with you aboard we'll be heading back home. If we have a choice, I'd rather be heading home, not buried along with the worms three miles down in some mud hole in the middle of the Atlantic. Feels better the closer you get to home, if you know what I mean.' He sniffed the salt air with the intensity of a man taking his last breath.

'How many men on a submarine, Captain?'

'A type VII-C like this? Around 50.'

'Times three. 150 men. To bring me back home.' He nodded towards the crew waiting on the U-boat deck. 'Do they know . . .'

'That's why they're all there. To see you. To honour you. To know what they might be dying for. That's all a soldier ever wants, isn't it, to know what he's dying for? I thought it only fair.'

'And I have become their Angel of Death . . .'

They were bumping alongside the hull, the dark waters of the Atlantic slapping its side, throwing the tiny rowing boat around and making it impossible for him to keep his balance, but there were hungry hands stretching down to grab him and haul him on board. As he found his feet on the slippery wooden deck casing he glanced around the men who were facing towards him, still saluting. He tried to look everyone directly in the eye, relieved in the near-darkness that he couldn't. He stood to attention but did not return the salute; he saw no point in saluting death, there had already been too much dying.

'Straight below, please. We're already taking more risk

166

than we ought to, sitting here. I think we've outstayed our welcome in Irish waters.'

It was only as they led him away that he turned for one final look at the shore and Sinead, but she was already lost in the descending night. He hoped she had already dried the tears and had gone.

EIGHT

It was around first light on what looked like being a filthy day when the asdic operator aboard the frigate HMS *Juno* picked up the fleeting echo. It was just as likely to be a shoal of cod as a 1,000-tonne U-boat, he thought, but his was not to reason why. He informed the officer of the watch, a punctilious if unimaginative youth from Yeovil, a former stores clerk made lieutenant who did everything by the book. The young officer had no hesitation in deciding to wake the captain; it was his first tour of duty as officer of the watch, and he was already mightily frustrated that the war would almost certainly be over before he had a chance to lob a depth charge in anger and play his own role in the annihilation of Hitler. He had no desire to add to that frustration by getting caught out, so he pulled his naval cap more firmly over his head and blew down the voice pipe.

The captain didn't complain, he was far too professional for that, but the croak in his voice indicated how tired he was. They had just finished a particularly rough passage from the Arctic and were about to finish a far longer war, and somehow the adrenalin wasn't pumping in the way it used to. He hadn't been in home port for more than three months, none of them had, and to be ordered to turn round just a day out and take up position counting whitecaps off Rockall tested the patience of everyone. Yet even the suggestion of a submarine still caused the turbines to turn and the blood to surge. Through tactics and technology the Royal Navy had largely won the confrontation with the U-boat packs yet no commander underestimated the potential and the toughness of any U-boat crew, particularly one which had survived this

168

long. The captain was on the bridge in less than a minute.

'Report, Mr Ansell.'

'Fleeting echo, sir! Indicating northerly heading. Trace very faint − asdic's trying to pick it up again,' the excited duty officer spluttered.

'Steady on, Mr Ansell, you've got time to take a breath,' the captain counselled. 'Now, no chance of it being one of ours, heading back home to Scapa? Don't want us snapping after our own tails, you know.'

'Definitely not, sir,' came the reply with a tone of hurt pride. 'No reports of ours in the area, I've double-checked. I've also alerted the other ships in our group.'

'Very well. We'd better try and pick them up again. Yeoman, form on a line bearing 270 degrees − course 030 degrees − ships 2,000 yards apart.'

'Further instructions, sir?'

'"Tally Ho!", Mr Ansell. "Tally Ho!"'

In the monochrome light that flooded U-494, the crewmen seemed already to be wearing death masks. There was a weariness about them even the tension couldn't disperse. Hencke discovered the crew had returned to Kiel after a gruelling tour of duty in the waters of the Bay of Biscay, torpedo tubes empty, one victim claimed, nerves shattered and duty done, the crew desperately hoping that this was the end of their war, when they'd received orders to sail immediately for Ireland. They hadn't even finished handing over their craft to the maintenance crew before they were instructed to refuel and were turned around; many of the crew hadn't had chance to set foot on shore. The days without sunlight, breathing air contaminated by diesel fumes and rotting food, listening to the monotonous, maddening drip of condensation, having had no bath in fresh water for weeks, not even being able to take a relaxed crap, all left their marks on the faces of the submariners. They were haggard, bearded, dirty and scared. They had been ordered back to sea on a Friday, the Thirteenth of April, and that was as bad a sign as an albatross building its nest in the conning tower.

Early on the first day out from Ireland they had been brushed by the tentacles of enemy asdic, but a sharp change of course seemed to have thrown that off. Perhaps they hadn't been noticed at all. On a normal patrol they would have taken a wide sweep round the Faeroes to avoid their notorious minefields before heading into the North Sea, but nothing was normal on this patrol. They had orders to take the short cut and risk the mines. It would save time. It might make them crab meat. But it also seemed to have fooled their pursuers. When finally they broke away from British coastal waters and into the North Sea the crew were allowed in pairs onto the conning tower bridge for a taste of night air to recover from the putrid atmosphere created by the tension.

Eling had wanted to head for one of the U-boat bases in German-occupied Norway, or even one of the isolated fjords along the Scandinavian coast, but his suggestion had been rejected. The High Command didn't want Hencke in some distant outpost of the Reich where their control was all but shot to hell and with local resistance fighters crawling out from behind every rock. They wanted Hencke home, in Germany. Eling's orders were specific about that. So once in the North Sea they proceeded south, risking the surface by night, submerged by day and hugging the deep trench off the coast of Norway where the darkest, safest waters of the North Sea were to be found. But they couldn't stay in the depths forever. Sometime, sometime soon, they would have to make a break for it.

'Then we're really going to find out how good a sailor our captain is,' one veteran spat. 'No torpedoes, no aircover, that stupid *Scheisskerl* Goebbels having told the entire fucking world what we're up to . . . Going to be a ride to remember, this one.'

'To where?' Hencke had asked.

'Kiel. Wilhelmshaven. Bremen. Probably to Hell. Wherever's open. And if not . . . as close as we can get.'

'He'll get us home? The Captain'll get us home?' The voice

170

belonged to a young sailor, on his first patrol, whose features had already been aged by the experience and the pale light as he sat in the shadows of empty torpedo racks.

The veteran offered no reply, preferring to study the dirt in his finger nails.

'I don't want to die,' the youth continued. His words lacked sentimentality; he was making a statement of fact rather than a plea of self-pity.

'No one wants to die, you bloody idiot. We don't get any choice in the matter,' the veteran responded. His words were sharp, but his tone understanding.

'But not yet. Please God, not yet. I . . . I haven't even had a woman,' he said. He was struggling hard to control the tremor in his voice, wanting to share. 'I had it all planned for when we got back to port. A shower. A beer. Then a woman. I had it all arranged . . .'

'Shit, you'd deserve an Iron Cross after going with one of those raddled old whores. They say they've had the clap so many times it's incurable, nothing can touch it. The Bremerhaven burn. Rotten way to go.'

It was coarse but not intended to be callous; the young seaman was now worrying about something other than dying at the bottom of the ocean, and anything was better than that.

'And what is it that you're so willing to die for, Hencke?' the veteran prompted, wiping the sweat from his brow with an oily rag.

'What makes you think I'm so eager?'

'You're going back, aren't you?'

'Only if you are.'

'I didn't get a choice in the matter.'

'Somehow war seems to take our choices and tear them into a thousand tiny pieces.'

The veteran looked at Hencke caustically. He wasn't in the mood for someone who talked in poetic riddles. He turned back to his young companion as his thoughts wandered off to their favourite hunting grounds. 'When we get back, son,

I'll take you to a proper place, not one of those crab-infested whorehouses you'd end up in. A proper place with real women who understand what pleases a man. If you're going to die, that's the place to do it. A long, slow afternoon's screwing with some gorgeous blonde who knows what she's doing, her lips all over you, the fire stoking up inside you, then one great, fantastic explosion – and it's all over. What a way to go!'

'So we *are* going to get back, you think?' the youth asked eagerly.

Once again, the veteran didn't reply but the insistent question disturbed him. He wiped his hands vigorously on the rag trying to rid himself of the frustration building up inside him, but no matter how hard he wiped it didn't work. His hands got grimier, his frustration grew. He threw the cloth impatiently into a far corner of the torpedo room and turned on the unwanted guest. 'What the hell are you doing here, Hencke?'

Hencke looked at the anger in the other man's eyes. 'Don't you want to get back to Germany?'

'You must be a brave man, braver than I am to want to go back. Or mad, like a lunatic trying to get back into the asylum. Or maybe you've been away too long and simply don't know what a bedlam our beloved Reich's turned into,' he continued bitterly. 'Each time we come back from a patrol everything's changed again. The buildings and bars you used to know have gone, half your friends are dead or disappeared, nothing works anymore. You try to find out if your family is still alive, but it can take you days to do that, by which time you're out to sea again on another bloody patrol. The orders get crazier, the odds get more ridiculous, none of the bloody torpedoes work properly, while the medals on the chests of those shit-eating Nazis get bigger and bigger. That's not the Germany that I signed up to defend!'

'But it's home, the only home you've got.'

'And we were there! A spit away from dry land. It would have been the end of the war for us. Then *you* came along. If it weren't for the fact that we're *Kriegsmarine* and we'd follow the captain to the other side of damnation, you'd still be sitting on some potato pile in Ireland and we'd both be on our backs getting laid.' He shook his head bitterly. 'I really wish you weren't here, Hencke.'

'Don't expect me to apologize. I didn't ask to be here either.'

'I don't want an apology, I don't want anything from you. All I want is half a chance of getting out of this tin can alive, and you can't give me that.'

Before he could continue, all conversation throughout the boat came to a stop. The submarine had changed course; it was noticeably bow-up and beginning to ascend. They were climbing out of the depths. They were headed home.

'Message from Admiralty. They've established contact.'

Churchill looked up from his chair in the Library. He had been in there an hour on his own, surrounded by the great men and events of history, wanting to be in touch, to draw strength, feeling at home amongst the memories. He had asked not to be disturbed unless it was important, and Cazolet knew that this was important. Yet the Old Man appeared not to have heard him. He sat in the light of a single green-topped table lamp, poring through the pages of an old book, bound in cracked leather.

'Carlyle,' he explained. '*History of Frederick the Great.* D'you know, Hitler is a devout follower of the old Prussian king. Almost mystical about him. Thought I might find some clues, some insight.'

'And. . . ?'

'Frederick waged war against all his neighbours, his armies rampaged throughout the land. He won great victories yet he reduced Prussia to poverty and starvation. And he took off his boots only once a year – on his wife's birthday.'

'So what clues do you find in that?'

'None, dear boy. Absolutely none. But there is more. There came a time, in the middle of a long winter, when he found himself surrounded by a great coalition of his enemies. Winter of '62 – 1762. There appeared to be no salvation.

173

Frederick himself was besieged in Berlin and considering taking poison, so desperate stood his cause.'

'That does sound familiar.'

'But then, *then* the miracle happened. At the height of his peril his enemy the Cazrina died, the great coalition ranged against him fell apart, and the sun shone on his endeavours once more.'

'A fairy tale.'

Churchill shook his head as though it were a huge effort, weighed down by nearly two centuries of history. 'It means he will never give in, Willie. He will live in hope of salvation until the day he dies. And this war will not stop until Hitler is dead. He will put his trust in ghosts rather than those who would urge him to give in, to bring the slaughter to an end. It must be by his death, Willie. Nothing else will do.' Churchill closed the book reverently, as if closing the pages on his own life. 'He'll never leave Berlin. Eisenhower was quite wrong to worry. If only . . .'

He couldn't finish, he didn't have to, not for Cazolet. Cazolet knew. There was a long period of silence between the two men.

'The submarine. They've made contact with the submarine,' Cazolet began again, but Churchill was waving his hand to cut him off.

'No, Willie. No more reports. Not until it's all over.'

As Cazolet left he could see the tears back in Churchill's eyes.

There was neither time nor opportunity for finesse. The odds against them were overwhelming. There was little opportunity for surprise and the forces criss-crossing the sea and skies above them would react quickly and expertly, as they had learned to do in grinding the once insuperable *Kriegsmarine* into defeat. They would have only one moment in which to grasp the initiative; after that it would be simply a matter of time and great torment before their luck finally ran out.

The plan was simple, for simplicity is born of desperation.

174

The captain had explained it to every man in the crew over the intercom. 'We've come this far together; you have a right to know what to expect.' They would be rendezvousing with the two other U-boats – if they weren't already at the bottom of the North Sea – just off the southern coast of Norway. It was Germany's doorstep; there was no other route home, and that's where the British forces would be waiting. At first contact the two other boats would go to full speed and head south and west, crossing wakes to make false echoes which might confuse the enemy, while U-494 slipped slowly south-south-east through the small hole in the net which the other boats had torn, hoping to get away before the deception was discovered, the hole was closed and their last chance gone. It was suicide, of course, probably for all three craft and certainly for the two decoys, but the fear was not new. Scarcely one in ten of their colleagues with whom they had started the war were still alive. They had been living on borrowed time for as long as any of them could remember.

U-494 hung back, electric motors turning the screws slowly, allowing her sisters to make the running and to drag off the cover. They were blind but for hydrophones, eighty feet down, but sound travels a long way under water and the hydrophone operator could follow the trail of battle as clearly as if he were a spectator in the arena. It began with the thump of screws as the two sister ships began forcing their way through the cold waters of the North Sea, followed only minutes later by the high speed whine of surface turbines, alerted by their own hydrophones and giving chase like greyhounds in the slips. The first submarine could be heard zigzagging, changing course, trying to find shelter in the underwater thermoclines which might hide and confuse the pursuers, but soon they could hear the crump of falling depth charges. You didn't need a hydrophone to pick up their unmistakable sound. That was when U-494 began to put on a little speed, hiding behind the noise of battle, slipping through the gap they hoped had been torn in the defences.

There was nothing for Hencke to do, there was nothing

175

for anyone to do, but pray. He tried to concentrate on distractions, even embracing his memories to stave off the fear and the tomb-like claustrophobia, while the sweat poured down his face and splashed onto the bare metal plates beneath his feet.

The second submarine was being attacked now, but all the time the sound of combat was drifting further away. And still no one had picked them up.

'God help those poor bastards,' the veteran muttered through clenched teeth as the cacophony of underwater explosions increased.

'But save a little for us,' whispered the youth.

In the control room the hydrophone operator was reporting the action of battle. 'Submarine engines stopped . . . can't tell whether they've been hit or are trying to shake them off . . . more depth charges . . . engines started again at full speed . . . more depth charges, there seem to be at least three of the bastards circling above . . .' He tried to clear the grit from his voice and swallowed his words along with it. But there was little need for his commentary; every man on board could hear the steady, insistent clamour of depth charges far away. When at last he looked up at the captain, his anguish told the story. The U-boat had been hit. Its race was nearing its end. 'Sounds like one of the engines has stopped . . . tanks being blown . . . they're trying for the surface but . . .' He could hear the futile, ragged whine of the U-boat's screw, more depth charges dropping on and around the stricken craft and, with an awesome finality, the sound of the pressure hull being crushed. He shook his head.

'OK,' cut in Captain Eling. 'Time to get out of here. Bring her up to snorkel height and engines to full!' he commanded. The air-breathing snorkel broke surface, allowing the powerful diesels to kick in, and there was an immediate surge of power as the *Diesel Obermaschinist* threw the lever that poured fuel down the throats of the engines. There was a pounding from the propellor shafts, the boat vibrated, even the crockery rattled. The pretence was over.

Eling flicked a switch above his head and spoke into a mouthpiece. 'This is the Captain. U-909 is gone.' A slight pause. 'Good luck to you all.'

'You marvellous bloody idiot!' the hydrophone operator exclaimed. 'Oesten's boat. He's making enough noise to wake the Bismarck!' He bit his lip to control his uncharacteristic excitement. 'He's doubled back, bearing north-west.'

The captain had grabbed the hydrophone headset, listening for himself. 'He's trying to draw them off and give us as much cover as he can,' he said, sharing with the rest of the crew, but quickly he grew silent, unable to find the words as the sacrifice was offered up and greedily accepted. Eventually he muttered between clenched teeth. 'They're on to him, caught him in their asdic. Two, maybe three of them.' The crump of depth charges was faint, in the distance, scarcely audible above the sound of the stretched engines. More minutes passed until he had heard enough. Reluctantly he handed the headset back to the hydrophone operator and moved across to the intercom. 'Gentlemen, we're on our own now.'

They had no time to grieve. It was precisely four seconds later when they heard the sound of asdic pinging across the steel hull of their craft, reaching out for them, grabbing at them, pouring ice into their hearts.

Josef Goebbels sat stroking the blonde hair of his youngest child, Heidi, not yet six. She had fallen asleep in his arms as he told stories of fiery dragons and shining knights, and she lay with a look of sublime peace, oblivious to the noise. Across the room her five brothers and sisters, directed by the eldest, Helga, were singing to the accompaniment of an accordion, and as their treble voices rose higher and higher the faces of their parents glowed with pride. The mood of celebration was being matched at many points around the Bunker and Reich Chancellery, although nowhere with such simplicity or innocence.

'They sing like angels,' he whispered.

'Didn't you once write that children were the bright ideas of God?'

He looked up to share a momentary smile with his wife, a rare event nowadays. They had long since ceased sharing anything of personal value, beyond the children. And their devotion to the Fuehrer. It was that which had kept them together – or, more accurately, his explicit refusal to allow them to part and his instructions to continue with their hollow form of marriage. He couldn't afford a public scandal amongst the Party leadership. So their spats and screaming rows and infidelities had been covered up – after all, who better than the Minister of Propaganda to ensure not only what was printed, but what was left out of the newspapers. It had always been an unlikely alliance, the diminutive stump-legged academic with the crooked teeth, pinched face and a body which looked as if it had been squeezed in a vice, matched against the highly-strung society beauty covered in expensive silk from the finest Italian couturière. But there were the children, it hadn't all been wasted.

'Josef, there can be no doubt, can there?'

They broke off to join in the singing of the chorus before he answered her.

'No, Magda. I heard it myself on the BBC and the news has been repeated for several hours. The American radio is playing solemn military music. There's no shred of doubt. Roosevelt is dead.'

'The Fuehrer is so happy, and I am so happy for him . . .'

Goebbels had heard the news driving back from an inspection of the front. He had immediately telephoned the Fuehrer, only to discover Magda already with him, celebrating. She often saw as much of the Fuehrer as he did, and had always had a more personal relationship. Again, as he had many times over the years, he wondered whether they had been lovers. He once overheard an adjutant in the Reich Chancellery joking that he could hear Magda's ovaries clanging every time she entered the same room as the Fuehrer. Goebbels had the adjutant posted to the Russian Front, but he couldn't dispose of his own suspicions so easily. On another occasion she had come back from one of the intimate tea parties, just the Fuehrer with Magda and one of the secretaries, and she had been flushed with pleasure and physical energy. She had insisted they make love and had been drenched in her own excitement before she had even taken off her clothes. And she had always been viciously jealous of Eva Braun.

But, no, decided Goebbels, it was probably not so, just an affair that had never grown beyond the idea and the wish. In any case, what did it really matter, when he and the Fuehrer were building the greatest Reich Europe had ever known and when, at their desperate hour of need, fate was once again smiling on them?

'It is a sign, I'm sure,' he continued. 'Roosevelt choking on all the blood he's spilled. And Hencke, a German hero about to become folk legend, on his way home. Death and Deliverance, the two mightiest weapons of war, all at once thrust into our hands.'

He looked at his wife. She was no longer the beauty he had married; the war and child-bearing had taken their toll on her nerves, which had never been robust. The pencil-thin eyebrows were now just other lines on her face, the soft hair which had lain on so many pillows was dull and brittle, and the lips had begun to sag. They had all of them become old and wrinkled, of course, but somehow in women it carried less well. No, if *Der Chef* wanted her, he was welcome to her.

'What was the Fuehrer doing when you left him?' Goebbels enquired, as the children struck up a new tune and Heidi stirred. He placed a gentle finger on her lips to soothe her back to sleep.

'He was reading a book,' his wife replied. 'Something about Frederick the Great, I think . . .'

They were almost home. Only a few hours sailing from the safety of the mainland and its air cover, when the final bombardment began. They had been fortunate up to that

179

point, driven along by the twin screws and their fear, every change in sea temperature and salinity confusing the enemy asdic, throwing him off balance for a few miles more, slowly eating up the distance between themselves and home. Somehow they had survived, the screws had kept turning, and for a couple of hours they had thought the sacrifice of their compatriots might be enough. But, deep down, they had always known it was hopeless. They couldn't evade the most experienced sub-hunters in the world, not for ever. The nearer they got to home, the shallower the seas, the closer they were forced to the surface and so their last hiding place disappeared.

The captain had ordered both engines to low revs in order to kill any trace of noise from the submarine, but the steel hull of U-494 had been caught by asdic in coastal waters with nowhere to run. Their hunters were getting closer, the insistent noise of asdic mixed with the thumping of turbines and propellor wash to form a cocktail of madness which each submariner feared would strip them of their courage and make them run screaming throughout the craft. But no one did, this was Eling's crew. So they waited to die. There was a crescendo of noise, a lip bitten to flesh, and the hunters were overhead and past. A whispered prayer. Could they have missed? For a moment without end there was stillness. As one, the crew took a sharp inward breath, knowing it might be the last. Instinctively hands reached out for support, a stanchion, a pipe, an instrument panel, anything which might brace them and help guard against the blow. Then it struck.

Hencke was thrown aside and his arms all but wrenched from their sockets as 250 pounds of amatol exploded 20 feet above the rear torpedo compartment, forcing the stern savagely down towards the bottom of the North Sea.

'It's OK,' shouted the veteran, clinging to a bed frame. 'Most of the force goes upwards. It's when they explode underneath that you kiss your ring goodbye . . .'

But already above the relentless and chaotic singing of asdic they could hear the splashing of further depth charges

180

being thrown at them. And in spite of the captain's manoeuvring they were getting closer. Hencke heard one canister bounce off the outer hull with a dull echo like the Devil knocking at the door. They were at 93 metres. The depth charge was set for 105. It detonated directly beneath U-494's engine compartment. Even so most of the plates and valves held, but most at 93 metres isn't good enough. The blast caused the craft to heel violently, ripping away Hencke's purchase on the torpedo rack and lifting him bodily before throwing him across the oily floor. Dials shattered and bulbs smashed as the pressure hull bent inwards, plunging the craft into complete darkness, and there was a ringing in his head so loud that for a moment it was beyond his brain's ability to comprehend. His ears felt as if someone were trying to drive six inch nails into them. When the auxilliary lights flickered on he found himself staring at the lifeless eyes of the young submariner, blood trickling slowly from the corner of his lips, from his nose and from his ears.

In the control room a few yards away he could hear the captain screaming for a damage report and feet began to pound along aluminium gangways; from above came the fading noise of the hunter completing its first pass. But there was another sound, as unmistakable as it was insistent. The sound of the craft dying. The savage hissing of gas escaping under pressure from somewhere nearby, the crackle of flame as smoke billowed from a control panel where the electrical circuit had shorted out, the explosive sound of bolts shearing, a raised voice reporting irreparable change to two hull valves mingling with the cries of the injured and the hammering of tools on paralysed controls. And beneath his feet Hencke could hear the terrifying noise of water beginning to slop its way through the bilges.

But he could hear no shouts of terror and panic as he might have supposed. Instead there were only shouts of instruction and command as the submariners, fear tempered by years of experience and discipline, scurried to salvage their crippled craft. Men began hurtling like acrobats along the gangways and through the small circular hatchways, there was the sound of banging metal as leaking seals were retightened and closed, and within seconds he could hear the drubbing of hammer on wood and steel as a team struggled to shore up buckled plates and stem the flood. Already the water was bubbling above the metal floor grille on which he was standing and the submarine had adopted a strange, unnatural posture, leaning to one side. Then another lurch, gentler this time, accompanied by the sound of compressed air being forced into the tanks as the screws beat desperately to gain purchase and force the submarine upwards, but the hydroplanes had gone.

For an agonizing time the boat seemed to hang suspended as the upward thrust of the engines was cancelled out by the weight of water pouring into the hull. Hencke's lungs were frozen, his body was no longer his possession and belonged to some other entity which was deciding his fate. And it seemed to be an age making up its mind. Slowly, imperceptibly at first then with painfully increasing confidence, the craft gained stability as the nose of the boat forced its way upwards. They were going to make it after all! The tension in Hencke collapsed and he began to breathe in deep relief, but he saw the veteran still clinging like a man possessed to the bed frame. He was shaking his head. He knew what was yet to come.

Perhaps the captain of the frigate was a touch too eager. Had he left it a few seconds longer there could have been no doubt but, in his anxiety to ram the submarine, he hit her just before she was fully surfaced. The bows sliced across the forward hull tearing a great gash, but the submarine bounced rather than being ripped instantly in two. She would die, of course, but slowly rather than in a moment.

Through the pandemonium Hencke could feel the craft beginning to settle rapidly bow-down. And still the water rose, up to his calf now, pulling at him and the others, trying to drag them under.

A face forced its way through the hatch which led from the

182

control room. It was a sub-lieutenant, with blood running from a gash on his forehead.

'Hencke to the control room!' he screamed. 'And secure all watertight doors!'

So that was it. The bulkheads were being sealed, the six compartments around which U-494 was built were being shut off from each other, transformed into their own private coffins. The most experienced hands prayed she would flood quickly and put an end to their inevitable agonies, the less experienced with their naive hopes of survival hoped it might flood more slowly, but everyone knew it was only a matter of time. Yet still the order of duty and command prevailed. The veteran grabbed Hencke by the arm and thrust him towards the hatch. Unceremoniously he was bundled through, smacking his head against some sharp metal edge, and as he picked himself up and turned he could see the veteran about to close the bulkhead door, with water already beginning to spill over the sill. The submariner's eyes were raging with anger.

'I wish to God you hadn't come,' he swore.

Then the steel door slammed shut, the wheel which secured the watertight seal was being turned, and he saw the veteran no more.

Inside the crowded control room Eling was standing by the intercom, barking instructions, eyes fixed on the dials and gauges as he listened to replies. But already he was giving instructions to sections of the boat from which no reply was forthcoming. As the chief engineer shouted in his ear that both aft torpedo hatches were flooding and water began seeping down an instrument panel, there was the unmistakable sound of the electric motors complaining, complaining again, and falling silent.

'Engine room! Report!' Eling shouted into the mouthpiece, but there was no response. He looked imploringly at the chief who stood soaked in a torn singlet beside the far watertight door, shaking his head.

With the dying of the engines and the closing of the hatches,

183

a relative quiet descended over the craft. Metal was still pounding against metal in a distant forward compartment, but soon that also stopped. The craft was settling nose-down in the water, and they listened to the submarine's death throes. A groan here, a creak there, the crying of tortured metal, the cracking of the internal wood fascias as they buckled and split, and always the slow, deadly sound of gurgling water. But from the crew there was only silence, the silence of men fallen into despair. The captain's gaze was fixed unblinkingly on the depth gauge, watching its hypnotic fall, great beads of perspiration trickling down his forehead. Then there was a heavy bump, hands once again reached out for support, and the submarine settled on the bottom.

The captain tapped the gauge. '120 metres,' he announced, his eyes glazing. 'Could be worse . . .' There was silence as everyone calculated the odds. 'Chief! Damage report,' the captain instructed.

'Engines dead, rear compartments flooded. I can't raise the forward torpedo compartment. The bilges are flooding so the batteries are gone and if they've not yet drowned they'll be choking on chlorine gas in next to no time . . . Sorry, Captain,' the chief apologized as Eling's stare gave him silent rebuke. This was still the *Kriegsmarine*, and there was a proper way to die. 'The control room is the only watertight compartment. For now.'

'How many men do we know for sure are still alive?'

'Just what you see, Captain.' It made a total of fourteen. Fourteen out of fifty. No, out of a hundred and fifty.

'Looks like we have them surrounded, eh?' Eling said grimly. He turned to Hencke. 'I'm sorry, Hencke. It seems we failed. I've got a dead craft and fourteen men left. As far as we can tell all other compartments are flooded, which means that anyone behind those doors is already dead. I *am* sorry.'

Hencke marvelled at this man who had been ordered to sacrifice his craft and most of his crew in order to bring one passenger home, yet who still felt the need to apologize.

184

'Is there anything to be done?' Hencke was surprised how calm his voice sounded, betraying none of the turmoil and twisted nerves within.

Before Eling could answer, from no great distance away came the echoing sound of an explosion, not a depth charge but something big. A grim smile of satisfaction flickered around the captain's mouth. 'So the dying's not yet done, and maybe the surviving too . . . That was a mine. One of ours. Ripping the bottom out of a ship. One of theirs. I took us into a minefield,' he explained. 'Seems to have paid off.'

'What will happen now?'

'They'll have trouble locating us on the bottom with all the junk and other wrecks around here. And now they've lost one of their own. . . ?' He shrugged. 'They'll probably call it a day. They won't want to thrash around in a minefield, particularly when they know there's a 95 percent probability they've sunk us already.'

As if in confirmation, from nearby came the explosion of a clutch of depth charges, one final gesture from the Royal Navy planted along the huge oil slick which was forming on the surface and which they hoped marked the tomb of another U-boat. One for luck, and farewell. The violent rocking cast the craft into darkness yet again and when at last some source of light was restored, even the rueful smile which the captain had managed to manufacture had been wiped away.

'Further damage report, Chief! Chief?'

But the chief did not respond. He was staring transfixed at the cabinet containing the emergency breathing gear. 'They're gone. There's not a single one left . . .' He turned in desperation towards the captain. 'The maintenance crew, at Kiel. They were stripping the boat down for overhaul, started here in the control room. They were unloading everything. Then we got orders to turn around, I threw them straight off board . . .'

No one spoke. What was there to say? In spite of the angry looks cast in his direction, it wasn't the chief's fault. On arrival in Kiel after weeks at sea they hadn't even had time

185

to break wind let alone check stores before they were ordered back out to sea. How could anyone have reckoned on some half-witted fitter being so forgetful? On all the emergency supplies in other compartments being cut off behind flooded bulkheads? On being caught out playing taxi service at the bottom of the North Sea?

As the silence dragged on Hencke could feel the eyes of some of the crew, particularly the younger ones, latching on to him, piercing him with accusation. The one who had brought them here. The one who had caused all this. The passenger . . .

'Do we have any prospects?' he asked the captain.

'Staying here and slowly choking to death,' responded Eling grimly. 'Or trying to escape without breathing apparatus from 120 metres and probably drowning. Take your pick.'

'It's no fun dying slowly, Captain.'

'I do so agree.' He gave a small Prussian nod of respect. At least the bastard wasn't panicking and screaming his head off; Eling couldn't have stood that. 'So. We make ready to abandon ship! Chief. Chief, where. . . ?'

The chief had disappeared head-first through a service hatch in the floor. When he hauled himself back up he was coughing and his eyes were full of terror. 'Chlorine!' he gasped. 'Chlorine!'

Sea water was leaking into the huge batteries which powered the electric motors, and the result was a chemical reaction which produced a gas as deadly as that found in any trench of the First War. And it was seeping uncontrollably around them.

'For God's sake flood the compartment and let's get out of here,' pleaded one of the younger ratings.

'Can't,' the chief spluttered. 'Won't be able to open the hatch until the air pressure inside has equalled the water pressure outside. 120 metres. At that pressure the concentration of chlorine in the lungs will kill us in seconds.'

'But it'll kill us anyway!' the rating responded. 'We stay, we die. We try to leave, we die. What have you done to us,

Chief?' The edge of desperation in his voice was beginning to infect the others around him. It wouldn't be long before there was a general outpouring of panic which would overwhelm them all.

'There's one chance.' It was Eling who spoke, very quietly, to reassert his authority. 'One chance, perhaps. Above our heads in the conning tower. There's room for one man. We close the hatch between the control room and conning tower, he floods the conning tower like an escape chamber, he opens the exterior hatch and escapes.'

'But what about the rest of us?' pressed a petty officer.

The chief interjected, desperate to bear hopeful tidings for a change. 'The first man closes the exterior hatch from the outside, we drain the conning tower, we do it all over again. Fourteen times.' But he didn't sound as if he had convinced even himself.

'No, Chief. It won't work. Not at 120 metres.' It was Eling. 'In order to shut the hatch from the outside he'd use up so much oxygen he'd never make it to the surface. If he forgets about closing the hatch he's got a chance. A small one. One man. That's it, and that's all of it.' A stillness of crushed hopes and despondency settled amongst the men. 'I'm sorry, gentlemen,' Eling continued. 'You deserve to know.'

'So which of us is it to be?' a voice enquired.

'Not I,' stated the captain.

'Nor I,' whispered the chief.

'Then who?' insisted the petty officer. 'Who's going to play God and decide which one of us gets it?'

'*Meine Herren*,' Eling commanded quietly. 'If there has to be an end, let us make it a good one, one worthy of the *Kriegsmarine*.'

'I've got a wife and five children,' the petty officer said. 'My end is no bloody use to them, good or otherwise.'

'You knew what your fate would be when you started on this war. The only thing you didn't know was how or when,' the captain responded. 'So now you do.'

'But who is to get the chance? I've got five children too . . .' another seaman lied.

'Let's draw lots,' another suggested.

'Call yourselves submariners,' the wretched chief engineer cried, almost in tears. 'Flood the whole damn boat and let's get it over with!' He lunged for a valve.

'No!' Eling instructed. 'Chief – *Take your hands away!*'

The chief looked at his captain through red eyes and slowly withdrew. There was still too much discipline in him, he couldn't refuse his commanding officer, not at the last, not after all this time.

'I cannot play God,' Eling continued in a low voice, forcing them to listen in silence, 'but in the *Kriegsmarine* we don't rely on luck or divine intervention, certainly not on the wisdom of our political leaders, but on *duty*. You've all followed that sense of duty from the moment you stepped on board this submarine, and that's what has got us this far. Through the ice pack off Murmansk. And the convoy escorts off the Azores. And back to home port time and again when other U-boats weren't so lucky. So our luck's run out. But we are still submariners! We started this mission with orders to do everything we could to get this man' – he waved at Hencke – 'back home. We still have those orders. You all know who should get the chance.'

'His life means we all die,' the rating said.

'Whoever gets out, the rest of us are going to die. Our only choice is whether we die like men or like rats. Not much of a choice, I agree. But it's the only one we've got.'

No one moved. It was the truth, they knew it, but no one wanted to accept it. Surely there was some other way? Then the chief stepped forward and stood by the conning tower hatch. He offered the captain a crisp salute. In turn, the captain faced slowly towards Hencke. He had bloodshot eyes and Hencke could see close up that he was scared.

'Do one thing for me, Hencke. Just get back. Make all this worthwhile.'

Hencke nodded. He said nothing; words would have been

188

inadequate, even insulting. He placed his foot on the first rung of the ladder into the conning tower and began to climb, assisted by one of the men.

As he disappeared what was left of Eling's crew came to attention as the captain barked the final order. 'Chief. Secure the hatch!'

'Thanks for agreeing to see me at such short notice.' Eisenhower's hand shot out from a crisp cuff and grasped the pudgy fingers extended towards him at the door of Ten Downing Street.

'Your visit comes as a welcome distraction, General – particularly when the matter sounded of such urgency.' Churchill led the way across the famous threshold, trailing cigar smoke. 'I have to admit, now that our armies are ploughing remorselessly through the remnants of the Wehrmacht, time seems to hang heavy. Not so long ago – do you remember when we were planning the invasion of Europe together? – every hour seemed filled with suspense and the need to take mighty decisions. Now I find that matters for my attention are not brought to me by commanders bearing brave ideas, but by bureaucrats who bear nothing but endless mountains of paper.' There was a weariness in the Old Man's voice, an emptiness inside where once excitement and intrigue had burned. His hours were increasingly filled with questions of fuel shortages, homelessness, depleted gold reserves and crippling foreign debts, and he had little appetite for them. 'Perhaps it is wrong of me, but I look back on those more perilous days of war with a feeling that they were the finest test a man could want. Where is the challenge to provide a suitable encore?'

'I ask myself the same question,' Eisenhower responded. 'What will the generals do when there is no more war to fight?'

'Why, do what generals throughout the ages have done – rejoice in the fruits of victory. Fornicate. And prepare for the next war!'

189

'Allelujah!' Eisenhower muttered to himself. Fornication had been much on his mind, ever since the few idyllic days at Sous le Vent and his realization that the approaching end of the war would strip away the excuse which had kept him so conveniently apart from his wife. The fruits of victory she would provide would be uniquely barren, and he did not relish the task of having to face up to his personal problems. He would return home a conquering hero, and conquering heroes didn't desert their faithful wives, not for a woman who was both twenty years younger and foreign, not if the conquering hero didn't want to be completely covered in crap and face a future selling second-hand tractors. So it would have to be goodbye, he couldn't duck it any longer. Hell, war was so much simpler . . .

He followed Churchill into the secluded garden of Number Ten, which was surrounded by a mellow red-brick wall covered in climbing plants and enclosing a lawn liberally sprinkled with daffodils and early tulips in abundant bloom. The cherry tree was coming into blossom, encouraged by the unseasonably warm sunshine. Churchill had put on a floppy Panama hat which he used when painting to guard against the sun, and beside the cherry tree stood a table with comfortable wicker chairs and two large china cups.

'And coffee. Scalding hot. Just as you like it,' Churchill commented as a secretary brought out a steaming jug to stand beside one of the cups, accompanied by a more modest pot of what Eisenhower concluded could only be that piss-tasting English tea. They busied themselves with the formalities of pouring and stirring. It was the first time they had met, even spoken directly, since that morning above Xanten and they were both taking care not to scratch at half-healed wounds.

'Your message was intriguing, General. "Face to face . . . not to be entrusted to any other means of communication". I have to admit that I have turned every corner of my mind to discover what could be of such magnitude as to bring you hurrying here, but to no end.'

Eisenhower sipped his coffee carefully, watching over the

rim of the cup as Churchill slurped away unselfconsciously, wiping a dripple of tea from his chin with the back of his hand. He waited until Churchill had replaced his cup in the saucer.

'It's about Berlin. And the redoubt. I felt I had to come and tell you personally.'

The Old Man's eyes were instantly alert, the glaze of weariness gone. They reflected disquiet, and anger. The hurt of their last encounter had not yet died but he said nothing, waiting.

'You know, I've been a military man all my life,' Eisenhower continued as if he were telling tales around a fireside. 'And I'm pretty damn good at it – one of the best. But the military is all about manpower and firepower and beating the stuffing out of the other man's army, and how you do it is almost secondary. That's why I've never been able to understand why you seemed so . . . passionate about getting to Berlin and rejoicing in the ruins.'

Churchill was about to intervene to protest that he had never described his ambitions in those terms, but decided against it. He wanted to hear what Eisenhower was trying to say. Anyway, it was true.

'But I've begun to realize that in one sense you were right. You can't judge an enemy solely by the size of the barrel he's got pointing at you. There are many more ways to die in war than simply getting blown to pieces . . .' The folksiness was gone, a sadness had crept into his voice. 'You know the reports we've been getting out of Poland of camps full of prisoners and bodies. I don't know about you; I always treated the reports with a touch of caution. Those camps weren't military targets, they didn't affect the way the war was being fought. Anyway, there was always the suspicion that they were exaggerated by Stalin's propaganda machine. And, deep down, perhaps I didn't want to believe.'

'The reports have been insistent, and growing in frequency. I dread to imagine what we might discover when the final curtain is drawn back on the Nazi stage.'

'No need to imagine any more. Four days ago I went to a place called Ohrdruf Nord, just outside Gotha which we captured last week. The local divisional commander called me direct. Said I must come. He was almost in tears. Believe me, it's all true and more.' He moistened his lips, his mouth felt parched, as if he could still taste the vomit. 'I saw bodies lined up in great avenues, hundreds of them, stacked one upon the other, just flimsy cast-off pieces of bone and skin lying out in the open waiting to be burned. Men, women, even children. Most seemed to have been gassed, but every single one of them had been starved and beaten. The mutilation was terrible, the scale of what has happened passed anything I could comprehend. I thought they had brought me to the gates of hell, that nothing could match what I saw there. Yet by the day we are discovering more camps. Places like Buchenwald and Belsen. As we drive deeper into Germany they seem to be getting bigger and far, far worse. Seems the Germans are running out of time and furnaces to cover their tracks. They simply can't dispose of that many corpses quickly enough . . .'

He was sitting tensely on the edge of his chair, leaning forward across the table. His voice was flat and deliberately unemotional but, as the general had raised the ghosts of his visit, Churchill saw the colour drain from his face.

'So I don't need any more lessons about war being more than just military objectives. How on earth do you put tens, maybe hundreds of thousands of tortured men and women into a military equation? How can you regard an enemy capable of such acts as simply another military opponent? Now I understand your passion. There's no man alive who wants so much to dance on that bastard's grave as I do, and if it meant leading a column to Berlin myself and digging the hole with my bare hands, I'd do it!'

'But I'll warrant you haven't come here to offer me second-in-command of this hypothetical column.'

The American shook his head. 'Nothing would give me greater pleasure. I can tell you with all my heart that I haven't cared for the . . . misunderstandings which have come between us recently. We shared so much in the months while we were planning the campaigns in North Africa and Europe together. I had come to regard you as a close friend.'

'You were right to do so, General.' There was a determined set to Churchill's jaw as he contemplated what he might say next. He was still battling inside with his hurt pride. 'This seems to be a moment for honesty. Well, let us not dance in the shadows. We have had no "misunderstandings", as you put it – we have understood each other all too well. We have shared differences of opinion which were profound and we both fought our cases hard. You have won, and I accept your victory with considerable regret. I fear that when Marshal Stalin gets hold of half of Europe, as he now certainly shall, it will be the prelude to a forest of concentration camps which will spring up through a long Siberian winter. The peoples of Eastern Europe will have exchanged one terror for another. But the die is cast. In politics, as in life, we must move on.'

Having conceded defeat as gracefully as he could, Churchill stopped to take a cigar from the flap pocket of the one-piece siren suit he had himself designed and had worn almost every day throughout the war. He had worn it today largely out of nostalgia; the war was almost over, it would soon be time to dispatch all such wartime trivia to the back of the closet.

Eisenhower leaned across to light the Old Man's cigar. 'There's more.'

'Thought there might be,' Churchill muttered, still full of hurt. 'Didn't have to come here to tell me yet again that I wasn't going to get Berlin.' He was staring moodily into the flame which rose and fell as the tightly packed tobacco leaves began to smoulder, his broad and upturned nose seeming to point at the General like an artillery piece made ready to fire.

Eisenhower's tone was as soft as his words were chilling. 'When I said I'd lead a column to Berlin to dance on his grave, I meant it. But he's not going to be there.'

The flame stopped dancing.

193

'The Germans have gathered all their leading atomic scientists in the Black Forest, just south of Stuttgart,' Eisenhower continued. 'They're also transporting a small pile of uranium and other supplies into facilities around Berchtesgaden.'

'Dear Lord, is it really happening. . . ?'

'And worse than we ever thought.'

'An Alpine redoubt. Endless war. And Hitler with an atomic bomb?'

'No one knows for sure how close they are to constructing a bomb, but sure as hell it doesn't look as if Hitler's ready to give up yet.'

'Now I see why you came yourself.' Churchill slumped back in his chair, cigar forgotten. 'General, I must confess that when I contemplate what my scientists tell me about the awesome power of the atomic bomb, I begin to believe the world is changing so fast and for such terrible ends that I no longer wish to play a part. Or perhaps I am no longer capable. I would have had you occupy an empty Berlin . . .' His head went back and he looked to the heavens. 'Roosevelt has gone. Hitler and Mussolini will soon have gone. The French Republic has been swept away. Poland, the country for whom we went to war in the first place, has for all practical purposes ceased to exist . . . There is a tide of history and it seems to have turned. Younger men wait impatiently in the wings, able and more willing to play these terrible roles for which the modern world calls. Sometimes I fear it is all passing me by, that I am just another stubborn old man getting in the way.' His head was raised towards the sky and the loose folds of skin beneath his chin stretched, like a condemned man offering his neck to the executioner's blade.

'So were you right about the Alpine redoubt? And was I all the time wretched and wrong?' Churchill continued. 'What must you think of me – what will history think of me. . . ?' His words faded. He looked aged and vulnerable, like a discarded rag doll, an old man in a child's siren suit, lost in the depths of his chair.

'You really want to know what I think of you?' the general enquired in a loud, belligerent voice. 'Well, I've lost count in recent weeks of how many times I've cursed and fretted, called you stubborn, cantankerous, cussed – and plenty of other things besides. You got in the way, you held things up, you went behind my back.' His diction slowed to emphasize his words. 'You've been a bigger pain in my ass than Sitting Bull was for Custer. *But* . . . Never once have I lost sight of the fact that if it hadn't been for you, your infernal stubbornness and your mule-headed refusal to accept defeat, then this war would have been lost long before we Americans even got here. You talk about a tide of history. Well, there are some occasions when one man seems to stand his ground and just refuses to accept getting washed away. That's how we arrogant Americans won the New World. And that's how you, Mr Churchill, have saved the Old World.'

There was a huge sob from the old man's direction as Eisenhower continued.

'If it hadn't been for you, by now the whole of Europe would be one vast concentration camp. Nobody's ever going to forget that.'

For a while Churchill continued to stare at the heavens, hiding what Eisenhower knew were tears, but they were no longer tears of anguish. When eventually his head came down his eyes were still moist but he had recovered, and there was a glow across his face. 'You once told me, General, that you were no politician. Yet it seems to me you have just made a very fine speech.'

'Thank you, sir.'

'No, thank you, my friend.'

Suddenly Churchill's whole body stiffened as if he had been stabbed, the look of pleasure wiped from his face 'Damn me for an imbecile!' His hand came crashing down on the table, sending the cups and their contents flying. 'I've only just realized. The Black Forest, that whole area, where Hitler is gathering his atomic secrets . . . That's all set out as a zone of occupation for the French. It's bad enough to let the

195

Russians have Berlin. But to let the bloody French have the Bomb. . . !'

Churchill's outrage was matched only by his astonishment as Eisenhower began a chuckle which turned to laughter that grew ever more uncontrollable until he was rolling around in his chair, his sides feeling as if they would burst, his knees rising almost to his chest. 'You'll . . . have to excuse me,' he spluttered, battling to control himself. 'It's just that I bet my intelligence chief ten bucks you'd react in exactly that way.'

It was now the turn of the American's cheeks to bear the trickle of tears. Churchill's face suffused with the colour of fury, but Eisenhower leaned across and grabbed the Old Man's hand to still him. 'Please. Forgive me. Don't worry. Oh, God, it hurts . . .' He recovered himself sufficiently to make sense. 'I've already given orders for the US 7th Army under General Patch to drive south and mop up those supplies and scientists.' He squeezed the Prime Minister's hand reassuringly. 'Don't worry, Winston. They'll get there long before the French. After this shooting match is over, Britain will still be the only atomic power in Europe.'

Churchill's nostrils dilated as he took in all that he had been told. He could have strangled this impudent upstart who seemed bent on humiliating him at every turn. Except . . . The French had been thwarted without ever knowing what mighty prize lay within their grasp. It was a loss which would cost them a seat at the great-power table after the war, leaving Britain pre-eminent amongst the European powers – and Churchill first of European leaders. And this great victory had been delivered to him, gift-wrapped and *gratis*, by a young American general.

Either way their relationship would never be the same. It was Churchill's moment for decision. Slowly his free hand stretched out and settled on top of the General's until they were clasped across the table in a brotherly embrace, the gulf which had opened up between them bridged once and for all. 'My dear Dwight, I am happy beyond belief to see that you have started fighting the peace as well as the war! I think you will go far . . .' He sniffed loudly before continuing. 'But one question. Pray, who was Sitting Bull?'

Both of them began shaking with silent mirth until they could restrain themselves no longer and sat, clasped together, two old friends with fresh coffee stains on their trousers and tears pouring down their cheeks.

On the other side of the North Sea, on a spit of sand which before the war had been a favourite loitering place of North Germans seeking sun and relaxation, a figure, scarcely discernible in the pale moonlight, was washed up on the shore. For several minutes it made no movement except for the languorous waving of the legs in the receding tide. Then it coughed and threw up before starting to cough again. Slowly and with obvious pain the figure began to claw its way up the sandy beach to the dry dunes and to safety.

Peter Hencke was home.

Part Three

NINE

'War sets the stamp of nobility upon the peoples.' He couldn't remember who had said it, the words were but a vague echo in his mind from one of the interminable pre-war wireless broadcasts. Nobility . . . He wondered how close the author could ever have got to the stench of battle. Never as close as this.

The journey from Hamburg to Berlin would normally have lasted only three hours, but already it had taken eight and they had still another sixty miles to go. In many places the autobahn was impossibly cratered or blocked by ruined vehicles and the stretches still open were being bombed and strafed regularly by British Mosquitoes. One moment they were forced to climb cautiously around potholes and piles of vehicular wreckage, the next manoeuvring past the bloated, gas-filled carcasses of dead horses, frequently being left with no option but to leave the autobahn altogether for the side roads that ran through the towns scattered along the banks of the Elbe. It was there the journey became even more hazardous and disjointed as they encountered a flood tide of humanity streaming towards them. The whole of Germany seemed to be on the move, shuffling west, away from the advancing Russians, carrying with them what they could. In two hours Hencke reckoned they must have passed almost 100,000 refugees, old women pushing barrows laden with linen and decrepit husbands; lines of young girls, many bare-foot, shuffling behind as they pushed prams or dragged carts; mothers struggling to carry wounded children who stared out of dirty bandages with enormous, frightened eyes. There were farm girls driving cows or pigs, or trying to round up stray chickens, women in fur coats covered in dirt, women in their best suits, women in rags and women in peasant costume still marked by the signs of toil on the land. But there were no men, at least none capable of walking, and there were precious few boys above the age of ten. They walked and stumbled, heads down, carrying whatever they had salvaged of their lives on their backs, resigned to the idea that whatever lay ahead could be no worse than what they had left behind.

These were the survivors, what was left of Germany, trudging away from terror towards a future which none could comprehend. And this was but one road, in one corner of the country, a small piece of a kaleidoscope of misery which was being repeated throughout the land as the German people were scattered like chaff.

The tide of shattered humanity was so thick that choking grey-brown dust rose in great clouds as far as the eye could see and no amount of bellowing, leaning on the horn or threats could part it. The shouts of the driver were met with red, exhausted eyes that did not understand, while in those few that did began to smoulder the spark of hostility as they saw the black Mercedes, clearly an official limousine complete with curtains and cocktail cabinet, trying to batter its way back to Berlin. Hencke sank deep into the red leather of the seats and his companion couldn't fail to notice the blaze of anger that spread across his face.

'I can understand how you must be feeling, you of all people. When you see sewer-Deutsch like that it makes you wonder why we bothered,' the other man sneered. 'In my book deserters like these should all be shot. Still, maybe they soon will be. The British front line is less than ten miles from here. That's why Reichsminister Goebbels sent his personal car for you. We couldn't afford to take the risk by plane.'

Captain Otto Misch sat erect and resplendent in his SS uniform with its FBK insignia, staring straight ahead and trying to avoid the hostile glances cast at him from the straggling crowd of refugees. He toyed nervously with the

Iron Cross pinned at his neck. It wasn't that he was afraid of the human flotsam outside his window, he simply didn't understand them and the lack of understanding made him uneasy. This wasn't the valiant resistance against the enemy which had been planned in Berlin and which he had been led to expect. As he twisted at the medal he noticed Hencke staring at his mangled hand.

'Moscow. I left the fingers in Moscow.' He waved his hand with a casual pride. 'I'm going back to reclaim them one day.'

'Not in this bloody car you're not,' the driver muttered as he swung the wheel sharply to avoid another crater, but his violent efforts succeeded only in running the car into a charred beam thrown across the road by recent bombing, and their progress came to a jarring halt moments before they would have run into yet another group of refugees.

'*Scheisse*, it would be quicker by bulldozer!' the captain swore.

'And a damn sight safer,' the sullen driver responded. 'The front wheel's gone. I'll have to change it. I'll need help.'

'Then get it!' Misch snapped irritably as an artillery shell landed less than a hundred yards away, sending up a malevolent plume of cement and brick dust. So close to the front not even Goebbels' bullet-proof limousine was safe.

It was dusk and they were on the outskirts of a small town, semi-derelict and ghost-like, over which a pall of brown smoke drifted as British artillery sporadically pounded what was left. Through the dust thrown up from the ruins of houses and by the tramp of a thousand feet they could make out a group of people gathered around a camp fire which stood at the centre of a crossroads; in front of them lay a tram which had been thrown on its side and filled with rubble. It was a primitive barricade behind which the defenders would be expected to fight tanks armed with little more than rifles and the one-shot *Panzerfaust* being churned out from back-street workshops and bicycle sheds – anywhere with a bench and a primitive set of tools. The driver set off towards the barricade in search of assistance, leaving his two passengers

203

listening to the radio which was tuned to pick up warnings of air raids in their sector. He was soon back, shaking his head.

'They say they're too busy to help – got problems of their own,' he reported glumly.

'Did you tell them that this was Reichsminister Goebbels' personal car?' Misch, instantly annoyed, slapped his gloves into his half-hand.

'Sure. They said if that was so it was the first official car they'd seen heading back towards Berlin all week.'

Misch ground his teeth in fury.

'I told them they were wasting their time with the barricade,' the driver continued laconically. 'That it would take the British only twelve and a half minutes to get past it.'

'Twelve and a half minutes?' queried Misch, taken aback by the exactitude of the estimate.

'Sure. Ten minutes splitting their sides with laughter, two minutes to bring up an artillery piece and thirty seconds to blow the whole fucking thing into the river.' Insolence was written all over the driver's face. Hencke noted that although he was in uniform, the driver hadn't saluted Misch once. This was not the German army he remembered. But this was scarcely the Germany he remembered, either.

Consumed by rage the captain slammed the door of the car and stalked off in the direction of the barricade. Hencke followed and found still more to astonish him in the new Germany. In the rapidly failing light the campfire threw lurid patterns on to the buildings surrounding the crossroads, all of which had been reduced by battle to empty hulks standing sightless and open-mouthed where once had been windows and doorways. Dust and smoke drifted like witches' breath through the gaping apertures, as the thunder of exploding artillery shells rolled all around. By the fire in the centre of this primeval setting stood an elderly man and a dozen boys. Scattered around them lay a motley collection of rifles of varying vintages, some from the First World War with fixed bayonets, and by the kerbside lay a canvas bag which appeared

204

to be filled with grenades. The man was perhaps in his sixties, the empty right-hand sleeve of his jacket pinned to his side. None of the boys was older than fifteen, all were filthy and covered in grime, a few were in the uniform of the Hitler Youth and one who had a split lip and a bruised temple was sobbing pitifully. Into their midst strode Misch and instantly there was silence. The old man looked up at the tall captain and his face filled with anxiety as he saw the unmistakable markings of the SS uniform.

'Heil Hitler!' Misch barked, snapping to a straight-armed salute which demanded a response. Immediately he flushed with self-ridicule as he noticed the empty sleeve, and his awkwardness did nothing to improve his temper. 'What the hell is going on here? I ask for assistance to repair my car. How dare you refuse!'

'I'm . . . sorry, Captain. I am the local schoolmaster, these are my boys,' the man stammered. 'We were having a little difficulty . . .'

Immediately the tearful youngster resumed his crying.

'What difficulty?'

'Nothing, nothing at all, really. Perhaps we can help you fix your car now.' But the schoolmaster's tone was a little too nervous, his words too rushed to hide his anxiety.

'What difficulty, you bastard? I want to know!'

A conspiratorial silence fell over the group, punctuated only by the youthful sobbing and the spitting of the fire. The old man, overwhelmed, cast his eyes down to the ground. Misch hit him hard, a single blow across the cheek.

'Tell me!'

Blood trickled down the old man's cheek where Misch's heavy ring had caught him and fear flooded into his eyes, but still he said nothing. Several of the boys were looking in the direction of the sobbing youth.

'As members of the *Hitlerjugend* you are all under military discipline. I order you to tell me what is going on here. You!' Misch pointed to one of the boys who already bore two medals on the breast of his uniform. 'Come here!'

205

The boy, who appeared no more than eleven years of age, ran forward.

'Tell me! No, don't look round at the others,' Misch shook him savagely by the shoulders. 'Tell me!'

'It was Hausser, sir,' he responded in a shrill treble. 'He . . . ran away. So me and Pauli had to go and drag him back.'

'Ran away. Where?'

'To his mother, sir. They were preparing to hang out a white sheet . . .'

Quiet fell across the gathering once again, but it was of a different, more menacing kind. Gone was the silence of conspiracy, replaced by oppressive guilt. All eyes were on the youth, tears still trickling down his cheek and mingling with the blood smeared across the adolescent down on his upper lip. Misch strode towards him.

'Get up, soldier.'

The boy made no move.

'Get up I said.' Misch kicked him hard on his bare thigh just below his shorts.

'There's no need for that,' the schoolmaster pleaded, rushing across to grab Misch's arm. 'Leave him alone. For God's sake what's the point? Can't you see? It's all over. *Verloren.* Lost. Lost.'

Misch threw him off and the old man fell heavily to the pavement. 'Nothing is lost while there are decent Germans still willing to fight!' he screamed. His face was blue with anger, his knee trembling; he was losing control of himself. 'It is only cowards and deserting pigs like this one who are losing us the war.'

'Let them all go back home, they're only children.' The schoolteacher stretched out his arm in supplication.

'They are soldiers defending the Reich. And this one is a deserter.' Misch looked around the group of boys, saw the look in their eyes which grew more haunting and fragile with every falling shell. He had seen it before, in front of Moscow, in the eyes of conscripts just before they turned and ran away through the snow and slush. It was why they had lost

Moscow. It was why he had lost his hand. And it was why they were losing the war. As the suffocating dust thrown up from a nearby explosion drifted across the scene, he knew that one more near-miss and they would be gone, blown away like autumn leaves even before they had sight of the advancing enemy. For Misch, and for the forces which had taken him as the hungry son of an unemployed printer and turned him into a feared and bemedalled warrior for whom people stepped out of the way and over whom women drooled, it was almost over. It was all crumbling away in front of him. A savage tremor ran through his body. He was about to be thrown back on the bloody rubbish heap, or worse. Because of cowardice like this!

'If any of you soldiers are thinking of deserting your posts, remember. There is only one punishment for vermin who choose to run away and leave their defenceless mothers and sisters to get raped!'

'This boy has already lost his father and three elder brothers in the war. For God's sake how much more do you expect him to give?'

'Shut up, teacher!'

Misch's voice had an edge of hysteria and his mutilated hand felt as if it were on fire. His revolver was already raised, pointing at the boy, who stared straight at him, face flooded with uncomprehension as he looked into the twitching eyes of this stranger. He still did not understand, even when the bullet struck him an inch above the right eye. For a moment his body twitched and froze, his eyes still staring straight at Misch, until belatedly and slowly his whole form seemed to crumple. He fell back, bouncing once off the bricks beneath him, and lay broken amongst the rubble.

No one moved, no one screamed. No one knew who might be next.

'Hang him from that lamp-post,' Misch ordered. 'As an example to anyone who cannot remember his duty.'

'As a monument to the Third Reich,' whispered the schoolmaster, still on the pavement where he had been thrown.

'You want to join him?' Misch turned the pistol on the old man and his hand was shaking violently.

'I no longer care to live. What is there to live for? You have murdered our future.'

Misch turned to the boys. 'Hang him! And put a placard around his neck which says "Deserter". And if you can't spell "Deserter" I'll shoot the teacher.'

No one doubted his word, and as one boy stirred from his petrification so the others followed. Not until they had carried out the orders to the full did Misch replace the pistol in his holster. He was nervous and uneasy, his pale cheeks unnaturally flushed, shocked with the realization of what he had done. 'Back to your posts,' he commanded. The schoolmaster nodded, and they returned silently to the building of the barricade, trying to keep their backs towards the lamp post.

Misch turned away and for the first time seemed to notice Hencke, who had stood silently behind him throughout. 'You'll understand, of course. After all you've been through.' Misch smiled nervously. 'The Fatherland means everything to me.'

'I think I need a piss,' Hencke responded, and clawed his way over a pile of bricks to the shell of a gutted building. He disappeared for a few moments behind a wall before reappearing. 'Hey, Misch. Come and see what I've found.'

He beckoned him over and Misch clambered after him until they were both hidden behind the wall.

'What's up? What have you discovered?'

Hencke turned to face Misch until they were no more than inches apart. 'I just wanted you to know what I thought of that little episode outside, Misch.'

The quizzical look was still on Misch's face when the bayonet which Hencke had filched from one of the boys' rifles caught him between the ribs. Then there was surprise, the pain hadn't yet hit him. Only when Hencke twisted the blade upwards, snapping two ribs and penetrating the heart, did Misch's eyes bulge as the agony forced him on to the tips

208

of his toes. He grabbed Hencke's shoulders with what was left of his rapidly ebbing strength until they were eyeball to eyeball, and Hencke could feel the fear and panic in Misch's hot breath as he began to choke on the blood rising in his gorge.

'But I thought you'd come back to help save us . . .'

'No, you murdering bastard. I've come back to kill Hitler.'

He gave another twist of the bayonet blade and Misch fell back dead at his feet.

TEN

Hencke arrived at his destination well after midnight. The RAF had finished with their nightly bombing attack on the German capital and there was a lull in the early hours as the survivors waited for the return of the American bombers by day. It was a routine with an awesome familiarity for Berliners. Somehow the city still functioned; hundreds of thousands went about their duties, baking, selling, stamping ration cards, clearing the streets, keeping the water and electricity flowing, distributing newspapers, even delivering mail – anything was better than sitting back to wait for the arrival of the Russians. Although there was a blackout the driver was able to see his way without difficulty; a choking cloud of soot and phosphorous smoke hung low across the city and the light from innumerable fires reflected back into the desolate streets, giving even darkest night a sickening edge of brightness. It was the fresh piles of rubble and unfilled crates scattered across the roadways which made the passage so difficult; wide boulevards had been turned into obstacle courses and several times they had to turn back and divert away from streets that were completely blocked or had turned into great tunnels of fire. More than once Hencke had helped the driver shift obstructions; they wrapped wet handkerchiefs around their faces to protect themselves from the hot, suffocating ash and fumes. At one point their way was obstructed by a body. The driver got out, grabbed the body under the shoulders and dumped it to one side.

'Was he dead?'

'Who knows? If we stopped for every body, we'd never bloody get there.'

Since Hencke had returned alone to the car, the driver had dropped any vestige of military discipline and respect. He had a job to do and he'd do it, but he didn't have to pretend to enjoy it. When Hencke explained that Misch 'hadn't made it' back from the growing chaos on the other side of the barricade, the driver didn't bother to ask why. It was too frequent an occurrence to arouse even his slightest interest; his only regret was that Hencke hadn't suggested they turn round and head westward with all the others.

They passed beside the Brandenburg Gate in the very heart of Berlin. It stood largely intact and shining in the glare of nearby fires, an awesome reminder of sights which seemed buried deep in a time when it had been illuminated by the torches of victory parades and the Fuehrer had taken the salute of adoring millions. But the military bands and the tramp of marching feet had gone; there was only the explosion of time-delay bombs and the shudder of collapsing buildings to interrupt the complaints of his driver and the low growl of the Mercedes engine.

They drove directly into the underground garage off Hermann Goering Strasse. Even by night and with many of its windows blown out or boarded up, the looming edifice of the Reich Chancellery was clearly recognizable. Teams were at work dealing with the rubble from the most recent aerial onslaught but it was no longer being taken away and hidden, merely pushed aside to allow access. Inside the building the upper stories had been vacated, parts of the roof and most of the windows having gone, but on lower floors and in the cellar there were still hundreds of people scurrying about their business. Indeed, as Hencke emerged from the garage into the heart of Berlin's main government complex, he entered a different world. While outside the great capital city lay in ruins, inside there remained at least a semblance of discipline and control. Even the driver had started saluting senior officers again. Telephones still jangled, commands were barked, soldiers scampered to obey. Yet as Hencke was led by an orderly through a maze of underground cellars and tunnels, he couldn't help but notice how fragile seemed this veneer of order. There was no hiding the weariness in the limbs, the ashen signs of exhaustion in the faces of men who had survived too long on too little sleep, the soiled uniforms which bore the dust and filth of excursions into the outside world and which no one bothered any longer to clean or replace. In many places the refuse of meals and drinking sessions lay uncleared, and Hencke passed two generals who were obviously drunk. Strangely their uniforms bore the least sign of battle grime, the only stains seeming to have come from spilt wine and soup.

Soon they were out of the cellar and up to the ground floor, where spartan utility gave way to the splendour of marble floors, rich carpets and even richer tapestries, all of which were spotted with the marks of fallen plasterwork. The lights burned brightly for the windows were heavily boarded and, as the orderly led the way down corridors and through rooms which echoed to their footsteps, Hencke was conscious of the soiled splendour of a once magnificent showpiece. Drawing-rooms had been transformed into sleeping quarters bursting with metal cots; where great receptions had once been held were piled man-made mountains of provisions and wooden crates; a burnished Steinway in the music room had been pushed aside to make way for an array of maps surrounding a briefing table, and everywhere there was a sense of desperate struggle to avoid the short descent into chaos. But still the heart of government was beating, even if the effort involved was proving colossal.

The orderly, a lieutenant, stopped outside a towering pair of carved doors and instructed him to wait. He knocked sharply and from deep within there came a muffled order to enter. He disappeared for a second and exchanged a few brief words before reappearing. 'He's ready for you,' was all he said before ushering Hencke through the doors.

The room behind the doors had once been a small reception-room – small, that is, only by comparison with the great halls through which they had passed. It was a good thirty metres long and decorated with gilded mirrors, oil paintings of traditional hunting scenes and a vast crystal chandelier which cast a delicate light across the inlaid oaken floor. Whatever furniture had once adorned the room had gone. In the middle now stood a large baize-covered table surrounded by chairs, sufficient for a briefing meeting of thirty, with a huge map of Berlin and its approaches pinned up at one end of the room. At the other end, beside an ornate fireplace whose mantel was covered in fine pieces of blue and white porcelain, was a vast pillared desk with a marble top which was all but hidden beneath neat piles of paper. And beside the desk stood the unmistakable, reed-like figure of Josef Goebbels.

'Hencke! Is it really you inside those rags? What a spectacle you make! But you are most welcome!' Goebbels paced stiffly across the room, his right foot pointing awkwardly inwards, extending his hand in greeting. A smile of amusement played on his lips as he studied his unkempt prize. While the under-sized Reichsminister was dressed immaculately in a conservative double-breasted suit with a pearl-white shirt, his dark hair brushed back and glossy with brilliantine, Hencke made a miserable sight. The change of clothes provided by the local police after his rescue on the beach had never fitted properly; now they were stained with the mud and dust from shifting obstructions and rubble. His boots and trousers had become soaked from the flooding of broken water pipes, a dark brown stain of dried blood clung to his left sleeve and around his neck still hung the grimy handkerchief he had used to protect his mouth from the burning air.

'Ha! I see you come well gift-wrapped,' Goebbels chuckled, clapping his hands in delight. He was clearly exultant. 'I am not a superstitious man, Hencke, but to have you delivered back to us, on such an auspicious day, is more than even my scepticism can take.' He saw the bewildered look on Hencke's face and led him towards two comfortable chairs which stood on either side of a low occasional table. 'Sit down, my dear

213

Hencke. We have much to talk about.' He poured coffee from a silver pot and began.

'Do you know what day it is?'

'Herr Reichsminister, I scarcely know what year it is. I have been in a prison camp, on the run, in fishing smacks on the Irish Sea and in a submarine at the bottom of the North Sea . . .'

Goebbels stretched over to grasp his hand and still him. 'The twentieth of April, my dear Hencke. The Fuehrer's birthday. I have organized a very special celebration for him. And a very special prize. Hencke, *you* are that prize!'

'I . . . am to be presented to the Fuehrer?'

Goebbels' saturnine face was unusually animated. 'Yes. Oh, yes. The arrival of perhaps the bravest man in Germany represents the return of hope and good fortune. My God, it will be better medicine than anything those quacks have poured into him in months.' The long creases about his face became suddenly harder and his voice lost its celebratory edge, becoming quiet, almost conspiratorial. He leaned close to Hencke as if afraid his words might be overheard, the blood vessels at his temples swelling as he strained forward. 'You must realize, Hencke, the Fuehrer may not be the man you remember. The assassination attempt at Rastenburg last year . . . it caused him grave damage. He was so close to the bomb it was a miracle he survived. His ear drums shattered, his hearing damaged, his sense of balance gone . . .' Goebbels was talking slowly, choosing his words with care. 'The worries he has borne over so many years on our behalf have taken their inevitable toll. He has given so much of his own strength to our cause, it is vital for us in turn to replenish it with our full support and encouragement. He is tired, unwell. He needs reassurance. While he has the will to carry on, so does Germany. Later today all of the party's leaders are arriving from their posts around the country to honour and strengthen him, to reinforce his desire to carry on in his great task. And that is why your arrival is so timely and so important. You are the embodiment of the German spirit to continue the

214

fight; he will regard your presence as an omen of good fortune, a harbinger of victories yet to come.'

'I fear I will disappoint the Fuehrer . . .'

'Hencke, you are Odysseus escaped from the clutches of the Cyclops and returned to Ithaca. This is no time for modesty. You have achieved more than any other captured German since this war began . . . But tell me, we know so little of you – no more than your name.' He was on the edge of his chair – like a cat waiting to pounce, thought Hencke. 'Tell me more about yourself.'

So they sat while Hencke talked, of his childhood in the Sudetenland, the German-speaking part of Czechoslovakia which had been almost the first of the Third Reich's territorial claims in Europe, stripped from the Czechs in 1938. Of his modest life as a schoolteacher, of his even more modest entry into the Wehrmacht as an ordinary infantryman, of his capture outside Bastogne on Christmas Day last as the Ardennes offensive turned to ignominious rout, of his incarceration and of his run for freedom. And as he spoke his mind was in turmoil. He'd only just arrived and already he was taking coffee with Goebbels – they were going to *push* him at Hitler! – could it all be so easy? Of course not. He needed time to think and his confusion and obvious exhaustion were causing his words to stumble. He took refuge in a yawn, mumbling an apology before Goebbels interrupted him.

'I have tired you enough. There is much for us to discuss still, but you must get some rest before our celebration this afternoon – it would not do for you to fall asleep on the Fuehrer! And we must do something about your gift-wrapping . . . Hencke, I am appointing you to the Leibstandarte Adolf Hitler, the most élite division in the Waffen SS. Its name is synonymous, as now is yours, with valour and dedication to the Fuehrer. I congratulate you! So, rest. There are a few hours before the Americans return to snatch our sleep from us and wake the dead. We can continue this later . . .'

Hencke's head swam from fatigue and the overwhelming atmosphere. He hadn't seen Goebbels give any signal, but when he looked up the orderly was waiting to escort him away. He rose stiffly with Goebbels' hand on his elbow for support. 'Sleep well, brave Hencke,' the Reichsminister said, assisting him towards the door. At the threshold he paused, taking Hencke's hand.

'I have never been able to fight in the front line, but you seem to have shown enough heroism for both of us. You're a very brave man, Hencke. Indeed, coming from the Sudetenland it could be said that you were part of this war even before it began.'

Hencke nodded. Goebbels didn't know how right he was.

'Tell me, where in the Sudetenland were you born?'

Hencke froze. The hand which held his, which had supported him across the room, had now become a restraint, a manacle holding him back. He knew their conversation had become interrogation and he would need all his wits about him. But his tired body no longer wanted to fight the fatigue and he felt paralyzed by the touch of the hand and the brush of the seemingly innocent words. Goebbels' dark eyes and lean, saturnine face had the hypnotic power of a swaying cobra, and for a moment it appeared as if Hencke could say nothing. He knew why Goebbels had asked.

'Eger,' he said softly. 'February the second, 1910. I was born just outside Eger.'

Goebbels nodded. 'They will be very proud of you. Well, goodnight, Hencke. And don't worry about a thing. We'll take care of you.'

And Hencke was gone. With a thoughtful look Goebbels walked back to his desk. He spent some time pondering over a slow burning cigarette before he lifted the phone.

'Bormann? Hencke's arrived. In Berlin. In the Reich Chancellery. Look, you're the man with the records. I want you to find out a little more about him. Schoolteacher. Born second February 1910 outside Eger in the Sudetenland . . . No, seems fine, but he's too valuable for us to take chances. I've arranged for someone to keep an eye on him, just in case. At times like these you can never be too sure . . .'

Replacing the receiver he checked his watch. He opened a large drawer in his desk and switched on the small radio which was inside, fiddling with the tuning dial before settling back to listen to the news service of the BBC. Nowadays it was the only way he could find out precisely what was going on. And Goebbels always insisted on knowing what was going on.

The orderly, who had not spoken a word on the journey through the Reich Chancellery to Goebbels' study, seemed to have relaxed. Once the Reichsminister appeared satisfied with his guest the tension had seeped out of the lieutenant, to be replaced by a stubbornness and even pugnacity. Hencke thought he could smell alcohol on his breath.

'How well do you know Berlin?' he enquired of Hencke.

'Not at all. I'm from the Sudetenland.'

'Rumour says you've come to save the city. That's nice of you, very generous,' the lieutenant continued, oozing sarcasm. He clearly had little time for heroes, particularly new ones. 'So let me show you a little of what you've come to save.' Without waiting for any sort of response he led the way along a back corridor and down a staircase. They were headed once more for the cellar. Soon they had left behind the lofty ceilings and soiled splendour of the upper floors and were down once more in the low, bare, monochrome world of hollow expressions and deep-sunk eyes rimmed red with fatigue. They proceeded along the corridor that ran through the cellar complex to a point where it became cluttered with bundles of blankets and rags. Inside the rags were soldiers, all badly wounded, some of whom already appeared to have given up the struggle and to be dead. There was a sweet, disgusting smell in the air and flies buzzed freely around. Up ahead Hencke could see doors and the lieutenant was headed for them, but barring his way was a broken, toppled figure, once a full man, now unable even to continue sitting propped against the wall. The body was hunched up, the eyes bruised and tightly closed, the only sign of life being a low moan of

217

despair coming from between swollen lips. Judging by the gaudy brass buttons that still clung to what was left of his uniform, the body appeared once to have been a young recruit from a naval training college. It was clear he would never return there. The lieutenant picked him up and gently leaned him back against the wall.

'Come on, old chap. Can't hold up progress,' he whispered in the lad's ear. He lit a cigarette to place between the puffy lips but the lad seemed to have neither the strength nor spirit to respond and the cigarette fell to the floor. The lieutenant crushed it angrily with his boot before looking back at Hencke. 'Looks as if you're too late to save that one. Never mind, plenty more inside.'

They went through the door, and the scene in front of them banished any last vestige of tiredness from Hencke's mind. Beneath a solitary lamp stood an officer and two women. The officer wore a barely recognizable uniform which was covered in blood, some old and caked, much of it fresh. The two women, scarcely less bloodied, were obviously nurses. On a high table between them lay a body with its stomach open and entrails pouring out on either side of the incision. The doctor was having trouble since the body was twitching and he was uttering curses about the lack of morphine. His eyes were as red and smeared as his uniform and his face grey from lack of sleep. One of the nurses was crying silently, not tears of weakness or fear but tears of compassion; the body before them seemed to belong to a youth no older than sixteen. Set back from the table, on a hard bench where he lay supported by a large stuffed cushion, was an old man. Even at a glance he was clearly not long for this world yet between racking bouts of coughing he was giving instruction and advice to the surgeon, who sought counsel frequently. Perhaps the man wielding the scalpel was not a qualified doctor at all. In one corner of the improvised surgery lay four other forms on stretchers, waiting their turn.

No one took the slightest notice of Hencke and the lieutenant. Not even when one of the nurses slopped something into a bucket and brought it over to the large bin close to where they were standing did she look at them. Hencke saw that the slops were yards of entrail, and the bin contained amputated arms and legs, some still with their boots on, in addition to much gore. He desperately wanted to vomit, but looking at the nurses made him feel foolish. He swallowed the bile and clenched his jaws until he thought his teeth would crack.

The lieutenant seemed unaffected; he had seen it many times before. 'Come with me,' he said, and dragged Hencke towards a door on the other side of the room which required them to push past the table. Still no one looked up. Hencke suspected they would still be there, bent over the table, even when the Russians came.

As he and Hencke walked through the door the lieutenant switched on the torch buckled to his belt, for whatever was on the other side was in semi-darkness. It was a large room, packed with beds jammed side by side which could only be reached by narrow passageways at their feet. There were well over 300 beds, all full, many with two patients sharing each narrow palliasse. In spite of the hum of a ventilation fan the stench was appalling, a rancid mixture of death, decay, gangrene, sickness and broken bowels. By torchlight a handful of nurses were floating about the room, ministering, comforting, cleaning. One was carefully unwrapping the bandages from a corpse, laying those which appeared the least soiled on a table for later use. The door of a medicine cabinet on the wall stood ajar, the shelves inside bare.

'I'm sure they'll be happy to hear you've brought them hope,' the lieutenant said. 'Still, a truckful of aspirin might have been more practical.'

Their journey was not yet over. Hencke was led along the side of the room, past patients who groaned with pain, some of whom reached out and implored them for a cigarette, many who seemed to lack the strength either to complain or to implore. Without knowing where he was going, Hencke hurried on. At the far end of the room was another door like the one through which they had entered and Hencke

219

approached it with a feeling of considerable relief. The lieutenant stood back to allow him through first, proffering the torch.

Hencke's first impression was that this was another hospital ward, for he could see rows of cots lined up in the gloom. But as soon as he took a breath he could tell this was not so; the stench was gone, or was at least different. He flashed the torch around and could see bodies on the beds.

'Turn off that fucking light, you fool,' a voice growled in the dark. Hecke shone the torch in the direction of the sound. In the beam of light he could see an overweight, pink body stretched out on a bed. It was one of the drunken generals he had seen earlier that evening. Astride him, her breasts bobbling up and down as she tried to get some rhythm going, was a young woman. He shone the torch away and played it quickly over the rest of the room. It needed no more than a second for him to realize what he had intruded upon. The room seemed to have been intended as a small extension to the main hospital ward, but the beds were strewn around in haphazard fashion. On many of the beds lay men entwined with women, sometimes with two women, either actively involved in sex or taking a break with a bottle or cigarette. To one side several beds had been pushed together, and on top of this platform Hencke saw the confused and contorted shapes of group sex. The men appeared to be mostly elderly, the women all young. 'Angels of the night,' whispered the lieutenant, 'who work just as hard as the girls next door. They call this the Recovery Room.' From somewhere in the gloom, accompanied by raucous laughter and much crudity, a young female voice began to groan and then rise, unintentionally mimicking the anguish of a wounded soldier. Hencke felt sick again.

'Join in if you want. You don't have to make reservations,' the lieutenant muttered. The angry snatch of Hencke's head gave him his answer. 'OK, if you've seen enough, follow me,' and they passed through a side back door into bright light. They were in a rest area, with comfortable chairs and sofas

220

arranged round coffee tables. It was yet another world, and officers sat exchanging conversation and bonhomie with each other and a variety of women, while orderlies passed between them dispensing drinks. Hencke shook his head to clear his thoughts, trying to ensure that what he had just witnessed was not simply the product of an exhausted mind beset by twisted dreams, but the stench of the hospital still swirled in his nostrils and he knew there was no mistake.

'I need a drink,' the lieutenant said, and without asking went across to a table that served as a bar and ordered two. He and Hencke tossed them straight down.

'Who are these women?' Hencke enquired.

'A mixture. Mistresses. Secretaries. Civilian personnel. Even housewives. Some are just spectators, here for a gawk and a good time, but many of them have run to the Reich Chancellery terrified of Ivan, fleeing from what they imagine is going to happen when he gets his hands on them. It seems that most of them after a drink or two prefer German hands, and plenty of them.'

The door behind them opened and the general, now fully clothed but with his uniform jacket unbuttoned, came through. He was pink with the exertions of his latest victory and raised a triumphal paw in greeting at a fellow officer who was drinking with three women. He strolled over to join them; there was no sign of the girl he had left behind.

'Down the corridor there's a dental surgery,' the lieutenant continued. 'You know, big black leather dentist's chair which can be adjusted to different positions. The latest trick is to strap a woman in it and tilt it to whatever angle you fancy. Two men often have a go at the same time. Then you stop for a drink, strap her in the chair some other way, tilt it to a new angle and start all over again. It's a particular favourite with the generals.'

'Rape?' Hencke was incredulous. He had thought himself no longer capable of surprise.

'Don't be a bloody fool. The girls are queuing up for it. Look around, do you see anyone complaining? It's like collective hysteria. There's nowhere else for them to go. They've probably lost their husbands or lovers in the war, they're alone and frightened. They come here and throw themselves at the nearest man with a pistol on his belt, desperately seeking protection and a way out. But after a couple of days and nights down here in the cellars they seem to catch the contagion. They call it *Kellerkrebs* – cellar cancer. As long as they can't see the war or hear it too well behind twenty feet of concrete, they manage to persuade themselves that it no longer matters, that Ivan's buggered off and they're safe. They drown everything in drink and fuck away all their cares. Live for today, for tomorrow we die . . . Who knows? When you think of what is going to happen, maybe they're right.'

He turned to order another drink and as he did so, three prettily dressed women wandered into the room, and the hubbub of conversation momentarily became subdued. They were in their late twenties or early thirties and appeared to be looking for a friend, for another woman detached herself from a group of senior officers and hurried to greet them. After exchanging a few moments of girlish laughter they all left together, and the conversation in the room resumed unabated.

'Who were they, Lieutenant?'

'Them? Doesn't pay to notice them, Hencke. Particularly not in this part of the Chancellery. Forget you ever saw them.'

'It seems there is a lot this evening I am supposed to forget.'

'No, Hencke. Don't forget the rest. I want you to remember all that sewage we've just waded through, because that's the Berlin you've come back to save. And if you're half the saviour Goebbels supposes you to be, it makes you the most dangerous man there is in this insane city.'

222

ELEVEN

Hencke awoke to the sound of bombing overhead. It was shortly before noon; the American air force had returned for their daily visit. Down in the cellar of the Reich Chancellery where Hencke had been billeted in one of the crowded sleeping quarters, the noise was like the rumble of distant artillery fire, the thick alluvial sand on which Berlin was built cushioning and deadening the effects of all but the most direct of hits. Yet after months of saturation bombing, almost everything had been hit, several times. The lamps overhead swung as if agitated by an imperceptible subterranean wind, fine plaster and cement dust settled on every surface and nobody seemed willing to talk as they listened for the one that had their name on its nose cone.

Underground the routine of bombing seemed the only way of distinguishing between night and day. People ate when they felt hungry, drank when they wished to forget, slept when they were too exhausted to stay awake any longer or, if they had the energy and desire, went in search of a signalwoman. Many, particularly those with no front line duties, had found reason to be there a very long time. The longer they accepted the shelter of the cellar and the less contact they had with the outside world, the more unreal it became. And Hencke was told that the Fuehrer had been in the cellar almost constantly since mid-January.

Before Hencke had managed to scratch the sleep from his eyes the lieutenant was at the foot of his bed. 'Knew you wouldn't sleep through this lot, not yet. Takes a couple of days before you no longer give a damn . . .' He held some clothes and boots. 'Try these. The boots are waterproof. Might come in handy, just in case you get caught short while you're busy saving Berlin.' As he mocked he threw the items on the end of the bed. They were the black dress uniform of the Waffen SS, complete with silver piping, distinctive collar markings, armband of the Liebstandarte Adolf Hitler division, and captain's shoulder flashes. Hencke looked at the officer's pips incredulously, rubbing them with his thumb to make sure they were real.

'Why, didn't they tell you, *Captain*?' the lieutenant goaded. 'Way things are going you'll be a bloody general by the end of the week. Or dead. Sir.'

Hencke decided not to argue the point – he wasn't here to argue, and he was too confused as to what was going on. The lieutenant enlightened him.

'Lunch – or, in your case, breakfast. Then you'll be taken to the birthday knees-up. Your big moment.'

'Where is the Fuehrer?' He hoped it seemed a perfectly natural question, but Hencke held his breath, waiting for the response. He couldn't afford to arouse suspicion.

'Where he always is. In the bloody Bunker, of course.'

'The Bunker? It's separate from the cellar?'

'The whole of this part of Berlin's been tunnelled out into several cellars and shelters. Under the Chancellery, Propaganda Ministry, Air Ministry. There's a little world of underground empires down here, all crisscrossed and interconnected; half the time you expect the bloody Minotaur to pop his head round the corner. But there's only one *Bunker*. No, I lie. Two. A *Vorbunker* where most of his personal staff bury themselves, and then down to the *Fuehrerbunker* proper. Twenty feet below sewer level, the underworld of Berlin. They say even the rats come out with a headache. Although the fact that the air conditioning doesn't work properly is supposed to be a state secret. Hey, they might even shoot me for telling you.' His face brightened for the first time that day.

'And the birthday celebration is there?'

'Good God, no. Too damned small. Get Goering and two

fat *Hausfrauen* down there and the rest would suffocate. No, the Fuehrer's going to honour us by coming up to face the daylight for once, and look Berlin in the eye for the first time in months.'

So maybe that would be it. His one chance of success. He wouldn't get more than one chance, and perhaps not even that. He washed and changed into his uniform. *The* uniform. He felt like an ancient knight donning armour invested with evil powers. The fit was immaculate, yet the collar felt unbearably tight as if it were trying to grip him round the throat and strangle him. As he fastened the last button on the tunic his chest heaved and he had trouble breathing – somehow the uniform seemed to be trying to take him over, to make him one of *them*. Only when he checked the leather holster and found the Walther 7.65, cleaned and with a fully loaded clip, could he begin to fight back against his anxieties and convince himself that he, not the uniform, was in control. Like everyone else he was sweating in the accumulating heat of the cellar, yet every few minutes a cold river of apprehension would flood down his backbone. *They were going to take him to Hitler.* Just like that. Could it really be that easy? Or had he already been sucked into this underworld of madness and illusion where nothing was as it seemed? He waited for over three hours, trying to control the writhing knot in his stomach, wondering if he would be forced to take the lieutenant's advice and use his boots.

He quickly discovered that nothing was going to be as easy as it might have seemed. When the lieutenant returned they walked several hundred yards without once leaving the Reich Chancellery. It was vast and very crowded, bustling like a railway station. The remnants of an entire city and several Wehrmacht armies had been poured into its cellar and lower floors until the building had filled and overflowed. Growing piles of suitcases and kitbags were tucked away in corners and there was the constant clatter of people arriving, and departing. Armed soldiers were everywhere and he thought it could be only moments before one of them spotted

225

the unmistakable blush of treachery which he was sure marked his face, but they all seemed too busy with their own affairs to pay any attention to him.

It changed when they ran into the checkpoint. They had arrived in the antechamber of the so-called Court of Honour and armed guards were everywhere, relieving guests not only of coats and bags but anything that might conceivably resemble or contain a weapon. No one was exempt, not even high-ranking staff officers. All had to give up side arms and briefcases, the women their handbags. The Walther on which Hencke had focused so many ill-formed hopes in the last few hours was taken and a record entered in a huge ledger which had once been used to keep the accounts of the Chancellery kitchen. Even ceremonial dress daggers were confiscated. No chances were being taken; nothing, it seemed, could get past.

Yet even that was not enough. Four more FBK guards were waiting as they left the antechamber, two to watch proceedings with machine pistols poised while the other pair saluted each guest before submitting them to a careful body search. Women were dealt with in a separate corner by two female adjutants who looked as if they could take on a whole parachute platoon and still be through by breakfast. Passes and identity cards were inspected and checked against a master list. When it came to Hencke's turn the lieutenant produced a sheet of paper which he flourished at the guard and nodded towards Hencke. The guard seemed impressed.

'Here you are.' The lieutenant handed the paper to Hencke. 'Your pass. Signed by Goebbels himself. For Chrissake don't lose it or they won't let you out this side of World War Three.'

Only then were they permitted to pass into the magnificent Court of Honour, the *Ehrenhof*, the traditional place for such celebrations. Never had it looked more incongruous. The chamber glittered with its finery of medals, bejewelled batons, party insignia and gaily bedecked womenfolk, but the pride of Nazi society milled around like cattle at pasture, penned into one section of the room behind a cordon of guards while those still waiting to join the festivities formed an obedient, shuffling line in order to pass through a final security check. The absence of people in much of the hall gave the proceedings an eerie, echoing quality. Only when he looked up beyond the lofty marble columns did Hencke understand why. Although the polished stone floor had been swept of debris since the last bombing run, full across the gilded ceiling ran two cracks wide enough to take a man's arm to the shoulder. The ornate chandelier of a thousand pieces of crystal was lit, but lurching at a sickening angle from broken supports. No one could be sure when it would come smashing down, only that it must, and probably before the coming night's air raid was over.

His pass was inspected once more, his face examined, but still no one detected any mark of guilt. At last he was amongst the guests and, as he looked round, the knot in his stomach gave another savage wrench. Almost beside him, sweat pouring down his face, was the huge, bursting figure of Goering in full Reichsmarschall's regalia, beaming broadly, sipping his drink and taking a regular, nervous look at his watch. He seemed like a man who had an urgent appointment somewhere else, his agitated eyes suggesting that he didn't mind it being anywhere else, so long as it was outside Berlin. Nearby stood the diminutive figure of Himmler, oddly shaped forehead, thick glasses, no chin, no trace of humour in his face, also looking distracted, unable to concentrate on the conversation of his companions, his eyes moving restlessly around the room. There was Bormann, and Speer, Ribbentrop, Axmann . . . The whole damnable hierarchy of the Nazi Party seemed to have gathered, yet Hencke could sense something was amiss. There were bursts of jocularity and laughter, but the appreciation of a neighbour's attempt to raise spirits was perfunctory. A laugh, an edgy smile, and the faces returned to grimness. A five-piece military band struggled to provide entertainment but their scratchy performance suggested they had been hastily gathered and never played together before. There were also cameras and a film crew, moving round the gathering to capture the scene for the instruction and admiration of future generations in the Thousand-Year Reich. All the formalities and substance of an historic celebration had been brought together, yet the spirit was missing. There was little attempt to circulate, few of the leaders showed even the slightest interest in talking to their senior colleagues, preferring to bury themselves in small talk and joking with more junior personnel or the women. It was difficult to escape the atmosphere of unease and mistrust. Only Goebbels, dressed in the freshly-pressed brown jacket of his party uniform, seemed intent on circulating, shaking hands, talking, encouraging, listening, nodding his head in approval or wagging his finger to emphasize a point. He appeared to be the only common factor, the only remaining link amongst the remnants of what had once been the most formidable political organization Europe had ever seen.

'Ah, Hencke. You're here. Come forward, don't be shy.' Goebbels had spied him, hovering uncertainly, and the Reichsminister raised his hands above his head and clapped for attention.

Hencke stepped forward, feeling like the pig being paraded in front of the revellers at *Schuetzenfest* before they fell on the creature and tore it apart. Their eyes devoured him, stripping him, probing, questioning, wondering what sort of man was this. The sea of bodies parted and he was drawn onward, his legs leaden with trepidation, his bladder screaming for his boots, certain that at any moment some accuser would step forward to denounce him as he followed the diminutive figure of Goebbels towards the far side of the gathering. The band's leader, nervous of his responsibilities and with no one to guide him, struck up the *Horst Wessel Song*.

Zum letzen Mal wird nun Appell geblasen! . . .

The signal sounds for one last charge!
We stand ready for the struggle.

228

Soon Hitler's flag will fly above all,
The days of slavery will be shortlived!

The words seemed apt, but the Nazi carol was a marching song intended for raised voices and the crashing of boot leather, and its strains played at slow tempo on clarinet and violin seemed ludicrously out of place.

Then he was there. In front of him. Face to face with Adolf Hitler.

The band trailed off in relief as Goebbels started to speak. 'My Fuehrer,' he began. His voice was gratingly loud, although he was standing close beside his leader. 'I have the pleasure to introduce the man who has scorched the feathers of Churchill's tail, who took on the English war machine and won. A proud German who knows his duty both to you and to the Fatherland, a symbol of Germany's indefatigable desire to continue resistance until final victory.' It all sounded like cheap theatre, but the entire birthday party was nothing more.

'I present to you Captain Peter Hencke!'

Slowly a hand extended towards him, and Hencke reached out to grasp it, raising his eyes to those of the German leader. As their hands touched and eyes met, Hencke felt paralysis grip his wits as confusion flooded through his senses. He remembered the Hitler of the newsreels and the great victory parades, the strut, the confidence and arrogance, the raised chin, the flicking hand gestures with which he brushed aside opponents and orchestrated the world. The man of legend who had devoured nations and terrified the world. Yet that was someone else. The man in front of him was a physical wreck. Every inch told of a body and a spirit in decay. The once smoothly slicked hair was unkempt, the crystal blue eyes which had charmed so many German women were watery and bloodshot, the cheeks unnaturally puffed, the complexion sallow from lack of daylight, the chin badly shaved, the moustache greying and limp. There was a slight dribble from one corner of his mouth. The body was hunched,

229

the shoulders slumped like that of a man many years older than one celebrating his fifty-sixth birthday. The once immaculate plain grey jacket he habitually wore was crumpled and marked by food strains and slops; his left leg was entwined around a chair as if to give support and balance. And the hand that clasped Hencke's was like ice, flabby, with no strength; it was trembling.

'*Mein Fuehrer,*' Hencke whispered, lowering his head.

'Speak up, Hencke!' Goebbels commanded. 'No need to let your voice get lost in the hubbub.'

But Hencke noticed that the entire assembly had gone quiet, and Hitler was leaning forward, stiffly, as if better to catch what was said, while still attempting to keep his leg wrapped firmly around the chair support.

'I am overwhelmed to be here, my Fuehrer!' Hencke raised his voice, and Goebbels nodded in approval. 'I bring you greetings from all your forces across the seas.' He wondered whether he had said the right thing, since practically all of Hitler's forces across the seas were stuck deep inside Allied prison camps, but Hitler responded with a nod of pleasure. Or was it merely an uncontrollable wobble of the head?

'I . . . am delighted, Hencke. Thank you.' The voice was weak, croaking. 'You are a very brave man.' He turned his head to signal and an aide was immediately at his side proffering something. Carefully Hitler took it in his right hand and reached towards Hencke. 'The Iron Cross, First Class. Wear it with pride.' The patter of applause began to rise, but Hitler was having problems pinning the medal on Hencke's breast. His left hand came up to assist, but the co-ordination between the two hands seemed remote. The medal was in danger of being dropped to the floor and the diffident aide stretched forward to help while the applause died away in embarrassment.

Hitler cleared his throat, and when he spoke again his voice had regained some of its powerful timbre. 'My friends,' he said, addressing the entire company, 'you have done me great honour, coming from many parts of the Reich. But there are armies to command and battles to be fought.' He seemed not to notice Goering's quizzical raised eyebrow. 'Continue with the celebration with my thanks. But I must return to my duties. So farewell to you all, until the next time.'

There came the clicking of heels and a series of salutes from around the room as Hitler prepared to leave and the band struck up the national anthem, but no one sang. He had commanded people to risk their lives crossing from all parts of the Reich to be at this birthday celebration, yet no sooner had he appeared than he was preparing to leave. Goebbels was at his elbow once more, whispering in his ear, guiding him towards one corner in which a small group of dirty street urchins had been standing, looking miserable and bewildered. They wore a kaleidoscopic array of stained uniform jackets and military caps, all of which hung on them loosely. They reminded Hencke of the group he had found at the barricade; none of them was older than fourteen. An orderly pushed them hastily into line as the Fuehrer approached, accompanied by the retinue of cameras. Goebbels' little play was not yet finished.

'My Fuehrer, these brave soldiers are all orphans of the savage war inflicted on us by our enemies. They have lost everything, but still they are proud National Socialists. They have come from many different parts of the Reich to celebrate your birthday, and to volunteer to defend to the very end this great capital city of Berlin!'

One of the boys began to pucker his brow and shake his head, either in disbelief or disapproval, but quickly decided it was not worth the effort and went back to looking sullen. Hitler shuffled along the line, accompanied by the cameras, taking each boy by the hand, not saying a word. One of the younger boys in the middle of the line had golden hair and a less weary expression than the rest. Hitler patted his cheek affectionately and turned to the next, but Goebbels intercepted him to whisper yet again in his ear. Again without a word, Hitler returned to pat the child's cheek, this time right under the eye of the hastily repositioned cameras before moving silently on. Then it was all over and Hitler was walking past on his way out. As he did so he grasped Hencke's arm, leaning on it heavily. 'You must have tea with me, in a little while. An orderly will show you down.' With that he departed, dragging his left leg behind him.

No sooner had the hunched back of Hitler disappeared than the conversation started once again, much of it the formalities of goodbye as many made a scarcely disguised dash for the exit. The exodus brought Himmler and Goering together for the first time.

'Must rush. Armies to command and battles to fight,' Himmler explained, his reedy voice dripping in sarcasm as he mimicked the Fuehrer's words.

'See you in hell, Heinrich,' Goering snapped, ignoring the proffered gloved hand.

Within seconds both were gone, and within minutes at least half of the remaining guests had followed. The boys still stood in line; no one had told them they could move. Hencke wondered how many of them understood what this grim little ceremony had been about, or why they had been brought from what was left of their homes to this place. And how many of them would be alive in a week? Perhaps they would all be swinging from lamp posts, like candles on a birthday cake.

'Bormann, I'm glad I caught you before you . . . disappeared for the evening.'

Martin Bormann, Hitler's personal secretary and deputy leader of the Party, didn't look best pleased at the interruption. He was leaning close to one of the secretaries and chatting in a tendentiously informal fashion as they prepared to leave the Ehrenhof. He was notorious for his double life. Within the Bunker he was the soul of efficiency, the most loyal and devoted of all Hitler's entourage who was a master at controlling the floods of paperwork and information that still cascaded towards the Fuehrer for his personal attention.

As such, even those who disliked him intensely – and they constituted a large majority – were forced to admit that he was invaluable to the smooth running of affairs, particularly when the city was falling apart. But once out of the Bunker he was a braggart, a drunk and a womanizer who spent long evenings lost in various corners of the vast Reich Chancellery cellar. By the way his hand was pawing the arm of the secretary, he had plans for this evening too, although as Goebbels advanced on him he was obliged to release her and with obvious reluctance wave her into a corner out of earshot.

'Any news of Hencke?' Goebbels enquired.

'Christ, you only asked me at four o'clock this morning. D'you think everyone in the records offices is an insomniac like you? What's the almighty hurry?'

'I want a double-check on Hencke. I'm not going to announce his arrival to the whole world until I know everything there is to know about him. I don't want to know if he scratches his ass, I want to know which hand he uses.'

'Why so picky? Hasn't just stopped you offering him to *Der Chef* like a tasty piece of birthday cake. Bit late to start having doubts, isn't it?'

'Some risks have to be taken to keep up the Fuehrer's morale. But that's no excuse to relax and forget what we're here to do.'

'Anyway, you're out of luck. All the record departments are having the shit blasted out of them by the bombing. The Wehrmacht offices received a direct hit last week, all their paperwork's in chaos. It'll take days to find anything in that mess.'

Goebbels sighed peevishly. 'Then check the civilian records – birth, school, university. He's a teacher, for heaven's sake, there's got to be some information on him. Get the Buergermeister of Eger out of his bug-ridden bed and looking for what we need. It's called using your imagination, Bormann.'

'OK, OK,' he muttered, looking ruefully in the direction of

the secretary. She would have to wait for a little while. 'You really are the most suspicious bastard I know. Can't you just trust in your good luck?'

'I don't trust to luck, Bormann, any more than I trust people. They have an unpleasant habit of letting you down. You make your own luck in this world, and your own mistakes. So I'm not going to launch him as the saviour of the German nation only to discover that he's some stinking Jew-lover or drowned his baby sister in her bath. I want him checked out. Now!'

'The Fuehrer is ready for you, Captain.'

Hencke started, as an orderly plucked him by the sleeve. 'Where are we going?'

'Why, to the Bunker.'

Hencke tried to compose himself as he was guided once more into the cellar and onwards through a bewildering maze of tunnels and underground corridors, but he found the task difficult. A lethargy had settled over his wits and limbs as Goebbels had performed the introduction, the tension swamping his faculties. He needed fresh air and a moment to think, but he was to get neither. As they proceeded downward, into the bowels of Berlin, everywhere there seemed to be checkpoints, guards armed with machine pistols and hand grenades, studying the papers and identity of all who wished to pass. They walked through a dank, bare concrete tunnel more than a hundred metres long which dripped with water and reminded Hencke of a rabbit's warren in autumn, while waiting at the end was another set of guards wanting to know who and why, double-checking everything. Every time his papers were scrutinized, his face examined, he felt another layer of his determination and fortitude being stripped away, leaving him like a rabbit trapped in a beam of light. Except rabbits have somewhere to run and for Hencke, in the tunnels, there was no way out. Every step further underground seemed like another step into his own grave.

Finally the orderly stepped aside to allow him past a heavy

234

steel door, and he was inside the Vorbunker, the staff quarters. He entered a narrow corridor which also served as the dining-room and rest area and, as he did so, he almost choked. The atmosphere was fetid from the body heat of people packed into the tight space. Twenty or so men and women, not all in uniform, seemed to be making strenuous efforts to recover from the general misery of the previous hour in the Ehrenhof by holding their own private celebration. Hitler was strictly teetotal and there had been no champagne served at the formal reception; down here the staff were making up for lost time. The clink of glasses and the music of a waltz being scratched out from a gramophone somewhere nearby mingled with a loud voice as one of the men related a story of the early days in Munich. The room had meagrely decorated walls and bare overhead lighting which blanched the faces of all colour. It resembled any of the low-life night clubs or dive bars Hencke had visited as a young man, particularly the unlicensed ones. But the memory served only to remind him how far he was from home, deep underground, surrounded by people with ghoulish, unnatural faces and with guards on every corner. He realized it was all impossible. It was mad-ness, had always been madness, an aberration. He knew now that he could not possibly succeed. Did it really matter any more? Perhaps he was already beginning to catch the *Kellerkrebs*.

With leaden spirit he continued behind the orderly. They were still descending, down a spiral metal staircase with yet more bulkheads and FBK guards at both ends, and they entered into a short corridor. He didn't need to be told, he knew this was it. The Fuehrerbunker. Several open doors ran off the corridor and through them Hencke could see how small and claustrophobic were most of the rooms, with low ceilings you could touch. Then another short corridor, another guard and yet more doors running off into tiny rooms. Shelves along the corridor were spilling over with a disorderly collection of papers, manuals, candles, bottles, uniform caps and other paraphernalia – but nothing that might be used as a weapon – and a twisted assortment of cables and hoses ran along the bare concrete floor, a sign of impromptu repair work to electricity and water supplies. From nearby, Hencke could hear the whine of a generator and could smell latrines. This was the Emperor's palace.

It was quiet down here, the atmosphere colder than the crowded Vorbunker, with no comfort of conversation or music to break the silence. It reminded him of a medieval castle near Asch where he had once taken a party of schoolchildren. They had descended into the catacombs, dank and oppressive, with a smell that brought a funny taste to the back of the throat and left even the bolder boys anxious to leave. The Fuehrerbunker gave the same sensation, parching his mouth, putting him on edge, filling his thoughts with dark memories. Suddenly Goebbels, always the stage manager, was there in front of him.

'Remember, Hencke. Don't tire him. And above all don't irritate or contradict him. Not if you don't want that Iron Cross shoved up your ass. Your job is to encourage him, that's all. Go in. He's ready for you.'

Hencke found himself in an office, scarcely ten feet square, decorated in simple fashion with blue Frisian tiles and a bare oak desk, upon which stood two well-burnt candles as might be found on a chapel altar. Above the desk, dominating the room, hung a large oil portrait of Frederick the Great. A voice beckoned from the far door.

'Is that you, Hencke? Come in, come in!'

He entered another room no larger than the office, furnished as a sitting-room with carpet, coffee table, blue and white velvet sofa and chair. On the table stood a small, feminine Dresden vase filled with fresh tulips and in the chair, beckoning, sat Hitler. He seemed more at ease sitting down than he had been standing, and his smile of welcome was genuine. He was scratching the ear of an Alsatian puppy which sat contentedly in his lap. As Hencke advanced he saw an orderly hovering in the corner kitted out in military uniform. Even in his inner sanctum, Hitler was not alone.

And the nearest thing resembling a weapon was the butter knife.

'Sit. Have some tea. A most refreshing drink. Probably the best reason for conquering the British Empire there is.' Hitler grimaced in self-mockery. 'They tell me you are a man of few words, Hencke. Good for you. Suggests a man of action. Take Goebbels, now he's a man of many words. But action? If I had to rely on shrivel-legged little runts like him to beat back the Russians I might as well shoot myself straight away. I only need one Goebbels but, oh, what would I give for a thousand Henckes!'

Hencke was taken aback at the greeting and sat silently on the sofa.

'You know, Hencke, you and I have so much in common,' Hitler continued, lowering his head unsteadily to meet a piece of cake held in an equally unsteady hand. 'We are both men of valour, holders of the Iron Cross,' he said, wiping smudges of cream from his mouth with the back of his hand. He pointed proudly to the medal, the only decoration on his tunic apart from his tiny gold party button, which had been awarded for bravery under fire as a courier, a mere corporal in the First War before he was gassed and invalided out. But that had been in the distant past, more than a generation ago, in another world.

He was muttering away through mouthfuls of cake. 'And me as an Austrian and you from the Sudetenland, we understand the need to build a Greater German Reich, to bring all Germans together – not like those feeble minds and faint hearts who nowadays flood out from every sewer to question why we ever needed to send soldiers across the blasted Rhine! They're like a plague . . .' His pale face coloured rapidly with indignation. 'All about me there are men who think they know better, who disobey my orders, who betray the Reich. The generals are the worst. I, almost single-handed, gave them the continent of Europe.' His voice rose, bits of cream cake spraying across the table. 'Everything but England, that puny island governed by the son of a pox-ridden aristocrat.

I gave it to the generals, Hencke, and what did they do? Prick-pullers every one. They've thrown it all away!' His voice had gained a remarkable strength for someone so frail. There was still passion in those glassy eyes, a flickering glow like a candle trying desperately to revive itself on the last traces of wick. The willpower and determination were still there, struggling to find some remnants of physical energy on which to cling. The puppy discreetly jumped down from his now-exposed position and waddled out the door. 'Not one of them knows what it is like to have been under fire, to have an enemy trying to shoot the balls off you, that feeling of exhilaration when you realize the bastard's missed. They've never risked their lives in battle, like you and me. They have betrayed us both, those aristocrats from their military academies. Why else were you left to rot in a prison camp? Why – else – am – I – here?' His hand beat down on the table, but the effort and animation were rapidly tiring him. His lips could no longer keep pace with his anger, and saliva dribbled down his chin, which he did not bother to wipe. He settled back once again in his chair, the flame subsiding.

'And the German people . . . I wanted so much for them, expected so much of them. But they have failed me. The Reich has turned into a great field of white flags for the Russians and Americans to harvest; and you won't find a single German who can ever remember supporting the Party, let alone coming to one of my rallies to cheer until they were hoarse. Do you remember, Hencke? Berlin, Nuremberg, Munich – rallies of more than a million wonder-filled people. Where have they all gone?'

His mood had become depressed and a look of anxiety crossed his face. His moustache and nose, swollen and pulpy in old age, twitched in agitation and he began biting one of his fingernails until it was red and ripped to the quick. 'Tell me, what was it like waiting to die, in that submarine? On the bottom of the ocean?'

Hencke couldn't see the purpose of the question; he didn't

238

know how to react. He decided to be honest, answering slowly.

'Terrifying.'

Hitler nodded, as if he understood. 'Different from facing death in the field, in the open air? Tell me, is there anything noble about . . . waiting to die. Stuck in an underwater tin can?'

Or stuck in an underground box, thought Hencke. So that's what is getting at him. Facing the Russians in his Bunker won't be the same as facing the French in the trenches; he's worried he may not be up to it. 'No, nothing noble.'

Hitler sighed, the breath rattling in his lungs. 'Hencke, look at me. As you see I am not a well man. I am not physically strong. There are those who see this and believe that the war is over. They wish me to make an end of it, here in Berlin. Particularly some of the generals. The war is lost, they say, but we can still save Germany if we end it properly, nobly.' His hand came up to tap his forehead and his bleary eyes stared directly at Hencke. 'But I have not lost my mind yet, Hencke. What damned purpose is served by dying like rats in a cellar, tell me that? Where's the nobility of a Russian bullet in your guts – or worse! Having your body dragged through the streets of Moscow behind some hairy-assed com-missar?' He leaned forward, his brow wrinkled with concern. 'And then there are the women to consider; it's not just me. They have served me so loyally, more faithfully than any man. They have stood by me when the men were trampling on babies in their rush for a seat on the plane to Switzerland. Would it be *noble* of me to leave them to their fates here, under the bellies of sub-human Russians who don't give a damn whether it's a dead woman or a dead sheep and will screw the lot? That's how my noble Prussian generals would repay their loyalty.' The flame in his eyes had found more fuel. 'They underestimate me, those cretins. I may not be able to fight at the front any more, but I'm not finished yet. No, not by a long way! Those cowards in the High Command

239

forget that Julius Caesar was an epileptic but it didn't stop him conquering half the world. I don't forget! I don't forget that no enemy ever defeated Caesar, his stinking generals stabbed him in the back!'

He reached over to grasp Hencke's hand but his fingers were so unsteady he had to use his other hand to quell the shaking. He was already breathless and wheezing painfully. 'Hencke, I have a plan. The war will not end. We shall stay in Berlin a few days longer and give the Russians a bloody nose. Then we shall fly to the mountains! We can fight for months from there, up where the air is sweet and the sun will shine upon us. We shall leave this shit hole of Berlin for the Americans and Russians to fight over. Jewish capitalists marching from one side and Jewish Bolsheviks from the other. Imagine! The mightiest blood-letting history has ever seen. They can lob artillery shells at each other over the fucking Reichstag, for all I care. We are *die vom dem Berg*, people of the mountain. We don't need vast panzer divisions and to hell with all those miserable, whingeing, double-crossing generals. Just a few thousand of us, carefully chosen. People like you, Hencke. We can stay up in Berchtesgaden until the Americans get bored and limp back home after they've stuck their bayonets up the bums of half of Russia. We shall have new weapons, deadly new nerve gases, Tabun, Sarin, atomic weapons perhaps. Then – will – be – our – time – again!'

He collapsed back in his chair, exhausted, unable to continue.

Hencke, too, was incapable of speech. Deep inside, in the parts where men cry and rant about the injustices of life, he cursed whatever forces had brought him to this underground bedlam. They had brought him into the lair to inflict his mind with further madness, shown him an evil beyond comprehension, filled him with such horror that he knew he would burn in hell if he failed to wipe out this evil. And yet he had been left powerless, stripped of means or ideas to end it all. He could see no shadow of a chance.

240

'It can work, can't it, Hencke?' Hitler asked, interrupting his thoughts.

The endless alpine war? Hencke had to admit to himself that, like so much madness, it just might. He nodded.

'I knew it. You are my lucky mascot, Hencke, sent to let me know that with valour like yours we can still achieve anything we want.' He shook his guest's hands limply and he had started to mumble with exhaustion. 'This is a happy day . . . very special one for us both . . . miserable bastards, to hell with the doctors and their suicide pills. They can shove them up their wives' . . .'

Suddenly Hitler halted his litany of abuse, and Hencke looked up to see that they had been joined by another figure, a woman, pretty, lithe, smiling, in her early thirties. It was one of the group of friends he had seen laughing in the cellar of the Reich Chancellery. Hencke expected outrage at this unannounced interruption, but instead Hitler gathered his energies and rose unsteadily to his feet, straightening his jacket, and kissing the woman tenderly on the hand. Gone was his rambling coarseness of a moment before.

'Hencke, allow me to introduce you to Fräulein Braun, a dear and trusted friend of mine.' Having effected the introduction, he sank down heavily in his chair.

'I came in to make sure you weren't tiring yourself,' she said to him. 'It seems I came not a moment too soon.' There was a scolding tone in her voice and her blonde, shoulder-length hair fell about her diamond-shaped face as she leaned over Hitler. She turned to Hencke. 'Captain, forgive me, but I think it's time for the Fuehrer to rest. He has so much still to do . . .'

'No, one last thing,' objected Hitler. 'Hencke, I have something for you.' From beside his chair he produced a red leather case which he thrust at his guest. 'Something special.'

Inside, Hencke found a solid silver photo frame. Inlaid into the metalwork was a small gold swastika. It carried a photograph of Hitler and there was writing, a dedication in practically illegible scrawl which he struggled to decipher.

241

Hitler hurried to cover the embarrassment of his growing inability to control a pen. 'It says: "To Peter Hencke, A brave and devoted follower. From your Fuehrer, Adolf Hitler". I don't give those to everyone, you know.'

'I find it difficult to know what to say.'

'Well, that's it. Time for a rest. Perhaps see you later, Hencke.' With that he pulled himself awkwardly out of his chair. Having straightened himself, Hitler bowed courteously to the woman and shuffled off into a neighbouring room. The interview was at an end. Hencke never had a chance.

The office was dark, the only illumination coming from a candle on the desk. The power had failed again. Bormann was in a foul mood. He loathed Goebbels, for his intellectual gifts which Bormann could never match, for the significant role he had played in the early days of the Movement, for the access to Hitler which this gave him, and for his role as *Der Chef's* oldest – and nowadays seemingly *only* – trusted counsellor. Over the years Bormann as the archetypal bureaucrat had outmanoeuvred and outlasted most of the others, but he had never learned how to handle the Reichsminister for Propaganda. Goebbels always seemed one step ahead. And Bormann seethed when he remembered how Goebbels had spoken to him, in the presence of the secretary, too. No one else would get away with that . . . So he was in no mood to tolerate the prevarication he was getting on the telephone.

'Look, I don't want a debate on logistics, I don't want to hear how busy you are and I don't give a damn if your pet dachshund keeps crapping on your best carpet because of the shelling. This is not an enquiry. Nor is it a request, you little jerk. This is a *Fuehrerbefehl*, an order direct from the man himself, and if it's not obeyed I shall come down personally to the Ministry and string you up on a meat hook with my own hands. So if you want to live to see tomorrow night I suggest you drop whatever else you are doing and get me some answers. Can I make it any clearer than that? . . . That's

242

right. H-E-N-C-K-E. Peter. Check his birth certificate, his university records, his teaching diploma, his collar size, his taste in music, everything . . . I don't know if he's married, cretin. It's your job to find out! By midday tomorrow. Understand?'

He was just about to throw another barrage of abuse down the receiver when the connection went dead. Bormann stared at the mouthpiece, unable to decide whether the phone had been put down on him or the land line had once again been cut. He was still looking at it when the secretary, kneeling directly at his feet, ran the tips of her fingers across her heavily rouged lips.

'Shall I continue now, you big bear?'

'Captain Hencke, I think you have come here to cause the most extreme havoc.'

Hencke froze and his brow creased in bewilderment as he saw the young woman's green eyes staring directly at him.

'Do you realize that four of my best friends are at this very moment threatening to murder each other in order to see which of them is going to be the first to be seen with you in Berlin?' Her face lit up in mischief and a peal of laughter echoed around the small Bunker sitting-room. As she laughed she swung her narrow hips, causing her silk dress to rustle.

'Fräulein Braun, I'm not sure I understand . . .'

'Come on, Captain. You surely don't think it's only the likes of Goebbels who take an interest in you.'

'I fear I would be a miserable disappointment for one lady, but for four?' He shook his head in self-condemnation.

'Don't fool yourself, Captain. You might have evaded the clutches of Churchill and the entire British Army, but I can assure you that you will not escape so lightly from my girlfriends. They have instructed me that if you refuse I am to get the Fuehrer to sign a personal order!' She laughed gaily once more, and Hencke was still wondering who this extraordinary woman was who had walked in on Hitler and then propositioned him on behalf of her friends when her

243

laughter suddenly died. Her face puckered and her hand came to her forehead.

'Oh, this Bunker! The atmosphere is so oppressive, my head is ringing. It feels as if the entire roof has fallen in on me . . .' She was in genuine distress.

'Perhaps some fresh air,' Hencke suggested. 'I would offer to escort you, but I'm lost beyond the end of the corridor.'

She studied him carefully for a moment. 'Would you mind, Captain? I'd be grateful. Let me show you the way.'

Left with little choice, he followed her out into the corridor and past the guard, but not the way he had arrived. She guided him in the opposite direction, past a foul-smelling latrine and through yet another guarded steel door, but this time no one stopped to check him, the guard simply saluting him – or was it her? – and stepping back. Then on to a concrete stairway, which rose four flights until he could feel the soothing brush of fresh air on his face. They emerged into a garden from underneath the cover of a huge concrete block-house, twenty feet high, with an unfinished pill-box tower looming beside it. A broken cement mixer leaned drunkenly against its bare walls. In the fading light he could see the garden was mostly laid to grass with a few trees, but the lawn was badly churned from the impact of bombs and shells and most of the leaves had been stripped from the trees. Even the high walls of the Reich Chancellery surrounding the garden had been unable to provide much protection. A greenhouse nearby stood sagging and badly shattered, and Hencke could smell the fragrance of jasmine wafting through the broken panes, made all the sweeter because of the acrid smell of smoke which hung across the city.

They started walking along a narrow gravel path. She breathed deeply of the evening air, and the creases on her forehead vanished as quickly as they had come.

'Where are we?' Hencke enquired.

'The Bunker garden. We've just come out of the emergency exit. You're not supposed to use it, of course, except with the Fuehrer. Or me. You must be careful, Captain. Here less

244

than a day and already taking tea with the Fuehrer and walks in his private garden. There are those who will grow jealous.' Her mood was light and easy, but he had the impression that her words should not be dismissed as idle chatter.

'Who?'

'You're very direct, Captain.'

'I've only just arrived, remember. And I doubt whether I've got time to learn all the subtleties.'

'Ah! Too direct, I fear, for this city. It's not the habit here. People prefer to talk in code or riddles and you need an interpreter or an astrologist to find out what they really mean. Why, only an hour ago I heard that tub of lard Goering profess that he had undying faith in the Fuehrer. Yet already he is on his plane flying as far south as possible. With such faith, whole Reichs could be toppled, eh?'

Hencke's brow puckered as he heard the bluntness of her comments aimed at one of the most powerful men in the land. Who was this woman of the Bunker? 'I'm confused. Forgive me . . . Who are you?'

'Me?' She smiled. 'Of course, you've never been in Berlin and Goebbels makes absolutely sure that nothing ever appears in the newspapers.' She shrugged. 'But you'll know as soon as you ask any corporal in the Chancellery, and you seem to prefer directness . . . I am Eva Braun.'

His expression told her that the name meant nothing to him.

'I am the Fuehrer's companion. His mistress.'

For a moment the look on Hencke's face mimicked the effect of a kick in the groin, but he recovered quickly. 'Then it would seem that you should beware of jealousy, too, Fräulein Braun, for you certainly have far better access to the Fuehrer than me.'

She clapped her hands with delight, her green eyes sparkled and her voice fluttered with laughter. She moved gracefully, athletically; her body was slim, almost boyish, her teeth were white and her lips naturally red, and she had a dimple in the middle of her chin. Although she could never be called a beauty there was an untainted naturalness about her which belied her age and her fashionable clothes. She seemed and sounded much younger than her thirty-odd years. 'You are not like the others, Captain. I feel I can be honest with you. They all play games and intrigue against each other. I hope you won't be long enough in Berlin to catch their disease.'

'You don't seem to like Berlin.'

'I hate it. I'm a Bavarian, from the mountains.'

'You must be looking forward to returning there.'

'It . . . would be wonderful.' Her words were wistful, as if she were describing a dream rather than the reality of a few days' time.

'I thought it was all decided, yet you sound uncertain, Fräulein Braun.'

'We have made so many plans, over these past years . . .' She trailed off, her gaiety gone.

Darkness had fallen and a chill was catching the air. There were goose-bumps on her bare arms but she seemed not to notice. She was wrapped in thought and her words came cautiously.

'I've had fifteen wonderful years with him, Hencke. Every year has been like a lifetime and I have been so happy. I'm not afraid to die, if I have to. If that's the price.' She was twisting a ring on her little finger, the only jewellery she wore, and it had obviously come from him. 'I know everything has to come to an end. Some time. I'm not complaining, really . . .' She was biting her lip hard, losing her carefree composure.

'You feel that much for him?'

'He's . . . been so kind to me. So considerate. I was only seventeen, an assistant in a photographer's shop when we met. He's older, of course, much older, and I'm such an empty-head where he's so wise. Like a father. He trusts me because I don't play games like the others. I don't discuss politics or push new military strategies. And I never argue with him – I daren't. We just relax together. He says that if he closes his eyes and reaches out he needs to know that someone will be there, not with a knife in their hand but with virtue and steadiness in their heart. And all the rest are liars, every one of them. Goebbels tries to manipulate him for his little propaganda games, Goering promises to defend the skies above Berlin with planes he hasn't got, and as for that disgusting toad Bormann . . . He hates me because I'm the one woman he knows he can never have. He tells fearful lies, even pretends that he's a non-smoker and vegetarian like the Fuehrer. Vegetarian! One night one of the girls found a salami hanging behind his pillow. And she says that's the least of his revolting habits. But even with an oaf like him I have to share the Fuehrer.' She sighed with resignation. 'I have to share the Fuehrer, with the whole of Germany at times. I shouldn't mind. I've been at his right hand all these years. That should be enough for any girl, shouldn't it?'

Hencke was the schoolmaster once more, listening to a girl pour out her heart and her confusion, and in spite of her protestations of loyalty he knew there was something missing. 'But it hasn't been enough. Has it?'

'All these years, at his right hand, but never properly by his side. Sharing him with so many. Worrying that the difference in our ages was so great he must take me for a silly chattering girl. Wondering what love was like for all the rest . . .'

Hencke tried to imagine the decrepit old man he had seen that afternoon lying beside this young, vibrant woman. But he couldn't. No matter how hard he tried. He realized it couldn't be, or couldn't have been, not for a very long time. So that was the problem. A young woman. Facing death. Alone. She deserved it, of course, for the folly of a loyalty so blind. She could be condemned for a love which was twisted, unnatural, obscene many would call it. But even as he shared in the distaste he knew that he, of all people, could not join in the condemnation. Not condemn her for her love, for love could never be a crime. He understood. They sat down in a gazebo which had somehow remained untouched by the assault on the city, and he reached in the dark to touch her hand, as he would have comforted one of his pupils. He did it instinctively, without thinking, and she did not draw back. He could feel the warm splash of tears on his skin. But no sound, no complaint. Damn it, she was fighting hard.

'You are such a good listener and I am nothing but a silly blabbermouth, but I have no one else to talk to.' She squeezed his hand in gratitude and tried a brave laugh, to pretend she wasn't hurting, but couldn't sustain it. 'Tell me. Is facing death difficult?'

In the semi-light she was looking at him with the earnestness of a young woman, spoiled all her adult life and who had never grown up, never had to, but who had the honesty to realize it. Now she was having to catch up for those wasted years, to mature, to deal with pain, to face death, all in a hurry. Even in this place he couldn't help but have sympathy.

'Facing death difficult? I've found facing life much harder. Death is just another challenge, and not the most difficult. There is no pain in death, the pain is all in the waiting. You can spend every day of a whole lifetime fearing something which will come only once and, when it does, be gone in a moment. Why waste our lives fearing something over which we have no choice? You have only one really important choice, and that's nothing to do with dying, it's all about living. How long we have is of little consequence, what we do with it is everything. That's what makes facing death difficult, the regrets. The things you've done or, even worse, the important things you've left undone.'

'Will you die with regrets?'

He paused. 'I hope not.'

The darkness had closed around them like a confessional. She had stopped crying, they were still holding hands.

'Have you ever helped anyone to die?'

He ran his tongue across his lips to moisten a mouth which had suddenly run dry as he considered how best to answer, or if he should answer at all. He began hesitantly. 'Once, many years ago, a friend asked me to help him die. He felt alone, victimized. His colleagues and family had rejected him. He was in despair. He felt he had nothing left to cling on to.'

'What did you do?'

'I gave him something to live for.' Hencke's voice was no more than a whisper, as if every word had to be carved from his soul.

'And is he. . . ?'

'No, he's dead now. The war . . . But I think he died with no regrets.'

'Then he was a very fortunate man to have such a friend as you, Peter.'

'Maybe.'

They sat in the gazebo for some while, in silence, joined in spirit and by the touch of their hands. Eventually they were brought back from their private thoughts by the sound of heavy boots making their way up the Bunker stairs towards the emergency exit.

'We have to go. My friends are waiting for me – for you, really; they'll be disappointed! – and I mustn't keep them waiting. I'm going to take a short cut through the gardens but you must go back through the checkpoints in the Bunker and sign out. But Peter . . .' There was pleading in her voice. 'Promise you'll help me, too.'

'Help you? How?'

'Help me to live, to die if needs be, with no regrets. Tomorrow. This time. Meet me. Help me.'

'Where?'

'The reception area in the Chancellery. It's always crowded. Don't come up and talk to me. Just follow me. Please?'

He had no chance to consider or reply before she pushed him in the direction of the Bunker entrance, while she ran off, disappearing into the night, leaving him bewildered. What did she want? How could he agree to help her? He felt the uniform grabbing at his throat once more and beads of perspiration gathered on his brow. Christ, Hencke, remember what you're here for!

As the sound of boots on concrete steps drew closer, he

discovered he was still holding the case containing the photograph. He turned it round on all sides, rubbing his thumb over the soft leather, knowing what honour the gift implied, remembering the inscription. 'A brave and devoted follower . . . From your Fuehrer . . .' He weighed it carefully in his hand, testing its weight before casting around to make sure no one was watching. Then he threw it down the jaws of the broken cement mixer.

TWELVE

'Hencke, Peter. Born when he said he was – Second of February, 1910. Born *where* he said he was, just outside Eger in the Sudetenland. Only son, father a local shopkeeper, gassed at the battlefront during the 1916 offensive at Verdun and died a few months later. Brought up by his aunt, also now dead. Left Eger to study at university in Karlsbad, never returned. No surviving relatives left in the area.' Bormann's bullet-shaped head looked up from the slim folder that held the notes of his conversation with the flustered Buergermeister of Eger. 'He checks out, your Hencke. He's all right.'

Goebbels sat, staring into the fireplace, the corners of his mouth dragged down almost to the bottom of his jaw as he concentrated, giving him an air of unremitting gloom. It was a while before he responded.

'What else?'

'Else? Nothing else. I said, he left Eger. We're now checking with the people in Karlsbad and Prague. But what's your problem? The creep checks out.'

'You're talking about nearly twenty damned years ago! Nothing since then. You call that "checking out"?' The tone was accusatory, the look that Goebbels threw at Bormann far worse.

'For God's sake, what's bothering you? Haven't we got bigger things to worry about? Three hundred thousand men just surrendered in the Ruhr, Russian tanks already driving along the autobahn around Berlin, the Fuehrer a stumbling wreck, the last opportunity we've got of getting out of this hole rapidly going up in smoke . . . and you keep fussing

251

about one lousy man. A man *you* brought here in the first place. What the hell do you think you're doing!'

Bormann's fingers were trembling, a flush creeping up his thick-set neck and across his bony features. He was angry, exasperated, frustrated, but Goebbels could see it was more than that. The man was afraid. A shaking leaf. It was as simple as that.

'Don't you see? It's precisely because we want to get out of this hole that Hencke is so important. If we just scuttle off to the Alps the whole of Germany will think we're running to save our wretched skins. White flags will sprout like weeds all the way across the Reich and the war will be over within days. Dammit, as soon as we start heading for the aircraft they'll be ripped apart by those being left behind. We'll look like deserters. But with Hencke, with the example of a man who's risked everything to fight at the Fuehrer's side, we might still make it appear like an inspired move to a new fortress, a brilliant plan to outwit the Russians. An example which might keep resistance burning throughout Germany.'

'You don't sound too bloody sure . . .'

'Of course I'm not sure, you idiot! What do you think I am, a magician? But I know one thing for damn certain. If we stay here we're all going to have our balls dangling on the end of Russian bayonets before the end of the week. So make your choice. Hencke? Or singing castrati for the Communists!'

Bormann made no reply. His head sagged and he looked mournfully towards the floor, while Goebbels took several panting breaths to regain his composure.

'So, my dear Bormann, check out in Karlsbad, check out in Prague, get them sifting through the records of the Wehrmacht, enquire anywhere you might find something about Hencke. Check, check, check. We need this bastard firmly under our thumb, because next to the Fuehrer, he may be the most important man in the Third Reich . . .'

The reception area of the Chancellery was crowded still, but something had changed since the previous day. There were fewer armed guards standing around than Hencke remembered from his last visit, the piles of packed suitcases seemed to have grown higher, more people were off in corners whispering anxiously between themselves. They appeared to be discussing more than where to spend their evening. The vast foyer retained the bustle and atmosphere of a railway station, but one in which the last train was about to leave with not enough room for all the passengers. A new form of greeting had become common around the Chancellery – 'How's your family? Where are they?' Anybody with sense was trying to get their families moved west, away from the advancing Russians, and those with influence were trying to join them. A major with responsibility for issuing transportation permits had been busy the previous day dealing with a long line of applicants, shouting down the phone to discover when the next train, road convoy or airplane was leaving; today the queue had gone and he sat listlessly by a silent telephone, head in hands. Nobody was bothering with permits any more, the transportation system was shot to hell and it was every man for himself.

He saw her descending the huge marble staircase. She didn't look up. She was wearing a bright floral-print dress with long sleeves, and carried nothing but her handbag. She wore no make-up. Her shoes clipped purposefully across the marble floor as she headed towards a side door off the reception area, her well-cut dress brushing across her legs. Once again he noticed the athletic grace with which her hips swung and her body moved. He also noticed many men casting similar furtive looks as she passed by but, unusually in this place, their appreciation remained silent. Nobody mentioned it or offered any of the usual ribald remarks.

She passed close by Hencke but gave no sign of recognition. He allowed a respectable distance to develop before following her out through the side door, striding after her as she led him quickly away from the central reception area with its crowds into increasingly remote areas of the Chancellery where many fewer people scurried around. He followed along anonymous corridors, up and down flights of stairs, through reception rooms, until he was completely disorientated. It was as if she were trying to lose him. He hurried around yet another corner to find himself in a bare corridor which echoed with emptiness. She had gone, disappeared. He'd lost her and lost himself into the bargain. He had no idea where he was or what she wanted of him. Why the secrecy? What was he doing here? Where the hell had she gone? He was stumbling mystified along the corridor, growing more bewildered with each step, when a hand reached out and dragged him into a doorway. It was Eva. Putting a finger to her lips, she pulled him into a small, windowless secretarial office with two desks and typewriters, and papers strewn across the floor. The room had been vacated in a hurry. She showed no interest in their surroundings and was leaning against the door, ear to its panelling, listening. He moved across to join her but once more she raised a finger to her lips, demanding silence. A few moments later came the sound of booted footsteps approaching from the way they had come, hesitating, scraping in uncertainty, then quickening and moving sharply onward. Before they disappeared completely the footsteps broke into a run, bringing a wry smile of satisfaction to Eva's face.

'I thought as much. They've put a man to keep an eye on you,' she whispered.

'Following me? Why?'

'I told you many would be jealous.'

'They suspect me? Of what?'

She smiled reassuringly as she saw the look of alarm twitching around his eyes. '*Everybody* is suspect in this city. It was only a few months ago that generals in the High Command tried to kill the Fuehrer. And you they suspect because you're different, you're new, dropped in out of the blue. They don't yet know what your vices or ambitions are. Everybody in Berlin has vices and ambitions, and they're all recorded somewhere on somebody's files. But not yours, not yet. Perhaps you should make it easy for them, present them with a written list,' she chuckled impishly.

He showed no sign of appreciating the humour. 'Who are "they"?'

'Practically everybody. No . . .' She paused while she considered her response, her ear to the door once more checking for further sounds of pursuit. 'Come to think of it, probably Goebbels or Bormann. The rest of them seem to have lost interest in what goes on here. Yes, probably one or other of that rotten pair.'

The lids closed slowly over his eyes and his lean face sagged as he contemplated the horror of his position. Under constant watch, with seemingly no chance of finding the opportunity he sought. Now locked in some mysterious conspiracy with Hitler's mistress. His eyes flashed open. 'What am I doing here?' he demanded.

'Come with me' was all the explanation she volunteered. She grabbed his hand and, after listening once more for sounds outside, proceeded to lead him through the labyrinth which made up the service areas and passageways of the Chancellery. Several times she stopped to ensure they were not being followed, but they were deep inside the disused section of the Chancellery, evacuated because of bomb damage, and there was no one about. They started to climb, up flights of stairs littered with debris, fallen chunks of plaster and the occasional brick or abandoned file. In one section the wrought-iron balustrade had fallen away and paintings sagged at drunken angles from the wall; elsewhere the lights had failed, but she seemed surefooted and to know precisely where she was headed, leading him onwards with the aid of a small torch she had taken from her handbag. They were several storeys above the inhabited section of the Chancellery before they came to a set of tall doors. She tried the handle, but the door refused to budge. Once more she tried, before appealing to Hencke. He turned the handle; the door wasn't locked, just jammed. He put his shoulder to it and it gave way with a shudder, covering him in a shower of plaster dust.

He was still brushing the dust from his SS uniform when she pulled him inside. Even in the darkness he could see they

255

were in a magnificent library, perhaps forty metres long with towering mahogany bookcases on all sides. Some of the bookcases were empty, their contents strewn on the floor or thrown into packing cases which stood abandoned in the centre of the room. Every one of the tall French windows was smashed, some hanging crazily off broken hinges, yet elsewhere the room seemed almost untouched. A sumptuous tapestry adorned the far wall and fine oil paintings still hung in their places between the bookcases. Beautifully carved chairs, desks and expensively covered chaise-longues were scattered around, and a tray of coffee waited on one of the tables. Hencke picked up the pot but it was stone cold and there was a deep ring of dust around its base. It hadn't been touched for several weeks.

'What on earth are we doing here?' he demanded once more.

'I wanted to show you the view,' she said, leading him to one of the windows. Outside there was a small balcony which afforded a panorama of the city. A huge sweep of Berlin was scattered before them in the early night, from the Brandenburg Gate and the wooded Tiergarten lying behind, to the ruined Reichstag which had burned in 1933, and onwards to the ministries, embassies and hotels that crowded along Unter den Linden. Many of them were burning now. Through the low-hanging clouds of smoke and dust that swept across the city they saw the silhouettes of great cathedrals, hospitals, monuments, boulevards and railway stations, thrown into stark relief by the fires that glowed all around. Away into the distance the whole city was lit by flame. In some places conflagrations burned out of control and consumed whole blocks where the firefighters had given up in despair; in others there rose the flicker of fiery geysers where a gas main had been breached and was burning, despite the order issued days before to cut off the last of the supplies. Elsewhere, on street corners and in courtyards, they could see the flickering campfires of the Hitler Youth, lit not so much for physical warmth as to comfort the spirit while they manned roadblocks and waited for the assault. Where buildings still stood they burned, where they lay in ruins they smouldered, and this once-great city of Berlin was cast in the light of its own pitiful destruction.

Yet it was the sounds of the dying city which made the deepest impact. There was no sound of warfare; the artillery bombardment had stopped for the moment, and although they couldn't know it the Anglo-American aerial bombardment had stopped too, for good. The Russians were now so close that the pilots of the British Lancasters couldn't be sure at night whether they were bombing ally or enemy. In place of the noise of battle came the sounds of the capital tearing itself apart. The screams of a battered city yielding to the assault were everywhere; the pathetic cries for help of the injured and maimed still trapped in the rubble, the drawn-out death rattle of buildings as they gave up the struggle and collapsed, the crackle of flame, the shattering of glass, the frantic shouts of alarm as a horse-drawn ambulance or rescue truck tried in vain to force its way through the chaos, the tears of children as they wandered forlornly through the streets in search of lost parents, the howling of dogs gone mad with terror. Yet, as in the madness of a nightmare, through all the cries of misery they could hear raucous shouts, screams and laughter as many of those who were left anaesthetized themselves in drunkenness, lust, depravity and revenge. While naïve civilians cowered in their cellars still praying for salvation, soldiers who had given up all hope wandered the streets looking for distraction. Occasionally a shot would ring out, whether as a sign of success or failure in that search there was no way of telling, but news of what was going on in the cellar of the Chancellery had spread like an infection and with it had been wiped out the last vestige of military discipline and control.

'I wanted you to see this, Peter. When I see what is happening to Berlin, I know it's nearly all over. Down in the Bunker the retreat to the Alps might make sense, but not up here. The whole world seems to have gone insane, and I don't think anyone can save it.' She stared out across the burning city. 'That's why I want you to help me die. With no regrets.'

'How?'

'By making me a real woman. By loving me . . .'

She had turned towards him and was holding both his hands. 'I'm not so much frightened of dying as frightened of never knowing what it is like to be properly loved. By a man. You're the only one I can ask. All the rest are liars and cheating swine. I don't want to end up as an item in one of their wretched files.'

'The Fuehrer. . . ?' he began, but she shook her head violently.

'Peter, please. We may be the only two sane people left in this world. It's just you and me. Because if that's the real world out there I don't want to live as part of it. But I don't want to die with regrets.'

Like an attentive pupil she had listened, and learned. He said nothing, looking down on her, as she grasped his hands still tighter to stand on tip-toe. Her head bent round, her blonde hair cascaded around her face, her slim body was pressed tightly into his and she kissed him fiercely. Then her arms were around him, pulling him even closer, and after what seemed to her an eternity she could at last feel him aroused.

'Thank you, thank you,' she said between kisses. She led him back into the great library, to the far end where a chaise-longue stood beneath the wall-length tapestry. The tapestry was a depiction of the Rape of the Sabines, vividly interpreted in the skilful weft and warp and standing in stunning contrast to the intellectual aspirations of the rest of the room. In the half light thrown through the windows she stood beneath the bacchanalian scenes and slowly unbuttoned the front of her dress, placing his hands on her breasts. They were small but well formed, firm and muscular, and the nipples sprang to life beneath his fingertips. Yet still there was a reserve about him, a reluctance to participate. What was he doing here!

'Your uniform,' she whispered, 'your uniform . . .' Her fingers were everywhere. The belt and its holster clattered to the wooden floor, the buttons of his tunic sprang one by one and her hands ran up inside his shirt. 'You're beautiful,' she breathed into his ear as her fingers explored the taut, sinewy frame of his body. He stood in front of the tapestry as she removed his shirt, her tongue loitering to play games across his hairless chest before she was into his trousers and underwear, pulling them from his narrow waist until they could go no further, and pushing him on to the chaise-longue while she wrenched at his boots. Then it was her turn. The dress, the chemise, the silk stockings, everything until she, too, was naked, her slender, almost boyish figure fully exposed. He was still sitting where she had left him, and she bent down to kiss him and let her tongue run tantalizingly down his body until she was kneeling at his feet making sure he was fully aroused. When he was ready she pushed him down and settled on top of him.

They said not a word. While he lay on his back she took all the initiatives, made all the running, did all the work, placed his hands where she wanted them to linger, flexed her athletic muscles and took him deep inside until she felt she would burst. When at last she did she let forth a great, tearing cry of passion which rang out to the far end of the library, echoing from the empty bookcases so piercingly he feared it would bring every Gestapo officer running from miles around. But it was just one more woman crying in the awful Berlin night.

As her sobs began to subside she collapsed across his chest but did not let him go, afraid to lose him, wishing it would never end. Yet he had scarcely moved.

'Oh, Peter. Are you . . . all right?'

'Don't worry about me, just yourself. You've got a lot of missed time to make up for.' His eyes were staring, empty, full neither of fire nor passion, but she was too busy sobbing with release and joy to notice. He could feel the warm tears trickling across his chest. She was no longer the predatory female, just another young girl filled with confusion and happiness, and at last he seemed to respond and put his arms around her to comfort and caress her.

'Are *you* all right?' he asked.

She nodded tearfully and vigorously, and began to kiss him like a puppy nuzzling her master. Eventually he tried to calm her frenetic kissing.

'Shouldn't you be getting back soon? Won't they miss you?'

'No. Not for a long time yet.' And she began all over again, working on him, arousing him, toying with him, this time staying with him until he, too, was spent. They lay together in perfect stillness for a while, until she rolled off to give him a chance to breathe.

'Peter, thank you. My truest, dearest friend,' she whispered. She ran a finger from his brow along the line of his face, loitering around his lips before tracing across his hard chest and to his navel. He was remarkably smooth for a man, so unlike the hairy swine her friends had told her about. 'In another life, perhaps we could have had more time.'

'Perhaps it is only the shortage of time which helps make this so beautiful.'

'Like a chrysalid burst into the most beautiful of butterflies, to enchant me for a moment and then be gone. Hold me, Peter. Make it seem like for ever.'

He took her in his arms once more, Hitler's mistress become his own. He didn't, couldn't talk. Inside his thoughts and emotions battled in confusion. He felt dirty, soiled by the selfish indulgence of the farmyard. And with Hitler's mistress! He could sense all those he had vowed to avenge looking on, reproachful, wondering if he had forgotten and forsaken them. Yet as he looked at this young woman clinging to him for support, trust filling her eyes, he knew he had given her something much more than physical fulfilment. Her tears on his chest were the tears of a woman escaped from confinement to fulfilment, a lonely and frightened

260

human being who had never hurt anyone, whose only crime had been to fall in love with the wrong man and who was waiting to die in the bravest way she could, with no regrets. He understood, sympathized, even cared. Yet, still, she was Hitler's mistress . . .

He was lost in the enormity of it all when their privacy was shattered by the explosion of a thousand brilliant flashes from beyond the windows. Lightning seared through the night sky, followed by a devastating and unending blast of noise. They jumped to their feet and stood naked, framed in the window, looking out once more into the night.

'The Russians. Those are Russian rockets and artillery. The final bombardment has begun,' she said quietly.

From around them came the crashing of falling shells as they erupted to pile new rubble on top of old, to seek out those corners of the city that had somehow survived and reduce them to ashes. They were back in the real world, the world of insanity and destruction which for a short time they had left.

'It will all be over soon, Peter.' Her voice was plain, matter-of-fact. 'But thanks to you I think I can face up to it.'

'Eva, take this.' Hencke was down on his knees, scrabbling on the floor in the semi-darkness for his belt and holster. The Walther was in his hand. 'Put this in your handbag. Just in case. It will get chaotic, very dangerous, neither I nor anyone else may be there when you need us most, to protect you.'

'To help me die, you mean.'

'Take it, just in case.'

She stretched up to kiss him once more, trusting, like a schoolgirl. She took the gun and placed it in her handbag.

'Time for me to go and for you to become a chrysalid once more,' she said, throwing his jacket at him.

He watched her dress in the flickering light of the bombardment. It had been worth it. He had gained a friend on the inside. And possibly, just possibly, through Eva Braun and

261

her handbag, he had broken the iron ring of security around the Bunker.

A few minutes before midday Hencke received the command to report to Goebbels in the Bunker. As he strode through the Chancellery it was clear that the established routine of the building had suddenly changed. No longer was it built around the twice-a-day pattern of Allied bombing; the bombers had left for good, and in their place had come the incessant and insistent pounding of Russian artillery and fire-belching 'Stalin organs'. The message of the barrage was unmistakable; there was no longer a time to sleep and a time to work in the Chancellery, only a time to die.

In the Vorbunker there seemed to be other ideas. Where before he had seen little but unrelieved grimness in the faces of its inhabitants, in its place had come a new tension, an excitement, a glow of hope in their eyes. Everywhere there were signs of preparation for departure. Packing cases were being nailed shut, suitcases locked, papers being sorted and discarded, crates being carried out. Instead of the maudlin atmosphere of the birthday celebrations there was purpose, energy, urgency, the noise of rushing feet echoing from the concrete walls.

'The Fuehrer has given the order,' Goebbels explained, eyes bright. 'The break-out begins!'

He paused from issuing instructions for the safe transportation of various cases and turned to study Hencke. Less than an hour ago he had received the report of the officer detailed to follow Hencke and who had lost him in the maze of the abandoned Chancellery. Why had Hencke gone there? Out of curiosity? Souvenir hunting? Yet the report had said he seemed to know precisely where he was headed, not tarrying to look. And it was certain that he had deliberately lost his tail. What had he been doing during those lost hours of the night? Yet what harm could he possibly do in the empty section of the Chancellery? Hencke was a puzzle, and Goebbels neither liked nor trusted puzzles. Particularly now.

Two of Goebbels' children were playing at his feet, a little girl with a doll and a boy with straight blond hair who was bouncing a ball. It ran loose towards Hencke and he stooped to retrieve it.

'To think they will be playing in fresh alpine air in two days' time.' Goebbels smiled as he took possession of the ball, looking directly at Hencke. He arched an eyebrow. 'And the Fuehrer has instructed that you will join us.'

Hencke remained expressionless as he tried to figure out the import of what Goebbels was saying. The little girl started crying and the Reichsminister stooped to gather her in his arms; only when he had finished comforting her did he return his attention to Hencke. He took from his pocket a dog-eared petrol-station map of Berlin and its suburbs, smoothing out the creases on the table.

'The Russians are rapidly encircling the city. Their advance troops are already in Koepenick and Spandau; in a few days there will be no way out. So we start. There is an emergency airstrip at Kladow on which we have gathered a variety of small planes to ferry us out to the Rechlin airbase – here.' He stabbed with his forefinger. 'They've assembled an entire fleet of Condors and Junkers 390s, enough to fly us to China if we wanted, more than enough to get several hundred of us to Berchtesgaden in a few hours. With luck they may be able to make two or three trips. The autobahn routes to the south and west are also still open for everyone else.' His carefully-manicured finger ran across the map, indicating the way. 'So we leave tonight! Hencke, the fight back begins!'

'Why are you telling me all this, Herr Reichsminister?'

Good question, thought Goebbels. Was it because Bormann had received fresh information from Karlsbad confirming that Hencke had studied at the university there, had no record of political agitation or other trouble, had kept his nose clean and graduated into a respectable teaching post in the small town of Asch? His story was checking out, but still Goebbels was not content. Something about the whole situation gave him the feeling of needles being stuck into the nape of his neck. And there was still no trace of Hencke in the records since 1938, since the annexation of the Sudetenland. Perhaps, Bormann had suggested, it was because all the record keeping systems had changed and the new records were kept separately. He was still checking, he was sure they would come through with the full story. But Goebbels remembered there had been trouble in Asch and other towns which had been 'liberated' by the Sudeten Freikorps, who had left a trail of blood and broken bones in their wake. It made him uneasy.

Or was it because he wanted to see how Hencke reacted to the news, to see if there were any clues in his response? If so, the Reichsminister was disappointed. Hencke's eyes remained unmoved and impenetrable. Perhaps it was because Goebbels, his faculties sensitized by his twisted frame and a lifetime of physical inferiority, knew that his own fate and the fates of all of them were inextricably linked with Hencke. Salvation or annihilation. Somehow Hencke would decide.

'I tell you, Hencke, because you will soon hear about it anyway. I shall broadcast news of the break-out to the world as we leave tonight. In six hours. It will be too late then for the Allies to react and stop us. The whole of Germany will know that the fight is not yet over, that resistance must still continue. A mighty new chapter in our history, Hencke, one which you have helped to write. Because I shall also announce that you are with us, by the Fuehrer's side, showing the world that Germany still has the will to resist. And I want you to say a few words of encouragement, too. What do you think of that, eh?'

'It goes far beyond my wildest dreams, Herr Reichsminister.'

'You are of great importance to us, Hencke. Next to the Fuehrer you may be the most important symbol in the Reich.'

Hencke swallowed hard, scarcely able to believe what he heard.

'Oh, yes. That is why I have to give you new instructions.

These are dangerous times, crucial times for our survival. We can afford to take no unnecessary risks. So I am giving you an armed guard, Hencke, to ensure as best we can that nothing befalls you. They will be with you day and night. Doesn't that make you feel better?'

Hencke felt a sharp edge of pain as the last window of opportunity slammed shut across his fingers.

Goebbels nodded to someone behind Hencke and there was an immediate crashing of boot leather as a guard snapped smartly to attention. 'Sergeant Greim here will look after you. He's one of our finest commandos, utterly trustworthy. You'll like him, I'm sure.'

'I don't know how to express my thanks, Herr Reichsminister.' As Hencke looked into Goebbels' dark eyes there was a flicker of contact and understanding between them. Goebbels knew. Not for certain and not the details, and not enough to order any immediate action against him, but he knew. It was written all over his crooked smile. Hencke was trapped, and any time after the evening broadcast he would become dispensible. Goebbels could indulge his instincts and drop him down the nearest crevasse. He might not even make it to the Alps. That's what Greim was there for.

'You will excuse me, Hencke.' Goebbels gave a condescending nod. 'I have a radio broadcast to write. I shall see you in six hours.'

Regrets. He had regrets, plenty of them. To have come so far and to have got so close made the regrets which flooded in on him all the more difficult to bear. He knew he couldn't make a good death of it, not now. He didn't have to die, of course. He could slip the guard and lose himself in the ruins of Berlin, taking his chance with the rest. But as difficult as he found the prospect of dying with his regrets, it was nothing to the prospect of having to live with them. The memories of the school and its burning books and broken bodies came back. He had sworn revenge, it was the only way he had been able to live with those nightmares. Yet he had failed, and he knew the pain of the memories would suffocate and destroy whatever life was left to him. There was no way out.

Almost blindly he wandered back into the Chancellery, pursued by the dogged Greim. They didn't talk – what was the point? The signs of growing chaos and collapse were everywhere, yet he could take no comfort from them. In a makeshift command post a general was conducting a furious argument with an engineer about the flooding of the subway tunnels. The Russians will use them to infiltrate right to the heart of Berlin, screamed the general. They are the only shelter for hundreds of thousands of Berliners who will drown if the tunnels are flooded, argued the stubborn engineer, and would not obey. The exasperated general stormed off in search of another engineer. The veneer of military discipline which had hung over the Chancellery in previous days had finally blown away. It was as if an apple had been cut open, only to reveal a writhing mass of maggots.

Hencke felt an overwhelming need to have something other than solid concrete above his head. Walking slowly down the steep steps leading from the Chancellery entrance, he saw makeshift barricades being erected out of tree trunks, wrecked vehicles, sandbags, anything which was heavy yet which could still be moved. Waffen SS troops were being stationed at every point around the Chancellery as if a direct attack could be expected at any moment. The troops were speaking not German but a mixture of foreign tongues – French, Norwegian, Latvian, even Russian. These were the foreign volunteers, skimmed from countries which the Germans had overrun, renowned for their ferocity and total indifference to casualties. They had little to lose, since losing their lives in battle was a far better fate than any they could expect if returned as prisoners to their native countries. Hencke wondered if anyone else saw the irony, the heart of the most racially pure Reich in history being defended by foreign mercenaries.

Choking clouds of smoke and dust swirled through the streets around the Chancellery. In spite of continuous shelling and high risk of death there were lines of women with buckets drawing water from standpipes. The city's water supplies had been shattered, and there was little left to drink and nothing with which to fight the flames or wash away the sewage. The stench was appalling. On another side of the street was stacked a pile of weapons, rifles of many makes and descriptions, boxes of grenades and ammunition, pistols and *Panzerfausts*, at which both men and women picked, equipping themselves with weapons and trying to find ammunition that matched. Several old men, armed with Italian rifles and a handful of bullets each, were being marched off in the direction of the U-Bahn tunnels while a detachment of Hitler Youth on bicycles collected anti-tank weapons before riding east. At every point along the broad boulevards was destruction. Shattered tanks, trucks, buses, artillery wagons, scattered like children's toys. A field gun lay twisted with its barrel resting on the ground in symbolic surrender. From the back of a nearby ambulance with its driver dead at the wheel came the screams for help of the wounded. There were bodies everywhere, young, old, women and children too. No attempt was being made any longer to collect or cover them, and many of those that lay in the roadway had been hideously crushed under truck wheels or tank tracks.

By the side of the Brandenburg Gate there lay the smouldering wreckage of a light airplane with its single wing pointing accusingly towards the sky, the victim of a desperate attempt to put down on the emergency airstrip by the Gate. The wreckage had been pushed aside by a tank to allow other planes to take their chance on the rubble-strewn runway. In the wooded Tiergarten beyond the Gate the trees stood stripped of all leaf and many branches. Hencke had to remind himself that it was spring, that they should all have been in blossom and bud. Trunks of uprooted trees were being hauled away by teams of men and horses to act as barricades, while from the branches of many of those still standing swung the bodies of Germans, some in uniform and some not, hanged

267

for desertion and cowardice by the flying squads of SS and SA troops who were combing the city in an attempt to stem the growing flood of capitulation. All around there were craters and shell holes, the fresh earth thrown up in the form of gaping mouths, like graves waiting to receive their dead.

This was the reality of Berlin, the reality which those in that madhouse of the Bunker wished to maintain and extend through endless war. Except Eva. She had seen through it, recognized the self-deception, the futility of it all. If only her infatuation and loyalty hadn't blinded her to what was necessary to end the madness. But there was no hope of that, she was devoted to Hitler. There was no more chance of her acting to thwart him than a shadow might trip its owner. Poor Eva.

Suddenly, in the midst of the battered Tiergarten, he came to a halt. A thought had gripped him and all but choked his heart. Impractical, impossible, but it represented a flicker of hope. And what had he got to lose, except his regrets? He started to run, back towards the Reich Chancellery.

'What? What's that you're saying? Speak up, I can't hear a damn thing. What about Peter Hencke?'

Bormann was bawling down the telephone, trying to make head or tail of the splutter pouring from the mouthpiece. The phone-lines from Karlsbad had all but collapsed, and it was the third attempt they had made to get through to him. The Czech city was surrounded by American forces who were pounding all hell out of the place. It might be only hours before Hausser's Army Group decided to ignore the *Fuehre-befehl* to fight to the death and started surrendering. It didn't help that Soviet troops were also scarcely twenty miles away, willing and eager to finish off the job if the Americans couldn't.

'Speak up, speak up!' Bormann screamed, but it was no good. The phone was dead. He rapped the receiver a couple of times; there was no response. He snorted contemptuously as he replaced the instrument in its cradle. If it were that

268

important they would phone back again. He resumed his packing.

All was confusion inside the reception area of the Chancellery. Hencke had to force his way past milling crowds of soldiers, rather more of whom seemed to be armed with suitcases and knapsacks than with rifles. There was little pretence left that effective control or defence of the city was still possible. At one desk, abandoned by its duty clerk, an officer was on the phone making arrangements for his departure. He was obviously talking to his mistress, instructing her to pack immediately. Another phone stood unused on the desk, and Hencke grabbed it anxiously, rattling the cradle for attention. He demanded to be put through to the Bunker switchboard, and was mildly surprised when the connection was immediately made. He was still more relieved when, as he requested, they connected him to Eva's suite. Either his name meant something to the switchboard operators or, more likely, they no longer gave a damn.

When she answered the phone he could hear the noise of children laughing in the background. He surmised she was playing with Goebbels' children and that there were probably other women in the room. She was coy, but there was evident warmth in her voice.

'Captain, you are well, I trust?'

'You've heard? About the break-out?'

'Yes, of course. I shall be leaving with the Fuehrer tonight.' There was little enthusiasm in her words. 'It's my duty,' she added. She clearly felt the need to explain.

'I have been instructed to leave also.'

'I know. I suggested to the Fuehrer it might be a good idea . . .'

'I don't want to go.'

'What? Why on earth not?' she exclaimed.

'I came back to Germany to fight for what I believe in. I think I can do that best by remaining here in Berlin.'

'But you are the Fuehrer's mascot, his symbol . . .'

'How much better a symbol will I be if I stay behind to help lead the resistance, to fight to the last. That's the sort of symbol that will keep the white flags from flying!'

'Peter, do you really want to die that much?' In her surprise and confusion she had dropped the discreet formality for a moment.

'No. I don't want to die. But this way I can die without regrets. Remember?'

'I shall never forget. You know that.'

Their words were guarded, anxious of eavesdroppers. Greim was drawing closer to him, clearly curious.

'Fräulein Braun, I have a favour to ask.'

'Anything, Captain. Ask it.'

'I want the Fuehrer to release me from his order, and allow me to remain in Berlin. And I want the opportunity to bid farewell to him personally. It would mean everything to me.'

'He doesn't see many people on their own any more. He says they only ask to see him alone if they have terrible news or want to tell him that the war is lost . . .'

'Help me! There is so little time left. I would ask Reichsminister Goebbels but he is too busy for such matters, and I know of no one else to ask. Could you, this afternoon, take me to see him? It would be my greatest honour.' Greim was edging nearer, in a moment he would be beside Hencke and able to hear every word.

'It's very difficult . . .'

'Please, Eva. Remember. It's an honour I'm willing to die for.'

The voice on the other end of the phone flooded with admiration. 'You are a very exceptional man, Captain Hencke. I'm so very glad I met you.'

Hencke was becoming desperate. He turned his back on Greim, as if trying to shield the receiver from the noise of the officer who was shouting on the next phone. 'The Fuehrer, Eva. Can you arrange it?'

There was a long silence. Greim, making no pretence as to

his intentions, came round and sat on the desk beside him, cocking his ear so he could hear everything.

'Tea. In my room in the Bunker. Four o'clock sharp. Don't be late.' With that the phone went dead.

He threw an evil look at Greim, but the sergeant's attention seemed to have been distracted. At the next phone the officer had abruptly ceased shouting and was staring with incredulity at the receiver. A moment before he had been talking to his mistress in the suburb of Wannsee, scarcely ten miles from the Reich Chancellery. Now all he could hear coming out of the phone was a guttural male voice gabbling in what sounded very much like Russian.

Greim followed Hencke like an unpleasant smell as they walked down the tunnels and towards the Bunker. The checkpoints were all in place; whatever other chaos was going on, the FBK still seemed certain of its duty. He was anxious that the security checks might delay him, make him late, but at last he entered through the final steel door and was in the corridor of the Vorbunker. She was there, too, smiling. He offered a formal nod of respect and she took his arm, leading him towards the stairs that led down to the Fuehrerbunker.

As they started to descend the wrought iron staircase there came the clatter of Greim descending after them. Eva turned to him.

'Sergeant, where on earth do you think you're going?'

Greim looked uncomfortable. 'I have instructions, Fräulein. From Reichsminister Goebbels himself. I am to accompany the captain everywhere and ensure his safety.'

She laughed gaily. 'I assure you that he will be perfectly safe taking tea in the Fuehrerbunker with me. Or do you suspect me of wishing to attack him?' Her tone was light but mocking.

Greim began to stammer with embarrassment. 'No, Fräulein, but my orders . . .'

Her gaiety had gone, she was becoming rapidly impatient.

271

'Sergeant, your orders do not require you to be either ridiculous or impertinent. I promise you the captain will come to no harm.'

Greim writhed, a picture of misery. 'But I shall have to report to the Reichsminister . . .'

'And if you continue your insolence I shall be reporting to the Fuehrer!'

She was staring angrily at him, defying him to continue down the stairs. Greim felt himself caught between the hot breath of a firing squad and the frozen gales of Siberia. He had to choose between Goebbels and Eva Braun, and knew whatever he decided he couldn't win. He looked once more into her indignant eyes. Shit! She was here and Goebbels wasn't. It was bound to be all right if he stood guard at the top of the stairs. As the slut said, what the hell could happen down in the Fuehrerbunker?

Greim turned on his heel and disappeared.

Bormann threw himself down the corridor as if the hounds of hell were at his heels, his face beetroot red and spittle-covered from the exertion and his growing sense of panic. The telephone call had got through while he was packing up his office in the Chancellery. The line from Karlsbad was as terrible as ever and held out for less than three minutes, but three minutes had been enough, and – curse the entire milk-sucking Signal Corps! – when he tried in turn to reach Goebbels in his Bunker office just a few hundred yards away, he found the land line chewed to pieces by a Russian shell and out of action. So he'd been forced to run. He was very unfit. The sweat was pouring down his face and he thought he was going to bring up a bellyful of salami and sauerkraut. Since the telephone call there had been a terrible pounding in his temples and for a moment he wondered whether he was going to have a heart attack; it seemed a far brighter prospect than anything Goebbels was likely to do to him when he heard. He forced his tired legs onwards.

The sight of a wild-eyed Deputy Fuehrer charging down

272

the tunnels towards the checkpoints unnerved some of the FBK guards – perhaps the Russians were already here . . . or Bormann had cracked, he was always the one most likely to . . . perhaps they should shoot him. But such was the bull-like charge that he was past them before they had a chance to think. He hauled himself through the bulkhead door which led to the Vorbunker, took a huge lungful of air and bellowed.

'G-o-e-b-b-e-l-s?'

A bewildered adjutant paused from his packing, eyed the deranged-looking Bormann with astonishment, and found himself utterly incapable of response.

'Where's Goebbels, you bastard?' Bormann screamed. He lunged towards the adjutant who had begun to tremble but, just as he was about to lay his huge paws on the wretch, the soldier waved towards one of the doors leading off the corridor.

'But . . . but he's recording his radio broadcast. He mustn't be disturbed.'

With a wild sweep of his hand Bormann threw him aside and crashed through the door.

Eva Braun's suite led directly off the Fuehrer's sitting-room, and was furnished in similarly frugal style. Only a coat of pale yellow paint on the walls differentiated it from the other dingy cubby holes of the Fuehrerbunker. Hencke sat in an armchair while she busied herself on the small sofa pouring tea, moving to one side the vase of fresh flowers on the table. It was a scene almost identical to that of the Fuehrer's own tea party for him. Except there was no orderly. And the nearest guard was in the corridor, out of sight and out of earshot.

'Thank you for your help, Eva.'

'It wasn't easy. I haven't had a chance to explain things to the Fuehrer; I've simply invited him to tea, our last time in the Bunker. He'll be along any minute. I hope he won't be angry with me . . .'

From within his black officer's tunic Hencke took a one-armed toy bear. It looked sad and exhausted, as if it had had enough. He placed it on the table beside the tea cups.

'My lucky charm. It's been with me all the way . . .'

'Peter, how sweet. You with a teddy bear! You really are the strangest man.'

She picked up the battered toy to examine it, glowing with pleasure like a girl sharing presents with her schoolfriends, trying to stroke fresh life back into its tattered fabric. For a moment she scarcely noticed that Hencke had got out of his seat and was by the small bureau near the door, where she had left her handbag. When she looked up again she saw he was opening the bag and reaching inside.

'Peter. . . ?' The smile had gone as she saw him take out the Walther. 'Peter, what is it. . . ?'

It took him less than two full strides to cross the room. He was leaning over her. He didn't want to, from deep down within him he absolutely didn't want to, but he knew she would leave him with no choice. Her mouth was open and she was about to scream when his hands went round her neck and he began to squeeze, choking off the cry of warning. Her right hand came up, clenched in a fist, striking him fiercely in the testicles and he winced with pain, but kept squeezing. She tried to kick but her feet were obstructed by the seat. Her face was rapidly changing colour and after another futile attack on his groin her hands were up trying to tear his fingers away from her neck. The harder she fought, the tighter he squeezed. Her body was shaking, seeming as light in his hands as a pillow, and her strength was ebbing fast. Her tongue was out, her jaw was slack, her lips pursed in a silent scream of fury, and her large green eyes stared up at him accusing, beseeching, uncomprehending. While they stared, he dared not let go.

It seemed for ever before he realized she was dead, that the eyes, still full of accusation, retained no life.

His own eyes filled with tears. 'No regrets, Eva. No regrets,' he whispered. With great tenderness he leaned down and kissed her on the forehead.

It was as he stood up that he heard someone enter the room behind him. He turned round to find himself looking straight down the barrel of a gun.

'Bormann, you oaf. Can't you see I'm recording a broadcast?'
'Fuck the recording. It's Hencke we've got to worry about.'
'Oh my God. What is it?'
'It's not Hencke, it's not him!'
'Make sense, man!'
'I've just had Karlsbad on the phone. They've found out more about Hencke. The reason we haven't been able to find any recent records for him' – Bormann swayed with breathless fatigue – 'is that he's dead. He died seven years ago.'
'How? Where?'
'Hencke was a schoolteacher all right, at the time we seized the Sudetenland, but some bloody idiot Freikorper threw a grenade through a window during the troubles. It exploded in the middle of his classroom, killing Hencke and half a class of schoolchildren.'
'You cannot be serious,' whispered Goebbels.
'There's more. Seems he never married and was living with another man, a Czech. Might even have been a bit of a pillow-biter some of the locals reckoned.'
'Then if Hencke is dead, who the hell is this one. . . ?'
As one they sprang for the door.

Hencke stared into the glazed expression of Adolf Hitler. The gun in the Fuehrer's hand trembled as he gazed open-mouthed from Hencke to the body of Eva Braun and back again. His wits seemed dull, his reactions slow and his attention unable to focus, to settle on either, as if hoping that by looking back and forth often enough he would discover his eyes had deceived him. Eventually, agonizingly, as he stood looking at his lover's lifeless body, the truth pierced through to his befuddled brain and his watery eyes turned to real tears. It was the first time he had ever truly cried.

275

Hencke watched transfixed as Adolf Hitler's heart broke into a million pieces.

'Where's Hencke?' Goebbels and Bormann shouted in unison as they burst into the corridor.

This time the adjutant was completely incapable of speech and it was not until Greim, disturbed by the commotion, put his head around the bulkhead door from his position at the top of the stairs that they got their reply.

'Hencke? He's ... down with Fräulein Braun,' Greim whimpered. 'They went to have tea ...' He trailed off in terror as he saw the look on Goebbels' face.

'You shit-eating scum!' Goebbels pushed past him. 'You're dead!'

The Reichsminister was hobbling, dragging his braced leg behind him, yet Bormann was in panic as to what they might find and gladly let the other lead the way. As they stumbled in their haste down the corridor, Goebbels trod on the head of a china doll with which his young daughter had been playing. It shattered into useless, unrecognizable fragments.

They clattered down the metal stairs, Goebbels forced to take them one at a time and slowing Bormann and the FBK guards who had joined the pursuit. They rushed into the lower corridor of the Fuehrerbunker, Goebbels shouting ahead to the guard stationed outside the entrance to Hitler's rooms.

'Where's the Fuehrer?'

The guard pointed through the door and Goebbels lunged frantically past. Inside the Fuehrer's sitting-room they hesitated, unsure through which door to look. A single shot rang out. It came from behind the door leading to Eva Braun's suite.

Goebbels already knew what he would find as he burst into the room. Hencke was standing over the body of Eva Braun, a gun by his side. Directly in front of them, slumped on the floor, his face pointing to the ceiling, lay the body of Adolf Hitler. There was a gun in his hand and a bullet wound in his temple. He lay as dead and as useless as the shattered doll.

There are moments when time stands still. It did so now for Goebbels as he took in the scene before him. The Fuehrer, a single bullet wound in the temple. Eva Braun, open-eyed, distorted lips, the agonies of death etched across her face. A small porcelain vase of flowers tipped over on the table, the water dripping mournfully on to the floor. A scene to be remembered for all time. Suddenly a pistol was thrust over his shoulder and Bormann was firing. The first bullet struck Hencke full in the chest and spun him round, but like a man possessed Bormann continued to fire repeatedly into Hencke's body until it was slumped against the wall, covered in angry, raging wounds, and Bormann had run out of ammunition. Yet still he pulled at the trigger and the hammer clicked against empty chambers until Goebbels forcibly restrained him.

In the icy silence that followed, nobody moved. Then one of Hencke's eyes twitched open, a flicker of flame shone from somewhere within, and through lips twisted with pain and effort he whispered: *'Nelipuje.'* A thin, triumphal smile brushed briefly across his face, and he fell back, dead.

'What did he say, what did he say?' Bormann asked, quivering with shock.

'It was Czech,' Goebbels responded quietly. 'Czech for "No Regrets".'

There was another long period of silence before they were distracted by the gathering of curious guards beyond the outer door.

'Keep them out. They have no business here.' Goebbels was calm. He seemed very much in command, almost serene. At last he turned to face Bormann. 'It's over. The end.'

Bormann shook his head, unwilling to accept. 'But surely we can fight on. There's still the Alps.'

'Without the Fuehrer? Impossible. Tomorrow we are dead.'

'No, no. We can still escape from Berlin.' There was fear in Bormann's florid face.

'Hopeless!' Goebbels snapped. He pointed at the corpse of Hitler. 'The head and the heart of Germany are here in this room. The war is over, Bormann. All we have left is the idea.'

'What the hell are you talking about?'

'The cause, it must live on. And for that we need martyrs and a noble myth, not some shabby little scene played out in an underground sewer, the Fuehrer dead beside the body of his mistress and some snivelling Czech laughing in our faces. Is that what you want future generations to remember, for God's sake?' Goebbels had grown animated as he struggled for one final time to rearrange the pieces of history.

'But what can we do?'

'I tell you what you do. You find a notary and get him to marry these two.' He waved at the corpses of Hitler and Eva Braun.

'But they're dead . . .'.

'Do you want the world to know that Hitler died with a whore? You get the notary, and once he's married them, get rid of him. We can't have anyone going round telling tales.'

Bormann blanched.

'Then you dispose of the bodies. Burn them. We can't have them falling into the clutches of the Russians.' He stood amidst the carnage, struggling to summon up the energy and adrenalin for his task, but it became all too much and somewhere inside him a switch was thrown. Shoulders sagged, the long face wilted and he closed his eyes for a moment, seeking composure. When he spoke again, his voice had taken on an uncharacteristic mellowness. 'You do that. And I will announce to the world that the Fuehrer has committed suicide, his new wife by his side, fighting to the last to defend the Reich capital of Berlin. An heroic death which will inspire great histories to be written. Only you and I will know, Bormann.'

'What of him, the Czech?'

'Place him in a side room for the moment, out of the way of prying eyes.' Goebbels paused to consider the man in whom he had placed so much faith and who had betrayed him with such devastating effect. He shrugged, the energy for hate gone. 'Then give him a proper burial. He died a soldier's death after all, whoever he was.'

'The last man to die, maybe?'

Goebbels sniffed in contempt as the other man's fear filled his nostrils. But what did it matter any more . . . 'You get out of Berlin, Bormann. If you can.'

'You, too?'

Goebbels kicked a one-armed toy bear lying on the floor. 'No, I don't think I'll bother . . .'

EPILOGUE

The sun was setting through the leaves of whispering ash trees, long shadows falling across the path of the old man as he wandered between the neat lines of memorial stones. They were white and carefully scrubbed, and Cazolet paused in front of each one, lingering on occasion to offer a silent tribute to the exceptional youth or valour of the victim recorded on the stone, but always moving on. They were mostly American and British, almost all airmen, with every once in a while an Australian, New Zealander, Indian or South African being remembered. There were even five Poles buried in the Allied War Cemetery in Berlin, but they were not what he sought.

He found it after almost half an hour, when the sun had all but vanished and a fine autumn mist was beginning to gather. He had tired himself greatly and bent heavily over his walking stick as he read the inscription, his frail body trembling as he did so.

An Unknown Czech Soldier. Died April 1945.

'So the Old Man's crazy, impossible plan worked. We got to Berlin after all. If only he'd known . . .'

Cazolet stayed for a long while, until it was twilight and the damp had begun to bite at his bones. He did not mind. At last, and for whatever time he had left, he could be at peace with his memories, the hopes Churchill had built at the time he sent this man, and the guilt that had eaten at them both when they felt forced to betray him. Cazolet could only surmise what might have happened to their man, but

281

since he had got as far as Berlin it seemed probable that he had gone all the way. 'The insurance policy,' as Churchill once called it, had worked. Nobody would believe the story, of course, not after all these years. So the memory would die with Cazolet, and soon there would be nothing left but a small, white marker in some crowded foreign field.

In the deepening shadows of evening the frail old man dug into his pocket and pulled out the medals and decorations awarded to him during a lifetime of public service. Leaning carefully on his cane, he bent to place them on the grave of the unknown soldier. He walked stiffly away, looking content. Now he could face up to dying. With no regrets.

AUTHOR'S NOTE

'Hencke' was not the last man to die.

After arranging for the disposal of Hitler's body, Goebbels and his wife Magda prepared their six young children for bed in the family's quarters within the Bunker. Frau Goebbels dressed them all in clean nightgowns and brushed their hair, before feeding them poisoned chocolates. The six tiny bodies were then wrapped in white shrouds.

Afterwards the parents went up to the Bunker garden where Hitler's and Eva's bodies had been burned in a shallow trench. Standing by the cremation site, Magda bit into a poison capsule. As she fell to the ground, Goebbels put a bullet in the back of her head. He then bit into his own capsule, shooting himself in the right temple as he did so. They both wanted to make sure . . . An SS aide poured petrol over the bodies from a jerry can and set light to them. The semi-charred corpses were discovered by the Russians two days later.

Bormann attempted to break out of Berlin the night after Hitler and Goebbels died. He got less than a mile from the Reich Chancellery before he disappeared. His skull, identified through dental records, was dug up by developers preparing the site for an exhibition park nearly thirty years later.

The notary who had performed the wedding ceremony, Walter Wagner, was shot dead the same evening.